ECHOES IN THE SAND

SHANNON BAKER

SEVERN RIVER PUBLISHING

Severn River Publishing
www.SevernRiverBooks.com

ISBN: 978-1-64875-506-4 (Paperback)

ALSO BY SHANNON BAKER

Michaela Sanchez Southwest Crime Thrillers

Echoes in the Sand

The Desert's Share

The Kate Fox Mysteries

Stripped Bare

Dark Signal

Bitter Rain

Easy Mark

Broken Ties

Exit Wounds

Double Back

Bull's Eye

The Nora Abbott Mystery Series

Height of Deception

Skies of Fire

Canyon of Lies

Standalone Thrillers

The Desert Behind Me

To find out more about Shannon Baker and her books, visit

severnriverbooks.com/authors/shannon-baker

For Dave
Every single day

1

The undergrad wore a sundress so short a whisper of wind could get her arrested for exposure. She stood outside the door of Social Sciences building at the University of Arizona and glared at me with the power of her youth and certainty.

Enjoy the confidence while you can, sweetheart. I squeezed the sweaty hand clutching my own and jerked Sami forward into a dancing spin under my arm.

She giggled and skipped next to me along the crowded sidewalk. Ten feet behind us, an undeniable sigh of disdain brushed against my back. "Mom, please." At twelve and in middle school, Sami's playfulness embarrassed Josie.

The undergrad kept her contempt aimed at me as we approached the entrance of the building. I shouldn't take it personally, though I might have liked to practice an illegal chokehold on her. My uniform didn't play well on a university campus. It looked official enough that she probably assumed I was a cop rather than an Arizona Ranger. College kids—who know everything and haven't been tested in the big world—don't tend to have much respect for law officers.

Pushing into the air-conditioned building and leaving the blaring sun and heat of the Tucson spring, I reached behind me to slip my arm around

Josie's shoulder and bring her to my side. I hadn't counted on the crowd in the hallway. It didn't lighten my irritation at having to make this stop on campus.

Josie folded her arms and set her face into that long-suffering attitude. "I need to get home. I've got, like, a ton of homework and we're supposed to watch the news for social studies."

I checked the numbers above the doors. Chris was speaking in a room that should be a short way down the hallway. I didn't like the congestion in the hallway, and I leaned close to Josie. "We're heading home as soon as I give Uncle Chris a check for Ann's pool."

She rolled her eyes as only a preteen daughter can. "You couldn't give it to him Sunday, when we'll all be at family dinner anyway?"

As much as I'd like to agree with her and explain I hadn't wanted to make this stop either, I wouldn't defend myself and give her the impression the world revolved around her.

Bodies packed the hall and I checked my watch. No, it wasn't between classes. This many young people didn't come to listen to a Border Patrol recruitment speech. Something else was going on here and it wasn't good. I hesitated and surveyed the crowd.

The mass of students gathered outside the room where Chris said he'd be giving his annual recruitment speech. Manuel Ortiz stood down the hall just beyond the huddle all but wielding a conductor's baton. Chris had told me only a handful of kids usually turned out and stopping by wouldn't be a problem. But seeing the crowd and Ortiz put this gathering in a whole new light.

I tugged Sami's hand and directed Josie back toward the door we'd entered.

Sami went along with anything, but when we popped back to the heat on the campus mall Josie faced me. "What's going on?"

I pointed to a cement bench in the shade of a Palo Verde tree. "You go wait over there. I'll be out in a second."

"Mom," Josie protested. "This is so lame. Can't we just leave?"

"Go." I used the Mom voice and only turned away when they'd started for the bench.

I hurried back into the building. Wherever Manuel Ortiz showed up there was sure to be trouble, and I was torn between getting the kids far away and standing with my brother. The kids would be safe outside the building. Josie might be a pain in the butt these days, but she was responsible and smart.

As spokesman for the Border Patrol, Chris could handle a crowd, especially after all the trouble they'd had a year ago. But the students milling outside the room under the direction of Ortiz could get unruly. Having another uniform standing with him might not hurt.

By the time I reached the edge of the crowd gathered outside the door of Chris's room, the murmurs turned into shouts.

"Not Border Patrol, more like Death Patrol!"

"You're an extension of the KKK!"

"Get off our campus!"

"This is our safe place!"

As the noise escalated, Ortiz stood at the edge of the crowd with a satisfied smirk. His face beamed until his eyes settled on my uniform. He might know the difference between an Arizona Ranger uniform and a Tucson PD uniform or not. He wouldn't be happy to see anyone of authority breaking into his demonstration, especially one with a gun.

I knew Manuel Ortiz. He wouldn't know me, though. The protesters kept up their harangue. Using my elbows and hips, I shoved into the throng toward the classroom. Those gathered looked like students, and more than half had their phones out to record the event. The protesters hadn't entered the room, but gathered outside, chanting and clapping. Maybe the Border Patrol being on campus hadn't been a big deal in previous years, but now that Manuel Ortiz played ringmaster in this circus, and he seemed to have it out for Chris, this performance could pop up anywhere.

I managed to work my way to the front of the crowd and squeeze into the open doorway. A few students stood inside the classroom with panicked faces, their bookbags flung over their shoulders. Tall and blond, with the good looks of an action hero, my brother radiated a controlled rage. He'd packed up the banner, shoved the flyers and promotional SWAG into his courier bag, and looked ready to slash through the demonstrators with his bare hands.

He didn't look happy when I fought my way into the room. "What are you doing here?"

I shrugged. "Looked like you could use some help."

Six students, all young men, huddled in the middle of the room. An older man wearing slacks with a button-up shirt and tie, looking every bit the college professor, frowned at me. "You're not campus security."

My uniform wouldn't fool him.

Chris snapped the clasps on his bag. By way of introduction he said, "I don't know what you think you can accomplish."

I glanced out the door at the protesters. "Two uniforms are better than one."

Dr. Bartholomew frowned at me, "I suggest you call campus security."

His face tight, Chris shook his head. "That's what he wants. The more attention he gets, the better for him. You guys stay here. I'll leave. They'll follow me and yell, but they won't touch me. I'm sure Ortiz has told them how far they can go and not to go any further."

The older man didn't seem to like that idea. "How can you be sure Manuel is behind this? I imagine it's a spontaneous demonstration. What with DACA and the wall being such big issues, the students are paying attention."

I looked Chris in the eye. "Ortiz is out there. This is his show."

His jaw jerked as if he clenched his teeth, then a low voice sounded like a warning growl of a cornered dog. "That f—" He stopped himself and started again. "I'm sure he's got this spreading on social media and has the local news called with their camera. Damned grandstander."

"There are a lot of cell phones out there," I affirmed.

Chris squared his shoulders as if for a fight. "Someday this bullshit is going to get him in trouble."

"Probably not today," I said. "I'll go with you. Two of us will look tougher."

"You stay here with Dr. Bartholomew and these guys." Chris took a moment to shake their hands, though they looked unnerved and not interested in politeness.

Not great candidates for the Border Patrol if they couldn't handle this small amount of pressure.

Chris said, "I'm sorry about those people. The Border Patrol isn't usually the center of attention like this. We do our job keeping the border safe. Now all these do-gooders who don't understand the issues are stirring everyone up. These clowns aren't helping anyone, they're just making themselves feel like heroes."

A clinking sound drew our attention to a small canister that landed in the middle of the classroom floor. It emitted smoke as it trundled along the ground.

"Tear gas!" Chris shouted and with a sweeping motion, he seemed to gather the students into a group and move them toward the door. The professor froze so I grabbed his shoulder and threw my other arm around his back. I shoved him behind Chris and we formed a wedge to cut through the classroom door and power our way into the hallway.

The gas smelled god-awful as it started to spill into the hallway. The protesters didn't need any more incentive to evacuate as well. The swell of bodies surged down the hallway and burst through the doors into the mall, spewing students who trotted off in groups, yelling and laughing in general chaos. My arm still around the professor, I hustled him away from the building toward the bench where Josie and Sami stood searching for me with worried faces.

"Come on," I said, not letting up on my pressure to get the old gentleman away from the crowd of people, still worked up and maybe going into mob mentality.

Josie took Sami's hand and they trotted behind me as I rushed the man through another few turns until we stood in the shade of the open-air student union.

I gave him a moment to catch his breath. "I'm Michaela Sanchez. This is Josie and this is Sami."

He inclined his head to us. "Dr. Regis Bartholomew, dean of the law college."

Dr. Bartholomew panted, his face pale. We'd escaped before being affected by the gas, so my eyes didn't burn and my throat felt fine. "How are you? Did you inhale any of the gas?"

He shook his head and tried to catch his breath.

I held on to him, letting him lean on me. Josie scuttled off to a nearby café chair and pulled it over. He sank into it and blinked at her. "Thank you."

I threw her an approving smile. This kid. Flip sides of a golden coin. Self-centered preteen one moment, caring young woman the next. A vending machine stood in the corner and I reached into my pocket for a credit card. I handed it to Josie. "Can you get him some water?"

She took the card and Sami followed her.

His breathing evened out and he sat with drooping shoulders. "It's getting worse than I ever recall. This division. I feared there would be trouble today and I went to warn Mr. Wright."

I squatted beside his chair. "You knew there would be protesters?"

He licked his lips. "I'd heard rumors. But Chris is a stubborn man."

I could attest to that. If he hadn't been so stubborn, I'd have never grown up with love and security and all the advantages of a stable home. I wouldn't be living the blessed life I had.

"Did you know Manuel Ortiz would be there?"

Josie returned, gave him the water, and me the card.

The old man sighed. "Manuel's got his sights set on Chris. I'm afraid that means media spotlight following him." He took a drink. It seemed to revive him, and he pushed himself to stand. "Thank you again. My office isn't far from here. I think I'll relax there in the air conditioning for a bit before I go home."

"We can walk you there if you'd like," Josie said, making me glow with pride.

He patted her head. "That's kind, but I'll take my time. You've been a big help."

We watched him shuffle away and turn from the union. A knot of half a dozen students spoke with excitement, no doubt recalling the protest. It had felt like a large gathering in the hallway, but probably not more than thirty or forty people all together. It wouldn't take long for the tweets and Snaps and all the others to zap around campus and students to gather. I hustled the kids away from the union toward the parking lot.

The tear gas upped the stakes and I wasn't surprised to see campus security gathered at the building. We passed a pair of Tucson PD officers on our way to the parking lot. And a couple more sirens indicated more cops on the way.

I itched to go back to the building and start interviewing witnesses and collecting information in case someone wanted to file criminal charges. That was my old life, though. Not the sensible one where I volunteered for the no-risk Arizona Rangers, drove my Mom-taxi Honda Pilot for hours every day, cooked nutritious dinners, helped with homework, and led the safest, most vanilla life on the planet.

Sami and Josie chattered on the walk to the Pilot. I wondered what happened to Chris, and if this would stay local news or somehow hit tomorrow's national news cycle, and what that might do to his career. He didn't need more controversy hanging over him.

Sami didn't even argue when Josie climbed into the front seat. She hoisted herself into the back and clicked her seatbelt, all the while stumbling over her words in her excitement about all the people running from the building and helping the old man.

Josie smiled and gave me a sideways look. "Just wait till Dad hears about it."

Deon's reaction to this incident was something I could wait forever to witness.

2

Deon worked late, giving me a reprieve from discussing the tear gas incident. Again. I kicked off my hot uniform shoes and changed into a sundress. The cool tile felt wonderful on my feet. The girls and I made pasta with lots of fresh vegetables they helped chop. We carried our plates to the table by the pool and I tried to relax as the sun cast artistic shadows on the Catlinas that stood guard over our neighborhood. The girls chatted about friends, softball, our upcoming plans to visit Deon's family in Mexico. Josie jumped on her favorite topic: the unfairness of the dress code at school.

These moments with them were priceless. They were growing up and very soon the three of us enjoying dinner together on a weeknight would be rare. Even now, Josie kept eyeing her iPad, which I insisted she set aside for dinner.

But restlessness nibbled at the edges of my laughter. The adrenaline rush when the tear gas grenade clanked into the classroom must be what a junkie feels when the needle pierces skin. Helping Dr. Bartholomew came naturally, and I'd known without thinking exactly what to do.

In a couple of days I'd go back to that same campus in my Arizona Rangers uniform to work the book festival. I'd saunter down the mall, watching for anything out of the ordinary. Probably help someone with heat or dehydration. Maybe reunite a kid who wandered from his parents. And after four mundane hours, I'd come home to my family and make dinner, go for a bike ride, maybe watch a little TV.

No bombs going off. No domestic disputes or robberies. No high-speed chases or anything to make my heart thump.

I focused on Sami, her six-year-old excitement over a chapter book she'd checked out from the library. Josie, now reaching for her iPad. They were the reason I lived a quiet life. *They are worth it.*

As if going into the house for more water, I rose and walked inside. From the top of the refrigerator, I pulled down three of the four Nerf guns I'd placed there a while back. I liked the parallel of hiding these here; my sister, Ann, always insisted our gun belts stay on her fridge. I loaded all three with five Nerf darts. With nonchalance, I opened the back door and approached the table. Sami saw me lift my weapon to begin firing and she screamed. Josie wasn't far behind. She tossed the iPad on the table. I dropped the other two guns on the patio and ran behind the grill.

They fired and I retrieved their darts. They got mine and the fight was on. Yelling, dodging, laughing. Josie ran into the house with me hot on her heels. Sami brought up the rear, more sound than shooting. Around the kitchen island we waged battle until Sami brought her gun up, knocked a glass from the counter, and shattered it on the floor at the same time the door to the garage opened.

"Freeze!" I shouted to keep either girl from stepping on broken glass.

Deon stood in the doorway, his eyes wide, briefcase in hand. No one spoke for a second. His face tightened into a frown. My husband likes order and peace. This chaos might unsettle him. He opened his mouth to speak.

Whap! Josie shouted, "Gotcha!" as the dart she fired bounced off his face and onto the floor.

I'm sure the girls didn't notice how he pulled back from an irritated response, rearranged his face into a grin, and held up the hand not gripping the briefcase. "I surrender."

After instructing Sami and Josie not to move, I ran up, grabbed flip-flops for us all, and got the girls safely out of the kitchen.

While I started to tidy the mess, Deon said, "I haven't eaten yet. I'm going to change and clean up the leftovers. Wait for me."

It wasn't as if I had anywhere else to go. Deon stayed upstairs talking with the girls and I made sure every speck of glass disappeared. I brought in our dishes and reset the table outside for Deon's meal and enjoyed the silence of our backyard, watching the ripples on the lighted swimming pool.

The girls would be spilling the same stories they'd regaled me with over dinner. They'd probably let him know about the tear gas incident. He wouldn't be happy about that, so I wasn't in any hurry to have him join me. I'd have to explain how the kids were in no danger and the whole thing was really no big deal.

My phone buzzed and I picked it up. Talk about an adrenaline rush. I rose from the table and quickly walked around the pool to the cinderblock fence in the corner of the yard, as far from the house as possible. Even with the windows closed upstairs and the air-conditioning on, I didn't want to risk being overheard.

I stabbed connect. "Hi. Deon's home."

Jared's voice sounded husky. "Okay, just quickly then."

I stared at the patio door, waiting for it to open, the blood zinging through me.

"You're all over social media," he said.

"What?" That punch had nothing to do with Jared's voice on the phone.

"The demonstration on campus. Students are posting it all over. We've been looking at it to see if we can find out who lobbed the canister."

Jared was TPD, a friend from the old days who had recently resurfaced. He was cute and smart and dangerous. Jared wanted me, that was no secret. Did I want Jared? Not really. Flirting with him was wrong. No excuses. No explanations. Wrong.

But maybe I could help TPD with this. I pictured the hallway on campus. "Ask Ortiz. That SOB has something to do with it."

Jared probably tilted his head in that way that made him look like Rob Lowe, his blue eyes considering. "He was too far away and the videos prove that."

Damn it. I'd like nothing better than to pin something on that jerk.

Jared's voice swung low. "But you were so sexy. You came busting out of that room with the professor. You looked like you could save the world."

The warm glow started at my head and spread, even though I told myself Jared calculated his words for a certain result. It still felt good to have someone appreciate me. To Jared, I wasn't wife and mother, though I can't deny Deon never seemed to take me for granted. But Jared acknowledged my skill at law enforcement and understood how I felt about it. To me, that was way more enticing than his dark hair, six-pack abs, and dimpled chin.

His voice sounded like a still lake at midnight. "Meet me tomorrow."

"No." Not only no, but hell no. Never. No way. Flirting was one thing. Not a good thing. But not this. I'd never cross that line.

He breathed the next words. "Only talk. Come on."

"I'm volunteering at Mi Casa all day."

"Leave early. Meet me after you drop your kids at school. At the Holiday Inn next to the airport."

The back door slid open and Deon appeared. He leaned into the night. "Michaela? What are you doing out there?"

"Please, Michaela. We need to talk."

"Fine." Anything to get him off the phone and keep him from calling back right away. I clicked off and slid the phone into my pocket. "Talking to Ann."

Deon plopped down in a chair at the table. "Sweet Ann. Has she solved all the world's problems?"

"No, but she's trying."

3

I poured cold seltzer water for me and Deon and sat down.

He took a bite and gave me a thumbs-up. "This tastes fantastic."

"Thanks." I heard the distraction in my voice and sat up straighter and looked at Deon, giving him my focus and trying to push thoughts of Jared away.

"What's new with Ann?"

The cover-up slid too quickly off my tongue. "She's working on a fund-raising campaign."

He ate quickly. "It's always a good phone call from your sister if she's not on a rampage about something."

I kept from jumping to Ann's defense. Deon must have had a tough day because he rarely said anything negative about my family. The truth was, even though loyalty made me always takes Ann or Chris's side, you never knew what to expect with Ann. Some days she was sunshine and light, and others, well, having a helmet handy was a good idea.

While he finished off the pasta. We talked about our trip to see his family in Hermosillo in a couple of weeks. We planned what supplies I'd pick up at Costco to replenish their pantry and what gifts they might enjoy. I waited for him to bring up the campus tear gas incident, but he asked about my supply of insulin for the trip instead. It was possible the girls had been excited about their own issues and hadn't mentioned it to him. It wasn't as if we were keeping a secret. But if he knew I'd been in the middle of a demonstration and the girls were anywhere around, he'd worry more than he'd need to. It wouldn't be a bad thing if he never heard about it.

Deon put his fork down. "Sami said she and Emily are fighting again. Is that normal?"

"Totally. They'll be friends again tomorrow."

He took that in. "I don't get that."

"You didn't go to school with a bunch of spoiled kids. You kept to your brothers and studied. Sami is a social maniac. It's a good day when her teacher doesn't tell me she's talking too much or distracting others."

He started eating again and kept his eyes on his plate. "Do you think it's a good idea to roughhouse with the girls like that? Like when I came home?"

"We were playing. And yes, I think it's a good idea to have fun when we can."

He pushed the pasta around. "When I was growing up, we tried to keep quiet. Everything peaceful. I guess I'm nervous when our household seems out of control."

So much sadness with his childhood. "It had to have been hard always being afraid your parents would be deported."

He hated talking about why his family lived in Mexico and he was the only one here. We both suffered our own brands of guilt. He reached for my hand. "I'm too serious. Good thing they have you."

The warmth of his words felt as good as his hand on mine. "You're much more fun than you used to be. And serious isn't bad, anyway. It's made you a damned good lawyer."

He looked grateful for that and sat back, letting out a big sigh. I didn't know if it was contentment or exhaustion.

Jared. What had I been thinking? I hadn't meant to tell Jared I'd meet him, but maybe it wasn't such a bad idea. Seeing him would give me a chance to stop this nonsense face to face. I'd tell him this thing we'd been doing, with me dancing way too close to the fire, was over. Done.

The front doorbell dinged followed by an immediate thudding of feet on the steps. Sami squealed and a man's voice said, "Hey, squirt."

I pushed back from the table. "Sounds like Chris is here."

Deon reached for my hand before I could walk away. "I'm beat tonight. I should have stayed at the office another couple of hours, but I thought it would be better if I go in early tomorrow after a good night's sleep."

I ran the fingers of my other hand through his hair and he closed his eyes with pleasure. "Go on up. I'll talk to Chris and get the girls settled."

He kissed my hand. "Sorry to leave you in the lurch like this. But I need to get this work done so we can go to Mexico, and I promised the girls I'd go to Sunday dinner."

I hugged him around the neck. Such a good father. "Don't worry about it. We'll have time together in Mexico."

I'd been feeling sorry for myself that Deon didn't appreciate my cop training and yet, I hadn't asked him what case had kept him late at the office. When was the last time we'd talked about his clients and the work that consumed most of his time and provided us with this comfortable life?

I made my way toward the hoopla in the family room, where Sami skidded toward me in her stocking feet. "Mom. See what Uncle Chris got?"

Chris stood at the entrance to the family room. He'd shed his Border Patrol uniform like snakeskin and wore an old T-shirt, shorts, and flip-flops. Through the open front door, I saw Josie jumping off the porch steps and making her way to the driveway. "This is sweet," she shouted.

He had me curious. "What did you do?"

"It's red and shiny. Come see." Sami grabbed my hand and I let her pull me out the door to see the Ford F150 SuperCab in my driveway. Indeed, the red reflected the street light.

Josie sat behind the wheel and Sami clambered into the passenger side.

"Well, this is a doozy." I walked around it. "It looks brand-new."

Chris followed me, grinning like a proud father. "It is. Picked it up this evening."

Chris lived in a cheap apartment. He didn't have many clothes, no new furniture, and didn't take expensive vacations. He was far closer to the hardworking ant than he was to the extravagant grasshopper. "This is the first new vehicle you've ever owned, isn't it?"

He admired it. "Yep."

A little squiggle of excitement burbled in me. About time for him to loosen up. "This is great. What prompted it?"

His gaze caught mine and the smile slipped from his face. "I wanted it. I'm not getting younger and I wonder what I'm saving my money for."

Not like Chris. But maybe he was evolving. A splurge of luxury would be good for him. But a brand-new pickup like this would be half a year's salary. He probably had a bunch of money saved over the years. With no kids, no mortgage, and few expenses, it seemed possible.

Not my worry. He was an adult and knew what he was doing.

Josie appeared beside us. "Let's go for a drive."

"I thought you had homework," I said.

She glared at me. "Just a short drive."

Sami jumped out of the pickup. "Please. Please. Please."

He looked me up and down. "I didn't come over just to have you admire my new wheels. I wanted to see if you made it out of there in one piece. Looks like you did."

Josie answered for me. "Yeah, we took that old guy to the union and got him water and stuff. He seemed nice."

Chris rubbed the top of her head, messing her curls, a move that if I made, would have sent her into a tirade. "Thanks. He's pretty feeble. Something like that couldn't be good for him."

"I'm going to clean up dinner. You girls can take a short drive with Chris then it's time for bed for both of you."

"Mom," Josie said with disdain. "I've got homework."

"You can stay up to take care of that, but in your room. And I'll keep the iPad."

I finished the dishes and they returned from their ride all excited by the bells and whistles of Chris's pickup. I had one more go-round with Sami about bed and a verbal tug-of-war with Josie over the iPad. Chris and I retreated to the patio. I sank into a chaise lounge by the pool and Chris pulled a chair close.

"Okay," I said. "Tell me what's going on."

He blew air out his nose to show me I was nuts. "Nothing's going on."

"I may be younger than you, but I'm not stupid. You've been out of sorts for a while, and today you were close to losing it. Then the big purchase, something so out of character for you I'm about to have you committed. Is it Manuel Ortiz?"

He stared at me. "Why do you say that?"

I stared at the aqua of the lighted pool. "The way you spoke about him before they tossed in the tear gas. I've never seen that much venom in you."

"It's not Ortiz."

"Okay." I left it open-ended and waited, not letting him off the hook.

His shoulders sagged and he exhaled. "You think you know me so well."

"Yes."

He looked into my eyes and I told him without words that he might as well cough it up.

He argued with my silent statement. "Damn it, Mike. You read me like a Border Collie reads sheep." With a second's more hesitation, he started. "I don't want to tell you because I don't want you to get involved."

"I won't get involved. I've got enough to do."

He laughed. "You won't get involved unless you think you can help. And in this case, you can't."

"So, tell me."

"Really, Mike, the less you know, the better."

"Really, Chris," I mimicked. "You're forty-seven years old and you haven't figured out by now you can run but you can't hide from your little sister?"

He stood up, shed his flip-flops, and walked to the pool, dropping down and dangling his legs into the water.

I pushed myself out of the comfort of my lounger and joined him, enjoying the cool weight of the water on my feet and ankles. I waited, knowing he was building the words.

Eventually, he started. "You've met a guy I work with, Andy Bentley?"

I gave it some thought. "Sure. The bald guy with the Fu Manchu and the attitude." I let that sit. "The jerk."

Chris let out a bark of laughter. "You are an excellent judge of character."

"What about him?"

One long pause. "He's taking bribes. From coyotes. Or from one, at least. I'd been suspicious for a few months and then heard him getting a message that a group of crossers were coming through the fence. Andy didn't know I'd heard. When we started to patrol, he directed us away from the spot of crossing."

My first reaction was to gasp, say "oh my god," and tell him he had to report this immediately. I held my breath while I searched for the right words. Then quietly said, "Are you going to turn him in?"

He stared at the ripples from our feet. "Yeah. Of course."

"But?"

He didn't look at me. "He's my friend. We've worked together for a long time. He's got kids and a wife. Turning him in would destroy his life."

"What he's doing is destroying others' lives."

"It's not like Andy's letting drugs cross."

"That's stupid—"

He didn't let me go on. "Yeah. I know. If I turn him in, it's going to bring a lot of attention to the patrol. People hate us enough as it is."

I kept the roil of emotions from coming out, sounding calmer than I felt. "You're more concerned with protecting the reputation of the Border Patrol than protecting people being harmed by human trafficking?"

He splashed. "No. You asked why I've been upset, I answered you. I'm going to report him. But I want to find a way to do it that won't do so much damage."

"Damage to your career?"

He turned to me. "Yeah. When I turn Andy in, I'm pretty much done. No one on the patrol will trust me."

He feared losing his job and yet, he just bought an expensive truck. He was suffering some kind of crisis, obviously. I'd have to find some way to help him, but for now, listening was the only thing I could do. "Can you do it anonymously?"

He stretched his neck. "I'm sorry to throw this on you. Try to forget about it, okay? I'll figure it out." He pulled his feet out of the pool and stood up. "I've gotta go. Going to meet some of the guys for a drink at the Hot Spot."

I followed him to the back door, our wet footprints tracking on the pool deck. "Tell Fritz hi." I wanted to say a lot more. Starting with, "I'll go with you to turn Andy in." Or ,"I'll turn him in." Or, "How can you just go out and have a beer or two with your buddies when your partner is doing this?"

Who was I to question Chris? He'd do the right thing.

Of course he would.

4

Deon left before the girls got up, so I again dodged the discussion about the tear gas at the protest. When I checked online, I saw the story hit the front page of the paper. The picture they used must have been taken by one of the students, no doubt culled from many, to capture Chris's expression of fury. The good news was that only my arm and a bit of my black uniform leg showed as I piloted Dr. Bartholomew down the hall.

I dropped the kids at school, my stomach tightening into a hard lump. Meeting Jared at the hotel sounded awful. We'd worked together years earlier and I knew him to be stubborn and single-minded. After a few months of this flirting thing, or whatever I called it, sending him a text message wouldn't be enough to stop him.

I'd meet him, break it off, give him time to curse me, and then I'd be out of there for good. I'd let this thing go too long. It's not as if I didn't know what he wanted and where he thought we were heading. I'm no psychologist, but it doesn't take one to understand I was thrill-seeking. Taking risks was not new to me. This time, though, I was gambling something too important.

For once I didn't mind hitting every stop light on my drive from north Tucson to the hotel in the south. I needed to get this over with. Rip the bandage off quickly. Jared had texted me the room number on the second floor. I parked the Pilot behind a semi in back and entered into the side door. Queasy and with leaden feet, I climbed the stairs and thudded down the hall, skirting the housekeeping cart. A young Latina vacuumed the floor while the TV inside was turned to cartoons.

As a teen, I'd worked housekeeping at a hotel. It wasn't a great job, but it paid for food and gas and my small expenses. At that time, I had no kids, no career, no husband, and only school to worry about. Returning to that time sounded good. But this young woman probably wasn't working for spending money. Vacuuming a hotel room only *looked* simple.

I stopped in front of the door, so tense my shoulders ached. I watched my fist come up as if in slow motion and I rapped the door with three quick flicks.

Jared whisked open the door. He wore his TPD uniform, but his utility belt was missing. Dark hair, the waves careless and natural, the cleft chin giving him the look of chiseled strength. And the eyes, blue as the aquamarine earrings Deon had given me last Christmas.

Deon.

Jared may be taller, more dangerous, and handsome as a movie hero. But he wasn't Deon. Not the father of my daughters. The man who had slept beside me for fourteen years.

Jared pulled me inside the room. The door closed but he didn't let me farther into the room. "You don't know how long I've waited for this," he said, breathless.

The hotel room smelled of cleaning detergent and slightly musty air from windows that didn't open. The air conditioning kicked and clattered, sending waves of chilly air across the garish bedspread.

I held my hand up. "Talk. We're only here to talk."

Jared grinned, straight white teeth and sparkling eyes. "Right. Talk." He stepped back and tugged at his uniform shirt to untuck it.

No. I do not want this. And yet, that thrill burst through me. The devil on my shoulder whispered that no one would ever know. Deon's face faded and Jared's eyes told me how much he wanted me.

"What the hell is going on here?" A shout outside the room felt like a bucket of ice water.

A quieter woman's voice answered. She sounded scared. "*Disculpame. No quise molestarte. Es mi hijo.*"

"Jesus. Can't speak English. You come to our country and take our jobs, the least you can do is learn the damned language. Do you even have a green card or whatever?" A bang hit the side of the wall.

It must be the woman with the vacuum. And some stupid American jerk.

Jared leaned in, apparently ignoring the commotion in the hall and intending to kiss me.

I pushed him away, already moving toward the door.

"Hey, what are you doing?" Jared reached for me.

I brushed his hand away, the spell broken. Anger flashed—at me, at Jared, but mostly at the asshole in the hallway who thought it was okay to treat another human being worse than a stray dog.

Jared tried again. "Don't get in the middle of that."

Outside the door, the woman spoke again. "*Solo estoy limpiando el cuarto. Toque pero no contestaste.*"

I closed my hand on the doorknob. "This is bullshit." I jerked open the door.

The man stood in a crisp button-down with a tie twisted loosely around his neck, as if he'd dropped it mid-knot. He wore dress trousers and smelled of newly applied aftershave or cologne, Whatever, it was too strong and cloying. His brown hair was slicked back in *Wolf of Wall Street* power style. Even if I hadn't heard him through the door, I'd have been repulsed.

The woman's hands rested on the head of a little boy behind her back, as if she'd placed herself in the direct line of fire to protect him. The boy clutched a Batman action figure that looked as though it had crossed the desert on foot.

The woman's dark eyes shone with tears. "*Lo siento. El no es problema. No tenía un lugar para que se quedara hoy. Por favor, no le digas al jefe.*"

He glanced at me when I stepped into the hall and back at the woman, dismissing me in my T-shirt dress and flip-flops.

Bad day to underestimate me, pal. I took two steps until I stood directly in front of him. "What's your problem, Skippy?"

Surprise. Guess he didn't think a little lady would confront him about a worthless *senorita*. He opened his mouth but didn't say anything.

He had two inches and more than a few pounds on me. Pounds he probably kept firm with a fancy gym membership at one of those places where trainers yell at you. I raised my chin and stepped even closer. "This woman is doing her job. She said she knocked and you didn't answer."

He recovered but went on the defensive. "When did she say that?"

"Since you chose to have this battle in the hall, I heard her politely explain it to you."

He raised his lips in a sneer. "Oh, you mean that gibberish she was spouting trying to save her ass."

"I mean that very understandable Spanish she calmly used instead of calling you the flaming asshole you clearly are."

He took a closer look at me, probably deciding he had the upper hand. "This is none of your business, honey."

"Think again. I'm an Arizona Ranger. I carry a gun. I'm authorized to arrest you or maybe shoot you if you pose a threat to others." Well, I would have been carrying a gun if I wore my uniform.

He laughed. "Well, I don't know where you're hiding your gun, baby. But if you are a ranger, you're supposed to protect citizens, and my guess is that Consuela here isn't a citizen."

Who needed a gun? I grabbed the guy's shirt front and slammed him against the wall, letting his head bounce behind him. Before he could get his wits and use his strength and weight against me, I grabbed his arm and swung it around, making him face away and wrenching his arm up. That smashed his cheek against the wall. When I thought he'd gained some respect, I pulled him back and marched him to the open door of his room.

"Finish primping for your business meeting and check out. I'm not going to haul you in for harassing this woman and we'll call this good. I think you've learned your lesson."

I gave him a light shove and pulled the door closed. The woman stood rooted in the hallway in front of the housekeeping cart, the little boy still behind her. Round dark eyes showed her fear and shock.

Time to get her out of there. I hurried to her and searched the cart to find the complementary pens and note paper. "I'm sure he's going to call the manager or the cops or something. Anyway, you're probably done here."

Tears stood in the woman's uncomprehending eyes.

Damn. Slow down. I struggled to translate. Understanding was so much easier than speaking. It came out halting and more like a fourth grader would speak. In Spanish I said—or hoped I said, "I'm sorry. I think I lost your job. Here is a phone number. We can get you help. Go now."

The woman, now shaking and holding back tears, took the paper. "*Gracias.*"

"*Lo siento.* Go, hurry."

I slipped back into the room before Mr. Wall Street charged back out of his.

Jared stood in front of the bed. He'd removed his T-shirt to reveal his muscular chest, looking every bit as sexy as I'd imagined. "What was that about?"

I pointed at the door. Not sure if I was more upset about the incident or Jared bare-chested. "You heard it. He was abusing her. And that little boy."

"But it wasn't your problem."

Really? "And why are you a cop? Because wearing a uniform gets you laid? Come on, Jared. She needed help."

"I thought you wanted to keep this ..." He pointed to me and him and back to me. "... discreet. If you go inserting yourself into fights with hotel patrons and employees, it's likely someone is going to wonder what you're doing here."

"There's nothing here to keep discreet. We aren't doing anything, and we won't be. Ever."

Jared exhaled in frustration. "Come on." He moved closer and lowered his voice to a caress. "I'm sorry. Let's just try to forget it and start over."

Here came the guilt in a rush so violent I wanted to throw up. "No. I came here to tell you I can't do this. It was a mistake."

His mouth dropped open. "What? After all this time, the back and forth, you finally say yes and now, because some illegal gets in trouble, you're ready to quit before it even starts?"

"It's never what I wanted. I don't know why I let it come to this, but it's over now."

He stared at me, clearly building steam to argue.

I'd done some stupid things in my life. But this time, I'd stepped way over the line. And for what? There was no denying Jared was handsome. Funny. Smart. Actually, he was everything that would be great in a guy.

Except I had Deon. And a life. Quiet. Safe. But a real life. No matter how many wonderful qualities Jared tallied on his side, he'd never measure up to what I had in my own home. In my own bed. "Don't call me anymore. We're done." I reached for the door.

"Come on. Talk to me. What did I do wrong?"

I stopped for a moment and looked up at him. His sincere blue eyes, his hair that begged for fingers to run through it. "Look. I'm sorry." I'd said that to the woman in the hallway, too. Always sorry. "I was wrong. And this is wrong."

He shook his head. "We've known each other for a long time. This isn't just a whim. At least not for me."

What a mess I'd made of things. Not the first time. Maybe I could fix it, or at least stop it before it did more damage. "We've been friends. And I don't regret that. I know you don't understand, but I love Deon. This would kill him."

"But you walking away now might kill me."

Damn it. Who thought he'd take it this seriously? "Did you really think it would lead to something more?"

Jared stepped close to me and leaned me back toward the mirror over the dresser. "Okay. For now. I won't bother you. But you're going to have to talk to me, Michaela. Or maybe I should talk to Deon."

I pushed him away, palms connecting with the heat of his bare chest. In three strides I stood in the hallway with the door slamming closed behind me.

What have I done?

5

I might have sat in the hotel parking lot all day if Ann hadn't called and wondered why I wasn't at the center. She told me my friend Jamie, who worked in a youth program, needed my help. Worrying about Jared wasn't doing any good. He was upset and embarrassed at being rejected. He'd get over it. Right? Nothing to do but go about my regular day.

In twenty minutes I pulled up in front of Mi Casa, a nonprofit that assisted immigrants. Ann bought the old stucco office building for a song ten years ago and had been repairing and fixing it up ever since. She lived for her passion to help the immigrants who rotated in and out of her world. I envied that purpose in her life. In a rough southeast neighborhood in Tucson, the center fronted a busy street with a small blacktop parking lot that didn't add a lot of curb appeal. It was built in a U shape with the base facing the street and the legs running back to create an open plaza protected from the noise and bustle of the busy avenue.

Ann and her husband, Fritz, owned a slump-block house behind Mi Casa, separated by a decrepit wooden fence that tended to fall in strong winds.

I opened the tailgate of the Pilot and reached inside for the flats of bottled water and juice I'd purchased for the center. The lobby provided relief from the blaring sunshine when I stepped through the glass door and into a large room. At some point, it probably housed the receptionist desk for a group of dentists or doctors. Or maybe a real estate firm. Now the linoleum-tiled room contained a low table for kids, some toys and craft materials, a few chairs and café tables, and several secondhand bits and pieces of living room furniture. It served as the hangout for the center, and right now it bustled with noise and activity. Two young women sat at the table speaking rapid Spanish. Three young children created their own chaos with the toys and games. The back doors were propped wide to catch a breeze from the courtyard.

"*Buenos dias,*" I said.

The two women stiffened and offered wary smiles and their eyes flicked to their children.

Jamie Butler rounded a corner from the wing of offices, her face serious, as usual. "There you are." She rushed over and slid the top layer of drinks into her arms and took off for the kitchen along the same hallway she'd emerged from. "I'm trying to get two students enrolled for high school but we're having trouble with the paperwork. They don't understand the questions and I can't understand their answers. I need you to interpret."

Jamie could be abrupt, but I'd liked her from the first time we'd worked together as Arizona Rangers. Jamie and I had both started our careers as cops, Jamie in Buffalo and me in Tucson. She'd left the Rangers a while ago. Like Ann, she'd found her passion and I appreciated her devotion. "I'm at your disposal."

The two kids, a sister and brother from Guatemala, had arrived a week ago. They wore clothes donated to Mi Casa and sat close together on the cracked vinyl couch. Ann had found a dishwasher job for their mother and was working on housing for the family of five. She'd called Jamie in to help get the teens into school.

My Spanish was serviceable, and it wasn't the first language of their tiny village, but we muddled through and they even loosened up enough to laugh at a few misunderstandings. It took over an hour to complete the forms and they left with anxious faces. Their futures opened with opportunity but also terrifying unknowns. I walked Jamie to the door.

"How are things with the Rangers?" she asked.

"Good. Fine." Even to me, it sounded like a discontented sigh.

She smiled, something she did more frequently than she used to. "That isn't exactly enthusiastic."

"It's fine. The same stuff. Courthouse security, crowd control."

She hesitated, as if wondering how to continue. "It's a way to fill up your time doing something worthwhile."

"Keeps me out of trouble."

She studied me for a moment. "Why not go back to the force? We've talked about it, how much we both loved being cops."

That old flame flared, but I snuffed it out. "Yeah, but I love Deon more. He hated it when I was a cop. He worried all the time. And the kids need me to be around."

She stopped at the door. "Your kids are in school most of the day. Seeing a mother engaged in life and doing a job she loves wouldn't damage them."

I didn't want to talk about me. "Do you miss it still?"

Her face softened. "Sometimes. But what I'm doing now is good, too."

I nodded. "See? Life's full of hard choices. Can't do it all."

She didn't look convinced. "I've got to run. Talk about mom duty. Cali is performing in a spring concert and she forgot her dress. And I'm meeting Rafe for a quick bite before it starts."

I watched out the glass door as Jamie rushed to her car. These last few months had transformed her from a shut-off woman who barely opened her mouth to an almost vibrant person caring for a teenager and having a relationship with one of my old friends.

This thing with Jared had given me a little lift like that. The feeling of something new and exciting. As long as it stayed with flirting, I'd reasoned, we weren't doing any harm. Except, I knew better. Why would I even risk the good life I had? What the hell was wrong with me?

"Mike." Ann's voice broke through my recriminations.

I swung around and walked to my sister's office. She occupied command central right off the lobby. From there, if her door remained open, as it usually was, she had a view of the common room and the front door. She sat behind a banged-up desk in an L shape. I was sure she rescued it from the sidewalk in front of someone's house. A couple of folding six-foot tables, another Costco purchase from me, lined two walls. Every surface held stacks of papers and folders, bankers boxes and binders.

Ann couldn't ride a bike or even walk across a room unaided, but she could run a marathon of paperwork for the people who came to her for help. She was a wizard at stretching a buck, convincing people to open their pocketbooks, and pulling strings. The good work she did at Mi Casa was nothing short of magic.

"What's new?" I said, plopping into a folding chair opposite her desk.

She shoved back from her desk and reached for her crutches. I knew better than to offer help. "Come look at this monstrosity Fritz is building in the backyard."

It took some time for her to work her way from her office and through the lobby, pausing to talk to the two mothers there. I didn't rush her as we trundled out the door, across the central area half planted in a garden and half open for a playground.

I unfastened the gate in the wobbly fence and held it open for her. She rested on her crutches and cocked her head to the mess in her backyard.

It hadn't been much of a yard, just a patch of browning, scruffy grass fighting for life in hard ground. But now, most of the space was taken up with a swimming pool. At least, it resembled a pool but not one I'd ever seen before. The walls of the pool stood five feet high and a ladder with a small platform created a lopsided A over the side.

"What's this?" Chris and I had pitched in to buy Ann a small above-ground pool because her doctor thought it would delay the atrophy of her leg muscles.

"My pool," she said, dripping with irritation.

With the pool so large, the walls had a kind of brace every five feet or so, constructed of rough lumber nailed at messy angles. It had a homemade, cobbled-together look. "But it's only supposed to be fifteen feet diameter," I said.

"Fritz had a better idea." She stared at it. "He thought we needed a bigger pool. So instead of using the money you gave for what you picked out, he found this one on Craigslist."

I walked toward the pool. A garden hose snaked up from the ground and over the side. Water filled it halfway. It looked deeper inside than outside. "Is it ...? Oh my gosh, he dug it into the ground."

She closed her eyes and her mouth tensed. "I wanted a small pool for physical therapy. Fritz decided to jerry-rig me this monstrosity deep enough to 'be a real pool,' as he says. Basically, it will be over my head. He just scraped it out, didn't even level it."

I tried not to laugh. "He's only trying to make you happy."

"Or kill me. I won't be able to touch the bottom."

"You know, you don't have to fill it all the way."

She frowned. "I suggested that. But Fritz is set on doing it his way."

"That's motivation to keep swimming."

She huffed. "Don't try to defend him. He got carried away and now he won't admit it's a mistake."

"I know we didn't give you enough money to pay for this. We can put more down. How much is it?"

She waved that away. "No way. You and Chris are not going to pay for what Fritz has done. Besides, we got a nice donation, so maybe I'll take a salary for the next couple of months."

A rustling directly behind me made me jump and whirl around, ready to pull Ann out of the way. Grow up on the desert and you learn not to hesitate when you hear something slither close by.

A man stood silently, no expression on his face.

My laugh sounded nervous. "Efrain. You scared me."

Efrain worked for Ann. He'd been at Mi Casa for close to ten years, about the time they'd bought Mi Casa, and certainly since he was old enough to earn a paycheck. He had a room in the center that kept him on site for when anything broke down. Since Fritz ran a bar and Ann couldn't do much maintenance, he was a godsend.

Much like Jamie, Efrain was socially challenged. Unlike Jamie, though, I'd never felt relaxed around him. Ann relied on him and he seemed always willing to help her, so that was good enough for me. We didn't need to be buddies.

Ann's face lit up. "I'm glad you're here. Can you fix that ladder so it will be longer on one side than the other? Fritz dug that pool three feet below ground level for the extra depth, but he didn't think about making the ladder work."

Efrain nodded. He reached into the back pocket of his baggy jeans and pulled out a phone. "You can give this back to Fritz."

Ann shook her head. "He got it for you."

Efrain looked at it. "I do not need it. It is hard to make work." He spoke English with a thick accent. I thought it might be because he hardly said anything, so didn't have much chance to practice.

Ann spoke gently. "He said it's for you in case I need you."

"I am always here," he said simply.

She softened. "Yes. But he worries about me. You keep it. Maybe bring it on Sunday and Mike's girls can show you how to work it. Kids know everything."

Efrain looked doubtful, but he put the phone back into his pocket and walked over to look into the pool. He cast Ann a worried expression then pulled the ladder from the side and hefted it over his head. He walked through the gate toward Mi Casa without another word.

"He always seems so sad," I said.

Ann gave me a disbelieving look. "Sad? No. He's shy. He's uncomfortable around white people."

"You and Fritz are white."

"Yes, but he's known us so long we're family."

Okay. But he'd known me a long time, too. Deon wasn't white and Efrain acted as weird around him as he did me.

Ann's next question distracted me from speculating about Efrain. "Do you think something's wrong with Chris?"

My knee-jerk reaction to cover for Chris kicked in. "No. Why do you ask?"

She leaned heavier on her crutches and I started to walk toward her patio chairs, hoping she'd follow.

She clumped after me. "Fritz said Chris has been hanging around the Hot Spot more than usual. Says he's acting weird."

We made it to the chairs and I took her crutches and set them on the ground while she sat, then dropped into a chair beside her. "Chris is a weird guy. Probably just stress at work." Big stress. Like whether he's going to have a job when he does the right thing.

"Could you quit protecting him and have an honest discussion for once?"

"There's nothing to protect him about. I haven't noticed he's any different than usual."

She shook her head in annoyance. "We have no idea what he does when he's on patrol. I've heard stories from the people here. The Border Patrol has done some horrendous things to these helpless immigrants."

"Not Chris."

"How can you defend him without even considering it?"

Now I was getting mad. "Because he's Chris and I know him."

"That's just it. We don't know him. He's been working out there for years. We don't know what he's seen that might have affected him. Changed him from a decent human into a violent man."

I opened my mouth to blast her, but a movement at the pool drew our attention. Splashes and a squawk came from below the side.

Ann braced her hands on the chair handles and tried to push herself up. "A bird's in the pool!"

I jumped and ran. In a moment I was at the pool, trying to reach over the wall to help the panicking creature that looked like a Gila cactus wren. He fluttered away from my grasping hand. With no ladder and the bird flailing helplessly, I grabbed the flimsy wall and hoisted myself up and in the water.

The pool's bottom was uneven and I imagined Fritz had rented a tractor, scooped dirt any old way, and laid the pool liner down. That was typical for Fritz. He meant well, but Fritz wasn't known as a detail guy.

It took a few minutes and several attempts to scoop the bird out. He landed in the dirt by the pool and lay there, his little heart beating hard enough for me to see. By that time, Ann swayed on her crutches next to the pool.

I climbed out, my clothes dripping and my hair wet. If the shock of the cold water hadn't numbed me, Ann's words might have.

"This pool is a killer."

6

I left in plenty of time the next day to make up for the mid-morning congestion caused by the book festival. One of the perks of being a cop was not having to contend with parking at events. When you had a light bar and a city seal on the side of your car, you got to park wherever you wanted. Not so if you wore an Arizona Rangers uniform. I found parking in a public garage a few blocks from the University of Arizona campus and resigned myself to the walk.

The Tucson Festival of Books filled the university outdoor mall with an army of white tents. Meandering people packed the walks, soaking up the sunshine and the offerings of every kind of book known to mankind. Not only books, but food booths with all the usual carnival fare.

My partner for the day, Gordy, and I met up at the Student Union. The whole campus popped and spread at the seams with people. Maybe some of them came for the food or the entertainment. But the majority of people —the paper estimated 100,000 each day—came for books. All those doom-sayers who said reading was dead ought to have been out patrolling this festival. Booths stretched along both sides of a wide grass mall down one side and up the other with more booths stuffed in the middle. Sure, many of the vendors had little to do with books, being the usual tradeshow type selling water systems or subscriptions to environmental protection nonprofits. But the majority of sellers left little doubt this place would make book lovers swoon with joy.

"Manuel Ortiz is speaking in the Latino Celebration tent. I think we should check it out. It's at the east end," I said to Gordy. The last thing I wanted to see was that face again, but if there was going to be trouble at the book festival, that's where it would be.

Gordy heaved his belly up and let it down in a heavy sigh. "Clear at the other end. Of course."

We started winding our way through meandering groups. Some nibbled elote—Mexican grilled corn on the cob—some sipped straws stuffed in giant cups or licked ice cream or shaved ice. It was like filtering through a midway at a state fair. I watched for anything unusual since I was on patrol, and resisted stopping to flip through some of the more interesting titles. It amazed me how many people milled around paging through the books on display.

There was no doubt we'd made it to our destination when we saw a knot of people spilling from the tent into the bright sunshine. The sun blasted, as it often did in early March. Festival goers wore everything from jeans and sweaters to sundresses and shorts. Plus I saw the occasional costume from entertainers or those selling kids' books.

As we approached, the mumbles and distortions from the mic came into focus and Ortiz's clear rhetoric floated out. "You want to build a wall to keep people out. They're not coming to rob you. They're fleeing very bad circumstances, poverty and violence. And they're met with hostility. Families are torn apart. Children are taken from parents and shoved into foster homes."

We pushed to the back of the crowd next to the tent walls and because of our uniforms, people squeezed together enough for us to get a look inside the big tent. An older woman with a fluff of white hair like dandelion seeds put a hand on the slumped old man next to her. His pot belly hung over khaki shorts, his white socks and tennis shoes completing the typical snowbird uniform. I moved closer behind them, keeping an eye on the tightly packed rows of folding chairs filled with the audience.

Manuel Ortiz stood at a podium with a moderator seated at his left. He wore a crisp white shirt and jeans, an enormous turquoise medallion hung from his neck and a wide silver band circled his wrist. Dark-skinned, with thick black hair, he looked like a Latino JFK with all the legendary charisma. He held the crowd inside the tent mesmerized. Those on the periphery in the sunshine, maybe not so much.

The old woman said to her husband, "It breaks my heart to think of those poor children. I can't imagine what it's like to have your babies taken away and you don't know where they are."

He shook his head. "No one invited them to enter this country illegally. They knew the risks."

I tried not to hear their discussion. The words from the loudspeaker rolled over the gathering congregation and those on the outside provided a low undertow of comments to everything he said.

"One of the largest holding facilities in the country is only a few miles from here. In Eloy. They keep thousands of immigrants locked up without proper medical care or decent food. The inside temperatures are held in the sixties and these people, women and young girls, are not allowed their jackets or even blankets."

Across the tent a tall blond man caught my eye. With his aviator sunglasses, he looked confident and defiant. Damn it. Chris. He shouldn't be here. I backed out of the tent, made my way behind the listeners, and wedged through the bodies to stand next to my brother.

I tugged on his arm. "What the hell are you doing here?"

He seemed surprised to see me, but not in a happy way. Under his breath he grumbled, "Do you believe this guy?"

I slapped at his arm because I had to whisper and couldn't shout at him. "You shouldn't be here. What's wrong with you?"

"I didn't plan to be here. That would be your sister's fault."

"That would be *our* sister."

He pointed into the tent.

Sure enough. Ann sat in her wheelchair in front of the podium.

I turned back to Chris with a questioning look. "I thought she hated him as much as we do."

His lip turned up in disgust as he eyed Ortiz. "That was before his pro-immigration campaign. She asked me for a ride here without telling me why she wanted to come."

"Why didn't she have Efrain drive her?"

He didn't take his eyes off Ortiz. "Maybe he was busy. My guess is because she wanted me to listen to Ortiz and change my heart."

That sounded like Ann. "Is it working?"

He spared a scowl for me. "I don't want to see children separated from their parents. Ann thinks the Border Patrol is the enemy here. But we're only trying to enforce the law. It's not my fault those countries are corrupt and dangerous, and people are fleeing."

A man standing along the tent wall a few rows up from me, in jeans and a long-sleeved T-shirt, squared his shoulders and drew in a breath. It appeared as though he was about to give Ortiz his opinion.

I looked for Gordy to see if he noticed. No Gordy. He'd probably gone for nachos or maybe found a shady spot to wait me out.

This is the kind of thing the Rangers had been sent to stop. We were supposed to keep order and make sure everyone had a good time. I left Chris and wormed my way forward, quickly moving around the couple in front of me. "Excuse me."

Manuel Ortiz said, "The structure of racism in this country must be dismantled. We need to quit rewarding white skin and punishing darker hues."

Heads nodded and an enthusiastic applause waved out of the tent to end in a smattering of claps on the mall. There didn't seem to be much dissent except the guy I was trying to reach. His vision lasered on Ortiz and he almost panted.

Ortiz was talking to a crowd of mostly liberal, well-heeled retirees. I'd wager many of them hired lawn services and housecleaning from immigrants, legal or illegal. They probably felt guilty about it, but also sanctimonious for giving them a job.

"The question you need to ask yourself is: What are you willing to give up for equality?"

Again, more applause. The man cupped his hands around his mouth and sucked in a breath to propel his voice. I landed my hand on his arm and he turned a startled face to see me in my uniform. He didn't resist as I applied pressure and lowered his arms.

Ortiz drilled an intense gaze into the audience. "Would you give up your home to an immigrant family? Would you pay more taxes to ensure that the underprivileged got education, health care, housing? Would you sponsor a family and pay for their support while they settled into our city?"

Less applause but he still had the crowd.

"How about putting water on the desert so those desperate to come to this land of supposed opportunity won't die. Will you show up at the Border Patrol holding facility and protest? Will you do whatever it takes to stop the Border Patrol from deporting and separating families?"

Ortiz's speech had strayed from the normal talk of helping immigrants and seemed to be heading into a call for action.

"I say to you, if you're not willing to put aside your safety and luxury to help these people, you are nothing but a bunch of white, privileged hypocrites."

Someone hooted in enthusiasm, but there was a definite amount of uncomfortable shifting going on. The crowd outside the tent had grown silent. Tension rose like an unpleasant odor.

"Does that make you cringe? It should. I'm telling you, we need to quit being patient while people in power are gunning down children at the border. Filling them with bullets because they tossed a rock over the fence. If they are shooting at us, why are we answering with lawsuits and legislation? This is war. And if you're not with us, you're against us."

A few more people held up fists and shouted. Most everyone else seemed to shrink. Some looked around as if planning escape. A few of those outside the tent walked away. Others took a step back.

Chris slipped forward into the middle of a row.

I wanted to keep him from opening his mouth, but I didn't have time to get to him.

"Mr. Ortiz, you can't be calling for violence against the Border Patrol? Do you seriously think the men and women who put themselves on the line to protect the United States from invasion deserve an armed militia out to gun them down?"

This stupid outburst of his might lead to another spate of death threats to add to those from last year. They may not bother Chris, but they scared the hell out of me. All it took was for one of them to be true.

If I could only get to him, make him stop talking. But too many people stood between us and now it was too late. As much as I wanted to throw myself between Chris and Ortiz, I could only watch, like a spectator witnessing a car on a railroad tracks with the engine bearing down, the horn blaring.

Manuel Ortiz squinted to the back of the tent to see the man who spoke. When he recognized my brother, he sneered. "Chris Wright. Protector of the United States, mouthpiece for the new KKK, what he likes to call the Border Patrol. But more accurately, it's the Death Patrol."

I spun around and ran into a pack of onlookers. Whatever happened next, I needed to stand with Chris. That idiot.

The moderator rose to the podium and nudged Ortiz aside. She spoke loudly into the mic. "Looks like our time is up." She sounded rattled. "Manuel Ortiz's new book is *Border War*. He'll be signing at the Koffler patio immediately after this."

Someone said, "Hey, we have fifteen minutes left. What about the Q&A?"

Manuel Ortiz and Chris held eye contact, as if a whole tent of grumbling book lovers and activists didn't sit between them.

Chris's voice rose above the rustling. "The Border Patrol is here for your protection. Not everyone crossing the border is an asylum seeker. There are drugs, human trafficking, terrorists. We're doing our best to keep the citizens safe. Not to mention saving the lives of illegal crossers who are dying in the desert because people like you are encouraging them."

People stopped talking to hear Chris's train wreck.

Ortiz rose to the challenge. "Is that so? You are helpful and altruistic. What about those who abuse their power? The officers who use excessive force? Those taking kickbacks from the cartels?"

Trained spokesman that he was, Chris displayed none of the temper from the classroom a couple of days ago. He'd come expecting this confrontation and had prepared for it. "You know as well as I do that no organization is perfect. But what you're talking about is rare at the Border Patrol."

Ortiz had worked himself up and spittle flew. "Why are you hiding behind official lines and smiles? Rare? Ask those poor immigrants who have been beaten for requesting water. Ask Andy Bentley. What are the perks of his position?"

I had one second to witness Chris's face drain of color before the troublemaker I'd hushed earlier erupted. Using his hands as a megaphone he shouted, "Go home. We didn't invite you here and we don't want you."

The tent exploded with shouting. People rose, mostly to flee, but some seemed to be making their way inside. There's always someone ready to throw a punch. I shouted, "Stay calm. Everyone calm down."

In the jumble of bodies, I searched for Chris. He stood where he'd been. Our eyes connected and a jolt hit me at the accusation in his. His jaw twitched and he spun around, striding past confused people.

I grabbed the arm of the man who started the melee. "Make a peep and I'll arrest you."

He took me at my word. Since most people were here to read books and not fight or form a demonstration, the crowd thinned quickly. Visible in my uniform, I convinced others to move along. Gordy, back from whatever he'd been doing before all this started, stood close to the opening of the tent, urging people to leave.

I looked around for Ann. She seemed safe enough by the empty podium, though she looked upset. The next event wouldn't start for another twenty minutes and the tent seemed much bigger without the people crammed inside.

Where were Chris and Ortiz? What had happened here? I didn't think it likely Chris had turned Andy in and that Ortiz had found out so quickly. Someone besides Chris must have known and told Ortiz. Gordy stood in the mall about fifteen feet outside the tent, making sure any lingering audience didn't stir up animosity among themselves. But people had dispersed.

Manuel Ortiz was long gone, spirited away to his book signing, no doubt. No sign of Chris with Ann sitting in her wheelchair. I walked up to her and took hold of the handles of her chair. "That was fun."

I couldn't see her face but could tell by her voice that her lips were pursed. "That fool. It's not enough he runs all over the desert chasing innocent women and children. Or that he's an apologist of the Border Patrol. But he's got to disrupt a civilized speech at the book festival for heaven's sake."

I pushed her out of the tent, not easy on the grass. "Ortiz was calling for violence against the patrol."

She waved her hand. "He wasn't. Chris is too sensitive."

I stood with Chris on this one but arguing would do no good. "I have a couple of hours left in my shift. I can give you a ride home after that. I'll leave you at the union."

"Where's Chris?" She didn't see any irony in having him do her the favor of driving her home. "Actually, will you take me to Koffler so Manuel can sign my book?"

"No, Ann. I will not wheel you over to let you get a book signed by a man who is out to destroy our brother." I kept pushing her toward the union, glad I didn't need to see her face.

She grabbed the wheels of her chair, slowing it down, and twisted to look at me. "Did it occur to you Chris and the Border Patrol might be wrong?"

I took my hands off the chair. "I love Chris. I love you. We're the Tamutals. Period. I refuse to get in the middle of this fight." Maybe by invoking the name of our childhood club I could make my point.

She seemed satisfied with that. "Good. Then take me to Koffler."

Gordy waved at me from the mall. I waved back, put my hands on the wheelchair, and changed directions to Koffler. I knew where I stood on this. Manuel Ortiz was a dick for attacking my brother and I hated him. But I didn't want Ann making decisions for me, so who was I to make them for her? "I'm not waiting for you to get your autograph. Call when you're ready to go back to the union."

It wasn't as hard maneuvering the wheelchair across campus as I expected. Mostly, when people saw us coming, they made room. Ortiz's line snaked across the covered portico of the massive building and I positioned Ann at the end. "Have fun."

Not that I wanted another glance, but I couldn't keep from giving Ortiz a deadly glare. Next to an inset doorway, a familiar figure standing in the far shadows made me focus.

Efrain stared at the back of Ortiz. This might be a good solution to Ann's problem of having to wait around for my shift to end. Without waiting to talk to her, I rounded the author's signing table and bee-lined for

Efrain. He must have noticed someone coming toward him with purpose because he shifted his attention to me. His eyes widened and he stepped back as if I'd scared him.

"Efrain. Are you here for the festival?" Stupid question, but I didn't really know how to get started with him.

He looked at his scruffy tennis shoes. "I came for a little while. Yes. I'm leaving soon."

Exactly what I wanted to hear. "Going back to Mi Casa?"

He nodded. I didn't think Efrain had a car, but Ann often had him drive the center's old van. I wasn't sure he had a license because I wasn't sure he was legal. But I never asked. "If you drove, would you mind taking Ann home? Chris brought her but he had to leave."

Efrain's gaze sought out Ann in line. "Yes. I will do it."

Okay then. Guess there was no small talk or passing the time with Efrain. I nodded. "Well, thanks."

He didn't answer and I left him as I usually did, feeling slightly on edge.

7

I found Gordy by the smoothie stand. He'd taken advantage of his uniform and slid up front to get a free drink. He met me at the side of the snaking line, ignoring the dirty looks from those who'd been waiting in the hot sun. "Want me to get you one?"

I pulled my monitor from my pocket and checked my blood sugar. In the last few months I'd become much less self-conscious about my diabetes. I'd rather have someone see me with the monitor than suffer another seizure in public. It looked fine. I reached for a bottle of water from my utility belt. "Gonna stick with water."

He gave me an innocent look. "I guess the important thing is to stay hydrated. I prefer mine with some flavor, that's all."

"No judgement." A lie, since I noted his growing spare tire.

We patrolled for over an hour, winding our way through the crowds, watching snippets of entertainment in the outdoor venues. The smell of kettle corn and grilled meat wafted around us in mid-eighties heat. People seemed happy and interested in the offerings, tent after tent of books on display, authors peddling like carnival barkers. The kids' area rang with shrieks and laughter as magicians and storybook characters wandered the mall.

I couldn't get the look on Chris's face out of my mind. He didn't think I had anything to do with Ortiz's knowing about Andy, did he? But it's the only thing that had changed since I'd talked to him by the pool. We had family dinner tomorrow at Ann's. I'd corner him then.

Gordy sampled a few more treats, including fresh-squeezed lemonade and a plate of tamales. I joined him for the lemonade, careful to keep my blood sugar in balance.

Gordy and I helped one five-year-old boy relocate his frantic mother and fetched bottled water for an elderly woman who looked like she was about to pass out. Other than that, the duty wasn't pressing.

When I'd first joined the police force, Rafe Grijalva, my mentor, told me the job was 90 percent boring and 10 percent "oh shit." The Arizona Rangers was more 95.5 percent boring and 4.5 percent running errands for the real cops. It's not that I minded patrolling the book festival or any of the other jobs they sent us on, it's that I missed the thrill of being a cop. When your life hangs in the balance, you really feel alive.

Deon, on the other hand, seemed perfectly content to play it safe. He didn't understand that adrenaline rush. And definitely didn't think it was worth risking the life of the mother of his children.

There are worse things than being loved and needed by a successful and caring man.

"Come on back to Tucson, Michaela." Gordy tapped my shoulder.

I grinned. "Right here, Captain."

Like many of the Arizona Rangers, Gordy was retired military. He'd sold insurance for most of his career, but after he and his bride of forty years packed it up in Wisconsin and hauled themselves and their motor home to Tucson, she'd insisted he find something to occupy his time.

We rounded the corner in the children's area and were met by a squeal of excitement and barreled into by Sami. "Mommy!" Sami threw herself into my arms. She stood back and, bouncing on the balls of her feet, started in with high-pitched chatter about the books and characters on the mall. I followed her conversation, but most people would have only heard something like a siren.

Josie stood a few feet back, arms folded, doing her best to shoot me flat eyes.

While Sami kept up her babble in front of me and I silently tried to tell

Josie to get over it with my expression, I caught movement from the corner of my eye. Someone in a black uniform zeroed in on me.

Jared. Damn it. What was he doing here? TPD didn't usually handle crowd control. The last thing I wanted was him around my kids.

Before I could think of how to avoid an encounter, Deon appeared behind Sami. His wide, bright smile still sent a shock of pleasure through me after fourteen years of marriage. Dark skin, black hair, those eyes of satin. But today's racing heart wasn't because of his good looks.

"Hey." He greeted me as if this surprise was the happiest event of his whole week. "I hoped we might run into you. How long is your shift? Thought it would be fun to go for a bike ride."

Deon was trying hard to please.

Jared kept moving toward us. Would he say something? Would Deon catch a whiff of what had almost happened at the Holiday Inn? I hadn't gone through with it, but just toying with the idea betrayed Deon and our marriage.

Gordy thrust out his hand to Deon. "Good to see you."

They greeted and spoke a few words. I focused on Jared, who closed in on us. I shook my head slightly, warning him away.

Sami kept up her chatter, jumping up and down in front of me to get my attention. "Mommy, Mom, Mom."

Jared's mouth formed a determined line and I knew he was going to say something. My world would crash here on the University of Arizona mall in the bright spring sunshine, in front of my daughters.

A vibration tickled my breast pocket at the same time Gordy's phone chirped, and Jared paused with a startled expression. Gordy and I grabbed our phones.

A dispatcher's voice gave a terse message. "All Rangers report to the Koffler Building ASAP."

Gordy and I exchanged alarmed glances. My heart jump-started with that familiar excitement.

Deon knew something was up. He gave me a questioning look. "Is there trouble?"

I slid my phone into my pocket. Gordy was already looking up and around. "Where's Koffler?"

Jared had disappeared, probably on his way.

I pulled away from Deon and spoke calmly. "You should take the girls home now."

Deon grabbed me again. "Wait."

I yanked my arm, more forceful this time. "Take them home. Just do it, okay?" My head jerked to the left. "This way," I said to Gordy.

Behind me, Deon faked a jovial voice, but I heard the tension underneath. "Let's go take that bike ride!"

We trotted across the thin grass of the mall, skirting crowds and tents. At a gathering this large in today's world, it was possible some lone shooter was picking off festival-goers. I hadn't heard shots. Maybe a hostage situation in one of the panels taking place in Koffler. Ann would be long gone by now.

The people hanging around or standing in line to get into the panels or have books signed didn't seem at all concerned by sight of two swift-moving Arizona Rangers.

Sirens sounded outside of the mall area and red and blue lights blazed as cop cars and two ambulances gathered on the side of the building opposite the mall.

That commotion brought some heads up and people started to give each other looks of concern. Jared and another cop joined us. A TPD officer hurried out of the building and spoke to the festival volunteers manning the lines.

He left them and rushed to us. "Good. We need you for crowd control. The doors are locked and people are being dispersed. You need to stand out here and patrol around the building to keep anyone from going in or coming out."

Koffler is an enormous building. The cop motioned for us to spread out. "You four take these doors from here to here." He pointed on either side of us. "We've got other officers to cover the rest."

Gordy stopped the officer before he could get away. "What's going on?"

The officer hesitated, probably trying to decide if the information was classified. "It's not official. But someone shot Manuel Ortiz. Looks like he's dead."

My stomach did a 360, spilling equilibrium on the way. I closed my eyes to get control. Manuel Ortiz. I'd just seen him. So alive. So vicious to my brother. If I hadn't said it out loud, I'd at least *thought* about how much I hated him. But I didn't wish him dead.

It took me a moment to refocus on the job at hand. "I'll take the north door." I headed off to an isolated door surrounded by shrubs. It was something of a private exit used mostly by faculty. I knew of it because I'd gone to school at UA. My sociology prof kept office hours at the end of the day and I'd spent some time in his office. More than once we'd exited together, out this door. He'd hoped I'd accompany him to his car and probably to a nice hotel room. I'd toyed with the idea but hadn't followed through. That brought back my morning at the hotel. God, I looped through the same stupid mistakes over and over.

This door wasn't used much and had no way to access the building from the outside. It was literally an escape hatch.

The lines of people waiting for the next session broke up, slowing my progress. I slipped through clusters of people, under the shade of the over-large portico. I spotted the door and was surprised to see it clicking closed, as if someone had exited a second earlier.

I jogged toward the narrow concrete pad on the outside of the building and squinted through the shrubs. Tall bougainvillea with bright fuchsia blossoms blocked my clear view, but they rustled, as if someone had brushed into them. I ran toward the hedge, sure whoever had exited the building had slipped through the flowers and I didn't want to lose them.

I tore into the brush, the sharp branches of the bougainvillea scratching my arms. On the other side a walkway meandered away, cast in bright afternoon sunshine. A young couple pushed a stroller. An older man steered his wife in her wheelchair. Several children held hands with balloons bouncing in the air above their heads. Other people of every description jostled along.

I search for someone retreating in a hurry. The crowd ahead of me parted and I caught sight of someone moving quickly.

When I recognized the man slipping through the people, I stopped and drew in a breath. I watched as Chris hurried away from me, putting distance between Koffler and himself.

8

Smells of savory meat from the grill wound around Ann's cramped kitchen. Sami climbed onto Fritz's lap and tugged on his beard. He bellowed, as she'd expected, which sent her into peals of laughter.

"Don't bother your uncle." I didn't add a lot of oomph to it because I knew I'd get overridden.

Fritz grabbed Sami around her waist and gave her a tickle. "I can take care of myself," he said.

"Hearing them laugh does me good. I can use something positive today." Ann pulled herself from the pine kitchen table and grabbed for her crutches.

She'd been staring into space, something I found preferable to her waxing on about the tragedy of Manuel Ortiz's murder. I straightened from where I leaned on the kitchen island. "What do you want? I can get it."

Ann scoffed. "What do you think I do when you're not here to wait on me?"

I hated to think about it. Their kitchen, like the rest of the fifty-year-old slump-block house, was crammed with furniture and countertops crowded together. It would be impossible for her to use her wheelchair in here. Even with the crutches, it seemed an obstacle course.

Fritz bounced Sami on his knee, and she let the movement rattle her voice. "What do you think of Auntie Ann's swimming pool?" he asked.

I glanced out the sliding glass door to the backyard and Deon's bent form over the pool heater. The pool, in all its Clampett-style glory (except even they had a real cement pond), hunkered twenty feet from the back door.

The scuffed dining table took up most of the room, leaving a three-foot border between the kitchen island, the scratched sideboard, and the sliding door. The other side opened into a four-foot-square vestibule with a hallway leading back to three tiny bedrooms and the living room on the opposite side of the front door.

With the vibration in her voice Sami said, "It's weird and I can't swim in it because it's too deep."

Ann nodded. "And the motor doesn't work."

Sami enjoyed the rattle of her voice. "Daddy will fix it. He can fix anything."

Having a breakdown gave Deon something to do while he was forced to attend Sunday dinner with my family. He never complained, but I knew hanging out with my brother, sister, and her husband wasn't his idea of a great way to spend his precious time off.

Ann rested one crutch on the counter and reached into the cupboard to pull out a drinking glass. "Josie, do you want some of that root beer Uncle Fritz made?"

Josie looked up from where she sat at the table scrolling through her iPad. "No, thanks."

Sami jumped off Fritz's lap. "I do!"

I gave Ann one of those exasperated looks.

She grinned at me, a welcome sight after her gloominess. "So, she'll eat her vegetables tomorrow. Today she's at Auntie Ann's and it won't hurt you to indulge her and me."

Except being at Auntie Ann's wasn't an unusual event and indulgences could get excessive. I didn't argue. After a lifetime with my headstrong older sister, I'd learned to pick my battles.

Fritz leaned back in his chair and watched Ann maneuver the refrigerator door and pour the root beer. Like me, he'd learned to keep his mouth shut and let Ann do things her own way. "Where's that no good brother of yours?" Fritz said.

I wanted to know that, too. He'd walked away from Koffler yesterday after Manuel Ortiz's murder and before I told anyone else, I sure as hell wanted to know why. With all the public animosity between the two of them, Chris being anywhere near the scene would look bad. He had an explanation, obviously, and I wanted it.

I wasn't sure if Fritz was speaking to me or Ann, so I let her take it. "He said he'd be here. Don't know why he's so late." In a mean voice she added, "Maybe he's celebrating Manuel's murder."

Wow. That seemed uncalled for. She really was in a bad mood. The kids didn't need to hear that from her. I tried to keep my voice light. "Tone it down."

"The brisket will be burned if he waits much longer," Fritz said.

"And that would be a tragedy. I say we eat without him," I said.

Deon walked in the back door and slid the glass closed before too much AC escaped. "The heater is the problem. I took the cover off and it looks like a packrat condo in there. I pulled out the nests. At least one burnt carcass."

"Gross, Dad!" Josie said. Followed by the echo from Sami. "Gross!"

Deon smiled at their reaction. "My guess is they've been munching on the wires. I can order some parts and see if I can repair it. Or you can call the pool guy."

Fritz inhaled an agonized breath. "Those pool guys will charge a hundred bucks just to come look."

"If you'd have let Mike and Chris do it their way, we'd have a pool we could actually use instead of a death trap too deep. The experts would have installed a motor the right way and we'd be enjoying a pool party today."

Fritz looked embarrassed and beaten. There was no reason for Ann to treat him like that, especially when he was trying to do something nice for her. Sometimes I wanted to give my older sister a time out, for ten years.

I took a second to remind myself to back off. Ann lived with pain and disappointment I didn't experience. If she exploded occasionally, the least we could do as her family was let her burn it off.

Ann took hold of her crutches again and made her way to the table.

"Thank you for checking, Deon." She lowered herself to sit and tilted her head to me. "You're so lucky. Not only do you live with a great legal mind, he's mechanical, too."

Deon tried to make Fritz feel better. "I'm not sure if I do either one of them that well."

Doing my part to lighten the mood, I said, "Just so you know he's not perfect, he leaves his dirty underwear on the floor."

Josie again: "Mom, please! TMI!" Sami, after gulping her root beer: "TMI!"

Ann gazed at Fritz for a moment, then back to Deon. "If you wouldn't mind, we'd really appreciate you ordering the parts and seeing what you can do."

Fritz stood. "It would be a big help, thanks. The PT thinks Ann is improving with the pool therapy."

Ann focused on the strawberry-shaped ceramic sugar bowl in the middle of the table. "I don't know if that's true."

Always one to avoid tension, Deon changed the subject. "I saw that new pickup of yours. That's mighty fine."

I jumped in. "You got a new pickup, too? Chris broke down and got one."

Fritz grinned. "Yeah. I got one just like it. Mine's midnight blue."

Ann said, "Well, technically it's not ours. We got a very nice donation for Mi Casa. Our old pickup died last year, and Fritz has been using his and it's nearly worn out, too. So we traded in his and got this new one. Fritz gets to use it, but Mi Casa has first priority." Ann was really feeling her inner bitch today.

Fritz's smile looked strained. "Yeah. It's Mi Casa's."

She eyed me and now it seemed like my turn to get run over. "I got a call from a young woman yesterday. Sophia said she met a lady in a hotel who gave her the number for the center. Was that you?"

My breath caught, though I'm sure my face stayed calm. With effort, I kept from looking at Deon but listened for him. I started to breath when he asked Fritz something about digging the pool. Faking mild interest, I said, "Not me. What was it about?"

Deon and Fritz talked about the parts needed replaced on their pool heater. The girls had already shifted their focus, Josie to her iPad and Sami to poking Fritz.

Ann studied me. "From what I understand, her daycare fell through and she took her son with to her housekeeping job at a hotel by the airport. She accidentally walked in on a guy who hadn't answered her knock and he went ballistic. But she said a very pretty blonde showed up and helped her. Gave her the number of the center and disappeared."

"There's a lot of blonde women in Tucson."

She nodded and kept her eyes on me. "True. But not that many who work with Mi Casa and write down the address and phone number without looking them up."

I thought of that woman, scared, helpless, with her son to care for. I shouldn't ask, but I couldn't help it. "Did you help her?"

"I got her a job at the Verde Plaza on the east side. She'll go in early mornings and clean up the common space and they won't mind if she takes her son."

"Is this a new place for you?"

Ann kept her eyes on Sami bouncing on Fritz's lap with that wistful look that broke my heart. So many wonderful things in my life that Ann couldn't experience, such as hiking, biking, thoughtlessly running errands or even grocery shopping, and especially having children. "I've placed people there before. Martina pays cash and doesn't ask questions."

Ann suddenly leaned close, upping her already high intensity. "What has Chris told you about Manuel Ortiz?"

I shot back quickly. "Nothing."

She almost sounded accusing, as if I held something back. "You two are thick as thieves. Always have been. Ever since you were little."

Ever since the accident, she meant. She didn't have to say it out loud for the meaning to weigh on me. Chris and I were close. I owed him everything.

Ann kept her eyes on me. I glanced at Sami and Josie. Sami sang to herself and played with the sugar bowl. The iPad had Josie's full attention.

"Okay, yeah. Ortiz wasn't my favorite person. He tried to ruin Chris, and let's not forget he's responsible for all the death threats."

Ann scoffed. "You know those were fake."

"No, I don't. Even though Ortiz was scum, neither one of us is glad he's dead."

"Of course not." She didn't look at me when she said it. "But it won't look good, Chris being at the book fair. Listening to Manuel."

"He had a right to be there. No one could think Chris had anything to do with the murder." Unless they saw him leaving Koffler.

Ann pursed her lips in that old lady way of hers. "He shouldn't have been at the book festival, not when Manuel was speaking."

"Then why did you make him take you?" This was so much like Ann. She twisted you into making some stupid move then turned it around and made it seem like your fault.

She looked surprised. "I didn't make him."

"You asked him to give you a ride to the festival."

She shook her head. "No. Fritz was going to take me, but Chris called and said he'd come get me. Said he was going to see some guy talk about water rights."

That's not what Chris had told me. Whose version came closer to the truth? "Did you talk to him after the festival?"

"No."

"He never even apologized for abandoning you?"

"He was really upset. I don't know why because he picked the fight. I'm sure he forgot me. It's not a problem. Efrain drove me home."

"Stupid," Fritz said, startling me. "After the trouble Chris was in last summer, he should have stayed away from anything to do with Manuel."

Both of the girls looked up and around to me, Fritz, and Ann, gathering clues about the conversation.

"Chris didn't cause the trouble. Ortiz did," I said.

Fritz showed more fire than he normally did. "He should have left Manuel alone. When all that was going on last year, Chris was quoted saying some pretty racist stuff."

No one got away with disparaging Chris, not even family. "He's doing the dirty work on the border. They have to deal with things we don't even know about. He's not racist."

The front door banged open. Chris burst in wearing his khaki BP uniform and utility belt.

9

Sami dashed from Fritz's lap like lightning. She threw herself at Chris before he had time to swing the door closed. "Uncle Chris!"

He caught her midflight. "Hey, squirt." With ease, he kicked the door closed and hoisted Sami to his shoulder. "Duck."

They maneuvered through the kitchen doorway. Even Josie set her iPad on the table and gave Chris her sweetest smile. Fritz high-fived him.

"Finally," I said. "We about gave up on you. The children need to eat."

He lost his grin but didn't look at me.

"Ha! The children," Fritz said. "We know it's you, Michaela. Always have to be fed on time or you get cranky."

"Or her blood sugar falls and she has a seizure," Ann said.

Guilt. Scalding and fluid. I know she didn't mean for it to hit me like that. But it did. Every time. Chris didn't give me a sympathetic wink, as he often did. It felt like an icy wind blew from him to me.

Chris lowered Sami to the ground. "I would have been here sooner, but we got some crossers south of Sasabe at dawn. Took me all morning to get them processed."

Oh no. Not the day for that comment. Ann's mouth tightened and she geared for a fight.

Deon's eyes lit on Chris for a split second and moved to Ann. "I'll go check on the brisket."

Fritz jumped up. "You need an expert to help you." He tapped Sami's head. "Come on, you. We'll teach you the finer points of bar-b-que."

Josie looked from Chris to Ann and she pushed back from the table. "Wait up."

The door slid closed.

Ann pointed to Chris's utility belt. "On the fridge."

Chris's Border Patrol uniform showed perspiration stains under his arms. Without protest, he followed Ann's rules. Neither of us were allowed to wear a gun in her house. She insisted we take them off and keep them out of reach on top of the refrigerator.

He plunked it down and opened the door. "Got any beer?"

"Root beer." I added a tease to my voice to try to get him to acknowledge me. He didn't. If he thought I had something to do with Ortiz knowing about Andy, I'd never be able to ask him about leaving Koffler.

He pulled out the bottle with the old-time stopper. "Is this Fritz's?"

Never one to let anything slide, Ann slapped her hand on the table. "Those people you captured this morning. Were they women and children?"

He found a glass in the cupboard. "I don't want to get into this with you today. It's Sunday. Family day. Let's eat your fantastic brisket and drink Fritz's disappointing root beer and enjoy each other."

"Good plan," I said, stepping close to Chris and reaching for a glass, even though I didn't want root beer.

Chris backed away when I brushed against him, turning from me.

Ann sat at the table, her back to him as he leaned on the counter. Her voice lashed out. "Someone shot him. Killed him! And you're out within hours dragging people from freedom. Did you even know Manuel Ortiz is dead?"

Chris placed his glass on the counter without drinking it. "Yes, Ann. I heard about it this morning."

This morning? He could hardly have missed it when he was on campus.

"And yet, you're back at it, ruining lives. Didn't anything Manuel said yesterday sink in?"

Chris's lips curled in a sneer. "Manuel was not the angel you think he was."

"He's helped more people than we could ever hope to. He was a great man and the world will miss him."

"The guy didn't know the meaning of altruism."

They were heating up and I didn't know how to stop this. "Come on, guys. Ortiz might have done a lot of good for the immigrant cause. But he went after Chris. That's family and I can't forgive that."

Ann scoffed. "Ask Deon. He loves you but he knows loyalty shouldn't get in the way of doing good."

What was she talking about? She loved to poke at me, hinting that she knew Deon better than I did. Most of the time I didn't take the bait. I wouldn't this time, either, though it irritated me. If Deon had some kind of side hustle going with Ortiz, I'd have to find out later.

Ann was on a tear as I had rarely seen her. Grief over Ortiz seemed to enrage her. "There is no excuse for people like you getting a paycheck for destroying lives and causing so many people to perish in the desert."

Chris's face set like cold stone. He kept his eyes on the back of her head and didn't answer.

"The man gave his life to help those people. Those homeless, desperate people."

Chris didn't speak.

Ann turned her wrath on me, even though I knew she meant it for Chris. "Talk to him. Tell him how evil it is to target these innocent victims."

I didn't move. This fight had gone on for years. Chris worked Border Patrol; Ann ran a center for immigrants, most of them undocumented. For long stretches, they let each other alone. But the differences always roiled closely under the surface. The rest of our clan, small as it was, knew to retreat if the swords came out. I felt I needed to witness.

Chris gulped his root beer. "No one is sorrier than I am that Manuel Ortiz is dead. No one should die over this. But he made his choices. He didn't have to piss off everyone. Even people sympathetic to his side. He made the wrong people angry."

Ann twisted in her chair to face him. "Wrong people? What is the matter with you? He was trying to save women and children. Families are being ripped apart. People are dying in the desert."

Chris pushed himself to stand. "Don't tell me about dying in the desert. You aren't the one finding carcasses out there. Dehydrated and picked over by vultures and coyotes. You don't carry that stench of death constantly in your nostrils."

"Then how can you work for the Border Patrol? You're defending the regime that is causing this."

"The US government is not to blame. Stop the corruption in Guatemala and Nicaragua. Disrupt the cartels and gangs in South America and Mexico. We're trying to protect Americans, not kill women and children. Get off that self-righteous wagon—"

A soft knock on the front door stopped him. I jumped up, relieved for the break and hoping it gave them each a moment to cool off.

I opened the door to see Efrain on the concrete porch. He carried an aluminum foil pan in both hands. He always came to Sunday dinner at Ann's. With a straight face, he held out the pan. "The tamales are here." Weird he'd used the front door instead of coming through the gate from Mi Casa. But maybe he'd picked up the tamales somewhere and the front door was closer.

Since her house was small, Ann heard him from the kitchen. "Come in! I was afraid they wouldn't be ready in time for dinner."

Efrain walked past me, and I closed the door and followed him. He slid the pan onto the counter. He focused on Ann. "How are you today?"

She looked into his eyes with the same devotion she showered on Sami and Josie. "Tired out from yesterday, of course. But I'm good."

She hadn't told us she was tired. In fact, she'd insisted we meet at her place for dinner today. The second Sunday of the month was usually dinner at Fritz and Ann's. The first and third were at my house, and the fourth was at Chris's, which meant grilling in the common area of his apartment complex. If the weather wouldn't permit it, we brought pizza. If there happened to be a fifth Sunday, it meant dinner at a restaurant. Sometimes the girls had ball games or recitals, or Chris or I had to work. In that case, we did the best we could. Whenever possible, and since the accident twenty years ago, we'd kept Sunday for our family.

Efrain tipped his head to Chris.

Chris picked up his glass. "Efrain." It didn't hold a ton of warmth. The two of them gave each other a wide berth. I never saw them exchange heated words and didn't know if their reticence had history. Maybe Efrain was undocumented and afraid of Chris. Chris might suspect he had no papers and not like having to look the other way. I just knew neither of them seemed to care for the other. "I've got to see this catastrophe Fritz built in your backyard."

Ann directed from her place at the table. "Efrain, get the dishes. Mike, will you grab leaves for the table from the hall closet?"

When I returned from the hall with the leaves, Efrain and Ann abruptly cut short a conversation. They didn't try to pretend I hadn't interrupted.

Under Ann's scrutiny, we extended the table, leaving very little space in the dining room. "If you finish setting the table, Efrain and I need to go over a few things." She let him help her out of the cramped dining room across the hall to the living room.

Sami fought to slide open the back door and Deon walked in carrying a cookie sheet loaded with brisket, browned and smelling a little like heaven wrapped in mesquite and chilis. Josie followed him in and reached for her iPad.

Sami pranced around Deon like a pony and his voice tensed. "There's no room for that, Sami." He glanced at Josie. "Put your iPad down. It's time to eat."

"Okay, Sheriff Dad," Josie said.

Deon's mouth tightened but he didn't say anything. He'd hit his limit of navigating my complicated family.

I shifted to see out the back door. Chris and Fritz faced each other. They didn't look their normal, joking selves. Chris and Fritz had been friends since grade school. Even when Chris started at UA and Fritz went to work at his father's bar, they'd stayed close. Fritz marrying Ann when I was still in high school seemed the most natural thing in the world.

Chris leaned forward, thrusting his face close to Fritz. Whatever he said, he spoke with anger.

Fritz shoved him back, a move so unlike his usual passive nature.

Ann thumped in, her crutches making that awkward syncopation in the cramped room. Efrain walked behind her, speaking quietly about someone named Julio who needed a root canal and how he'd found a dentist who would charge less than usual.

Ann stopped and watched out the window. "Well." She leaned heavily on her crutches. "Wonder what that's about."

Efrain put a hand on Ann's arm. "Here." He pulled a chair from the table. "Sit."

She let him help her into the chair, not taking her eyes off the two men outside. They kept up their argument.

Deon wiped his hands on a towel. "Come on, girls. Get cleaned up for dinner."

Sami put up some resistance. Josie said, "I'll tell Uncle Fritz and Uncle Chris dinner is ready." As soon as she pushed the door closed, Chris and Fritz whipped their heads to the house. They both stopped talking.

"What's going on?" I asked Ann.

She sounded curious. "I have no idea. But I'll bet it has to do with Manuel Ortiz's murder."

"Why do you think that?"

"Manuel is one of the few things I've ever seen those two boys disagree about."

"I've never heard them fight about Ortiz."

She took her eyes from them and looked at me. "No. I don't suppose you would."

It seemed I wouldn't hear about it today, either.

Chris gave Fritz one last scathing look and stormed toward the house. Josie stepped back, her eyes and mouth in circles of surprise. Deon sliced brisket with his back to the door and Ann sat at the table watching. Chris whipped the door open and didn't stop to close it. He banged into me when he reached for his gun belt on the fridge.

"Chris, wait." I wanted to talk to him. About Ortiz. About Koffler. About Fritz.

He strode past Deon and wrenched open the front door. I ran after him.

He'd already crossed the small front yard and made it to his shiny red pickup when I scrambled toward him. "Chris."

He paused. Stared at me and shook his head. "I thought I could trust you."

In a second he was inside his pickup, the engine started and he drove away.

10

Dinner had been a grim affair for everyone except Sami. She kept enough chatter going with stupid knock-knock jokes that we were able to get through without too many awkward pauses. The brisket was a little tough, but the tamales saved the meal.

Ann asked Josie to help Efrain with his phone and the two of them huddled together. Josie showed a great deal of patience and the two of them spoke in a mixture of English and Spanish.

After dinner, Ann pushed herself to stand. "Let's see about getting the dishes done."

Efrain scooted his chair back. "You should not worry about the mess."

Deon clapped his hands. "The girls and I will take care of the kitchen."

My stern Mom-face anticipated some rebellion, but to their credit, both girls seemed more than willing to help with the cleanup.

"Well, if you really don't mind, that would be wonderful," Ann said.

I stood and picked up a couple of plates.

Deon nodded to me. "You go relax with Ann."

Fritz threaded an arm around Ann's ribs and half carried her to the living room on the other side of the front door, opposite the kitchen. Their living room had the same overstuffed feel as the dining room/kitchen. Two small couches, both worn and needing to be replaced, formed an L, with an overstuffed chair facing them. Various tables and bookshelves lined the walls and filled any open space. The shades were always drawn, giving the whole room the dreary appearance of an old hoarder's hovel.

Fritz helped Ann sit on the end of one of the couches. He perched on the arm of a couch and patted his stomach. "I could eat those tamales every day."

Ann tilted her head up to look at him. "Shouldn't you be helping with the cleanup?"

He jumped up. "Right. On my way." He hurried into the kitchen and we heard the back door slide open and closed.

I sank into the chair. "I wonder where Efrain gets them? A relative, maybe? I wouldn't mind buying some."

Ann closed her eyes. "Efrain doesn't have relatives here."

"No family?" He'd been working for Ann and Fritz for years, always seemed to be around, but I knew nothing about him.

Ann rubbed her forehead as if weary. "We're his family."

By "we" I doubted she meant Deon, me, and the kids. Efrain might be nice, but there was just something that made me edgy about him. Efrain wasn't the subject on my mind, though. I glanced across the front foyer to the kitchen.

Deon had put the girls to work loading the dishwasher and wrapping up the leftovers.

I leaned closer to Ann. "What did you mean when you said to ask Deon about Manuel?"

Ann stopped rubbing her head. "Never mind. I was spouting off. Didn't mean anything."

"Bullshit. Tell me." I didn't often get tough with Ann, so she must have known I was serious.

She sighed. "Deon is assisting on a case for a couple of women I've worked with. Manuel is ... was lending his name to the case and helping out some."

Deon hadn't mentioned it. But why would he? He knew how much I detested Ortiz. "What's the case?"

"Workers versus employers. These powerful business owners taking advantage of scared immigrants."

I gave her a chance to take a breath and wind up.

Ann dropped her hand to her lap and found renewed energy. "This situation's been going on for years. We finally have two women willing to put themselves at great risk. I mean great risk. They've already lost their jobs and could lose their work permits in the country. Maybe even be deported."

I gave Ann little encouragement to go on, but it didn't matter, she probably couldn't be stopped. "This is only the tip of the iceberg. Lupe and Angie have been working for these employers for seven years. Weekends, overtime, holidays. Not only below minimum wage, but no overtime or holiday pay. And when they finally got the courage to complain, they were fired. Fired! Without the wages they were owed."

I knew this to be common. "I'm glad something is being done."

"I'm worried about Angie and Lupe. After they started this case, I haven't been able to get them a placement. They have no income. Manuel was trying to find them something while they deal with the lawsuit."

"I'm sure Deon will take care of it." I wasn't sure. He hadn't even told me about the case. Because I hadn't asked about work or deliberate lies of omission?

Ann's mouth pursed. "It would be great if he'd tell you, because he won't talk to me. Manuel kept me updated. Deon won't say anything."

"There is attorney-client privilege."

She huffed. "These companies think they can treat the undocumented —and even those here legally—like chattel. Just because these immigrants are confused and frightened. And in many cases, don't know the law."

Sadly, this story wasn't new. Sophia, and many like her, kept working those jobs because it was all they could get to feed their families. Deon taking on this case, obviously pro bono, made me proud. But working with Manuel Ortiz ... That grated on me.

Ann looked through the hallway to the kitchen. "I'm grateful to Deon. Really. But we're going to miss Manuel and his support."

That couldn't stand. "Support? What about Chris?"

Ann frowned. "Chris is a big boy. He knew what he was getting into."

"So what? That makes it okay for Ortiz to try to destroy him?"

"Manuel was doing so to shine a light on the immigrants' plight."

"But he didn't have to attack Chris to do that."

"People don't listen unless there's violence. I don't know, maybe Manuel's death will bring more attention to the matter than he could have alive. People love a martyr."

Wow. This stopped me cold. She'd accused Chris of being happy about Ortiz's murder, but it sounded as if Ann saw benefits. My whole family was nuts today. One more reason to blame Ortiz.

Deon appeared in the doorway. He cleared his throat. "We've done about all we can do in the kitchen. Efrain is in the back cleaning up the grill."

"Thank you," Ann said, dropping our discussion.

"Are you ready to go?" Deon asked.

I rose and gave Ann a quick peck on her cheek. "Josie's got a game tomorrow."

Ann waved me off. "On my calendar."

We left her in their darkened living room and stepped into the blinding sunshine of a desert afternoon. My phone buzzed. Deon and the girls walked ahead of me and Fritz and Ann were behind their closed front door. I slipped the phone from my pocket.

Damn.

I hit decline and cut Jared's call off. I'd ignore him and he'd stop. Ghosting. It was trending, right?

The girls stood by the back doors of the Pilot, their home away from home as I chauffeured them through the week. They'd wait until Deon powered it up and had the air blowing before they climbed inside. I slid into the passenger seat, the heat a heavy curtain wrapping around me.

We drove from the south side to our neighborhood in the north with the radio turned to an oldie's station and we stayed in our own thoughts.

Sami leaned forward. "Mom, are you and Uncle Chris fighting?"

Good question. "Uncle Chris has a lot of things on his mind. But we're good."

"So he's not mad at us?"

"Nope. We're the Ta-mutals, like always." I used the term to ease her worry.

Sami giggled. "Tell me why you call yourselves that."

She knew why but loved to hear stories. "When I was about three years old, Uncle Chris loved the Teenage Mutant Ninja Turtles. He used to make me dress up with a scarf across my forehead. It's such a mouthful, the best I could do was Ta-mutals. Chris thought it was funny, so he started called me and Ann and him the Ta-mutals. Those things can stick."

That seemed to satisfy her chatty mood and she shifted her attention out the window.

My stomach churned. Fighting with Chris wasn't normal. When could I talk to him? He didn't miss many of Josie's games unless he was working. I'd get him aside tomorrow and ask why he was so mad at me and what he was doing outside of Koffler.

Deon's serious face turned to the road. Maybe he concentrated on driving, maybe he thought about the cleaner's case. The one he worked on with Manuel Ortiz, my family's enemy. We were going to talk about that, but not in front of the girls.

He must have felt my eyes on him and he turned. He flashed a brilliant smile, the one reserved for me alone. "I washed your car this morning."

Man. I hadn't even noticed. "Oh. That's great. Thank you."

Josie snarked from the back seat. "How hard is it to get your own car washed? You're letting her get away with being a queen."

I raised my eyebrows in amusement.

Deon leaned over and pecked me on the cheek. "She is my queen."

"Eyes on the road!" Josie shouted. Sami giggled.

Deon laughed and reached into the cubby under the GPS. "I left this in the car the day of the book festival and forgot about it until I cleaned it."

Curious, I leaned forward to peer into his open palm. When I saw the tiny wooden sculpture, I cracked up. "Where did you find that?"

He handed it to me. "There was this old guy whittling in a booth at the west end of the mall at the book festival. I asked him if he could do a St. Christopher. He took it as a challenge."

I turned it over. "I take it he isn't Catholic."

Deon laughed. "I doubt it. I had to describe it, and this is what he came up with."

"It doesn't look much like St. Christopher, but he got close enough I could make a guess." I studied it. "I love it. It might be my favorite one, yet."

This would be settled in a place of honor on the mantle in the family room, atop to a lovely bit of driftwood on which I displayed a half dozen St. Christopher medals.

Sami fidgeted in her seatbelt. "I forget, why do you have the St. Christophers?"

"You didn't forget," Deon said.

Sami blessed him with a grin showing off her dimples. "Honest. I don't remember."

She wasn't fooling anyone. She could probably tell the story better than us, but I didn't mind indulging her. "It has to do with how your dad and I met."

Josie wailed. "I forgot my iPad. We have to go back."

"Hard to tune us out when she can't keep track of her expensive gadgets," I said to Deon.

"Guess she's heard it enough times," Deon said. He lifted his chin and addressed her reflection in the rearview mirror. "Have Ann bring it to the game tomorrow."

"Daaaaaaad." She made it into a five-syllable word.

Sami rocked against the back of the seat. "The story."

Ignoring Josie's protest, I started. "I had just graduated from college and a bunch of friends and I hiked way back in Sabino Canyon. It was a gorgeous day and the water was running high. Just right for swimming."

"Brrr," Sami said. We'd taken the girls hiking there last summer and they'd expected swimming pool temperature water, not runoff from mountain snows.

Deon took up the tale. "And I had finished the first year of law school and hiked up there to celebrate."

Sami nodded along, her eyes bright. "All alone because you were an old stick in the mud and didn't have any friends." Yeah, she couldn't remember the story ... only my exact comments from earlier versions.

"He's lightened up a lot since then," I said.

Deon looked at me with a conspirator's twinkle. This is the part where we skirted the entire truth. "Some other kids were already up there. They were not using good judgment." That was Deon's object lesson to this cautionary tale. "Instead of stepping into the water, they were sliding down a narrow crevice in the rock and falling several feet into the pool." He teased me with his eyes. "So obviously an accident waiting to happen."

The real truth is that I was the one not using good judgment. I'd been going up there all my life and had never seen so much water. It seemed like the only thing to do was to use the rocks for a slide, because I knew I'd never get a chance to experience it again.

I grinned at Deon. "Your father thought he should warn the kids about the danger. He told them they needed to quit doing that because it was dangerous and someone could get hurt. The trailhead was eight miles down the canyon."

Sami rolled her eyes at her dad. "Fun-hater," she teased. "You're always bossy."

Deon glanced in the rearview mirror. "Not bossy. Just smart."

Deon's announcement that day didn't sit well with me. In defiance, I'd taken the slide again with no ill consequences. Not wanting a girl to out-do him, one of my friends followed me. He hadn't been so lucky. Instead of a smooth drop into the pool, he'd lost balance and ended up hitting a shallow rock squarely on his tailbone.

Deon said, "In this case, I was right. One of your mother's friends got injured. He couldn't walk, so your mother and I carried him to the trailhead."

"Eight miles carrying one hundred eighty pounds of whine," I said, and planted a kiss on Deon's cheek. That elicited an "ew" from Sami. "And I fell in love with your father."

Deon winked at me. "I never met a girl who could take care of someone like that without complaining. She won me over."

"So why the St. Christophers?" Sami asked.

Deon caught my eye. "Just to remind your mother to always be careful."

I shook my head. "That's not it. St. Christopher protects people, and your father thinks I need protection."

Sami nodded. "You do need protection, Mom. When you go out and work at Arizona Ranger stuff."

Now she'd bring up the campus tear gas story and I'd have to defend myself. "I don't do anything dangerous. No need to worry."

She brightened. "I don't worry, because Dad gives you the medals so you're protected."

Deon turned onto a tree-lined street. In our neighborhood, tall eucalyptus and palms shaded the houses. Yards maintained neat landscaping. This was our first, and only, home, purchased when we got married. We'd grown up along with the neighborhood, knew most of the neighbors and their pets and kids. We didn't spend as much time at the little park down the street as we used to, but we still closed off the street every year for a neighborhood potluck.

We pulled up in front of our house. A bushy mesquite tree shaded the front walk, with grown oleander and tall honeysuckle bushes providing color. Deon and I spent time keeping the weeds down in the rock yard and making sure the bushes and shrubs stayed trimmed and neat. Working together had never been a problem for us. Childcare and chores. Money, work, and play time. We seemed to coordinate our lives without the conflicts that plagued many of our friends. When Deon wanted me to quit being a police officer and stay home to take care of the kids, I'd agreed without protest. By then, he'd made partner and earned enough to support us.

If this is all good, why were you in a hotel room with Jared?

The kids popped out of the back. Sami danced and sang her way to the front door, while Josie followed, a frown lining her pretty face. Josie took after Deon's side. With smooth, almond-colored skin and deep brown eyes that seemed to see way beyond her years. Just a bit on the curly and coarse side, her black hair kinked in the slightest humidity.

Sami, though darker than me, favored my side more than Deon's. Her hair was smooth and straight, a medium brown, and her eyes were more hazel than Josie's brown. She was a mix of Deon's Mexican heritage and my blond, blue-eyed coloring. Of course I thought both girls were beautiful, but Josie would end up a stunner.

I caught up to Josie and popped a hand on her head. "What's bothering you?"

Sami punched in the door code and flew into the house. Deon made eye contact with me before following her in. He'd want to know what Josie and I talked about.

Josie kept her plodding pace toward the door and didn't look at me. "Nothing."

"Not nothing. Are you upset about Uncle Chris leaving?"

She hesitated a moment. "Well, yeah. I mean, what the heck? I know something happened with Manuel Ortiz last year and now he's dead. But that isn't Uncle Chris's thing, is it?"

I set my jaw. "No. It's not."

She looked at the open front door but didn't make a move for it. "Last year when Uncle Chris was in trouble, you and Dad wouldn't tell us anything."

"We didn't want you to worry."

She faced me and thrust out a hip. "Okay. I get that for Sami. She's still too little to know what's going on. But I'm in junior high now and can kind of make my own opinions. I know you and Uncle Chris don't like Manuel Ortiz, but I do. He came to an assembly last winter. He talked all about DACA and the border wall and how parents and kids are being separated from each other."

I pulled back on my instant irritation. "You never told me Manuel Ortiz was at your school. Didn't you need to get a permission slip signed to see him?" Her principal tried to bring in speakers of different opinions to teach the kids critical thinking. She also wanted to drive home the message of diversity and inclusivity and other lofty ideals.

"I told Dad and he signed the slip."

Maybe Deon simply forgot to tell me about it. More likely, Josie had strategically targeted Deon to sign and he'd consciously not told me. "Are you worried Uncle Chris is a villain who supports family separation?"

She shrugged. "I love Uncle Chris. He's fun and funny and takes care of me and Sami."

"But?"

Her gaze skittered away and she waited a beat. "He got in all that trouble last year and I read it in the paper."

"The paper?" Since I had an online subscription, she wouldn't have been able to casually read it at home. She'd have had to seek it out.

"At school. I read what other people said about it."

Part of me felt proud she'd taken the initiative. "What did you find out?"

She chewed on her lip a moment. "So, what I read is that a sixteen-year-old Mexican kid was shot to death at the border for throwing rocks."

"Essentially. There is more to the story, but yes."

She watched me. "And Uncle Chris is the spokesman for the Border Patrol, so he was the one who talked to the reporters and was on TV and stuff."

"He was in a really tough position. On the one hand, he hated that a young person died. And yes, the boy was only throwing rocks. On the other hand, the agent who shot swears he thought the boy had a gun." I had an opinion about the tragedy but, as Josie said, she was getting old enough to evaluate the merits on her own. I kept my assessment to myself and focused on Chris. "Your uncle never said the boy deserved to die. He defended the function of the Border Patrol." And because of that, he'd received a fake bomb in the mail and numerous threats and letters filled with hate. All from people who professed love and care for the immigrants.

She looked troubled. "How is it ever okay to shoot a kid like that?"

"I don't know what happened that night. What I do know is that your Uncle Chris and many other agents like him drive around with cases of water in their trunks. And diapers and boxes of food like nuts and crackers and things to give to people they find on the desert."

Tears threatened. "They said … the people in the comments said Chris is a devil and he should be taken out and shot. All kinds of bad stuff."

"It's name-calling." And Manuel Ortiz was the best of them. Unfortunately for Chris, Ortiz's audience included people watching the Sunday morning talk shows. "We don't listen to them."

"So, Uncle Chris isn't a racist?"

I wanted to believe that. "Uncle Chris and the other agents are trying to protect the border and uphold the laws. I'm not going to say that sometimes he doesn't get frustrated. He's made mistakes, I'm sure. We all do, especially in dangerous situations."

"So he is a racist?"

Damn it. Kids and their black-and-white view of the world. "What I know is how Chris has treated me and you kids. There isn't anything he wouldn't do for you. He's done everything for me. He's a good man." I believed that to my bones. A good man.

She nodded but kept her eyes on the ground. "I guess. But he seemed pretty mad today."

I hadn't helped her at all. Maybe Deon would be able to talk to her. He saw the world slightly differently than I did. Family loyalty ran deep in him, too. He'd never say anything bad about Chris.

We walked into the house. Here in our neighborhood, with shade trees and palms, green shrubs and flowers, it always felt so much cooler than Ann's. Again, guilt that Deon and I could afford a better neighborhood reared its head. Ann wouldn't want me to feel bad for the success we'd had. Well, mostly Deon. It was a success he'd worked hard for, starting in the same circumstances as many of Ann's residents. No one worked harder than Deon.

Stairs to the right of the front door ascended to four bedrooms. Downstairs a bright hallway passed an office and led to an open living area of family room, dining room, and a sunny kitchen with an island. A breakfast nook looked into the backyard and the sparkling swimming pool. I tried to assuage my guilt by reminding myself we'd bought the house fourteen years ago, when prices in Tucson hadn't been high. We'd added improvements slowly, always paying as we went along.

I loved our home. But I spent time volunteering at the center with Ann and knew others had so much less. I'd never be able to reconcile my great good fortune with the dire circumstances of others. The question dogged me constantly. Why me?

Banging and thudding from above told me Josie and Sami were in their rooms.

Deon watched me check my blood sugar monitor then opened the refrigerator. "Want a beer? A glass of wine?"

I crossed my arms. "No. I want to talk about the case you're working on with Manuel Ortiz."

He closed the fridge with deliberate calm. "Okay. Let's go outside."

Maybe he thought I'd raise my voice and didn't want the girls to hear us argue. We sat in chairs under the shade of an orange tree. "Why didn't you tell me you were working with Ortiz?"

He spoke softly. "You know I do a certain amount of pro bono work each year. Ann asked me to take this on. It had merit."

"You could have told me.

He smiled. "And we would have fought about it. This is an issue that needs to be addressed and I wanted to take the case. Us fighting about it wouldn't have changed my mind."

"So it doesn't matter what I think? You don't care if Ortiz set out to make Chris look like the devil. You're going to do what you want. But you won't tell me because you don't want to fight about it."

He leaned back and crossed his legs, as if trying to seem relaxed. "You're getting upset because of Manuel. He wasn't my favorite person either, but the workers are what's important. I can look past the man. You can't."

His calm scraped at my nerves. "It's not right to keep things from me because you think it might upset me."

His eyebrows shot up. "Not like a near riot on the UA campus where tear gas was set off in the vicinity of my children."

Busted. "Can I get that beer now?"

A smile played on his lips. Sometimes he approached disagreement with a pleasant face, as if neutralizing negative feelings. "I won't lie. Knowing this happened and you not saying anything hurt me. Okay, made me mad. We used to tell each other everything."

A dull knife sawed inside my chest. I blinked away the image of the hotel room. "It's always been easy between us." I searched his face. "I've taken that for granted. Maybe it's going to take some work now."

He looked sad. "Is something wrong? With me? With us?"

With me. I shook my head. "It's just, I feel ... you're not—"

The screen door opened and Sami hollered with all her six-year-old restraint, "Mom. Efrain is here."

Deon frowned. "What's he doing here?"

"I'll see." Efrain at our front door wasn't normal.

Josie and Efrain stood in the entryway. She held her iPad up. "Look. Efrain brought it."

"Thanks," I said. "I know Josie is happy about that."

He blushed and looked at the ground. "It is not a problem."

I looked beyond his head out the open door. "How did you get here?"

Efrain looked behind him as if he'd forgotten. "Sophia is a new resident. She gave me a ride. We are going for ice cream with her little boy."

"Are they in the car now?" I asked.

He nodded and seemed surprised when I brushed past him on the porch.

Sophia sat at the wheel of a dented blue Cavalier that had seen its best days a decade earlier. A shy smile greeted me.

"*Cómo estás*?" I said.

The little boy strapped in the backseat yelled, "*Hola*," with such enthusiasm we both laughed.

Sophia spoke Spanish in a quiet voice. She thanked me for sending her to Mi Casa and said how grateful she was for the job and a place to stay.

Efrain followed me out and stood by the passenger side. An awkward silence descended and we passed around uncomfortable smiles until Tomás started to chant in English, "Ice cream. Ice cream."

"I'm glad it's working out," I said and backed away so they could drive off.

Efrain shuffled around the small car until he stood in front of me. He looked at the ground. "I am wondering. How is Chris?"

I must have looked surprised.

Efrain explained, "He was mad when he left. Is he okay?"

What was this about? "I'm sure he's fine."

Efrain nodded and kept his gaze on the driveway. "I saw him at the festival."

My skin froze. When he hurried away from Koffler? Would Efrain tell anyone?

He raised his gaze to mine. "He must be careful."

Careful? Why? What did this mean? I opened my mouth to ask questions.

Efrain spun around and hurried to the passenger side. He threw himself into the car.

Sophia looked confused but put the car in gear. She and Tomás waved as they pulled out.

It seemed clear Efrain used the iPad as an excuse to come here. I tried to hear Efrain's voice again. Was it a threat or a warning?

11

Monday's late-afternoon sunshine bathed the ballpark with harsh light that no sunglasses filtered completely. If heat and light are a problem for you, Tucson is not your place. Four diamonds backed to each other and games were underway at two of them. Josie had come earlier with another of her teammates. Sami ran ahead to join the brothers and sisters of the players creating their own shenanigans at the far end of the field, where parents could keep an eye on them. I wandered over to find my regular place in the bleachers.

I loved the games. Loved watching Josie racing across the infield as shortstop, coming into her own grace. Her face full of determination and concentrating on her teammates. She might not be the best player on the team, and I didn't harbor any dreams of scholarships, but she held her own and thrived in the sport. I even enjoyed Sami's games, though I didn't expect she'd stick with the sport for more than another season or two. She was more interested in singing and dancing with her friends in the outfield than keeping track of the ball.

Mom hadn't missed any of my games until the accident. She'd taught me how to throw and bat in our backyard. She'd yell encouragement from the bleachers at every game and win or lose, she'd always be my biggest fan. Those memories hovered close to my heart when I smelled the grass and watched the kids with faces red from exertion. When I kissed grass-stained and bloodied knees.

I had memories of Mom and Dad from other places, but the ball field were my favorites. Dad made it to plenty of games whenever work allowed. But Mom was there every time until I was twelve, and I felt her with me today. She'd love to see her granddaughters and hear their laughter.

I made it to our side of the bleachers and paused at the fence with Amber and Jasmine. I knew most of the parents on our side. Regulars, like me. We cheered and commiserated. Sometimes we second-guessed the coach, but she led our girls to more wins than losses and didn't create unneeded drama and stress, so we didn't get too critical.

Sami played some kind of tag with complicated rules she'd explained to me several times. Her pack ran and jumped like beans in a hot frying pan.

Amber pulled off her ball cap, brushed back her short hair and stuffed it back on. "I hope Bella decides this is her last season. I'm so danged sick of sitting out here in the sun every week."

Jasmine grinned behind giant sunglasses. "I'm going to grow roots and be here through eternity. Three more kids after this one."

We started talking about the other team when a shrill hello interrupted us.

All three of us turned to see a dark-haired woman hurrying over and grabbing Jasmine's hand. "I thought that was you."

Jasmine didn't seem as enthusiastic in her greeting. "Moira. Do you have a kid playing?"

Moira waved her hand. "My daughter is captain of the Busy Bees. She's the tall one. The pitcher."

We all nodded. "Oh sure." The mean one who'd called Amber's daughter a skank during warm up.

Jasmine's voice sounded tight. "Moira, these are my friends, Amber Brown and Michaela Sanchez." We said hello and Jasmine continued. "Moira goes to our synagogue."

Moira's smile seemed more prideful than friendly. "Michaela. I've always loved that name."

"Her brother calls her Mike," Jasmine said.

She cocked her head. "Why would he do that?"

I didn't owe her an explanation, but I hated to make it uncomfortable for Jasmine. "My brother is ten years older than me. He wanted a brother and when they brought me home, he pretended I was a boy. He's always called me Mike."

Amber laughed. "I can so see you as Mike."

"What have you been up to, Moira?" Jasmine asked. I knew her well enough to hear the reluctance in her voice. Obviously, Moira wasn't a favorite of Jasmine's.

"Oh, this and that." Moira started in with chatter and I tuned her out. Sami seemed to be directing the game on the end of the field. I pulled out my phone to check the time. Deon was going to try to knock off early to see the game. If he didn't hurry, he'd miss it. We hadn't told either of the girls about his plans. They didn't need the disappointment if, as so often happened, he was a no-show.

I stuffed the phone back in my pocket, found Josie in the huddle with her team, glanced over at Sami again, and caught sight of a uniformed man.

My heart slammed against my ribs. Jared. No. Not here. Not now. Why couldn't he leave me alone?

He stood at the curb by the parking lot and looked over the field, probably trying to spot me. I never thought he'd follow me around. It wouldn't be hard to figure out my schedule. He could not be here. My skin crawled with regret as if I stood in a red ant pile. Somehow I had to figure out how to get rid of Jared for good.

I turned my back and tried to slide around Amber, who had a couple of inches on me and might hide me from view. She hadn't moved away, far more polite than me.

She stepped back to make room for me to join the discussion. Or rather, the monologue.

As far as I could tell, Moira hadn't taken a break to let anyone else speak. "So I took the kids to the book festival last weekend. They have such fun at the kids' section. Got their faces painted and they insisted they wanted to see R.L. Stein, you know the guy who wrote *Goosebumps*. I never understood what people see in those books. I mean, people actually die. It's too scary for kids, but whatever. So the line was so long I left them there and popped over to another tent and I'm so glad I did because it's the last time anyone will ever hear Manuel Ortiz speak again. And I was there."

I'd been concentrating on not turning around to see if Jared approached, hoping my eyes didn't look any more glazed than those of my two friends. Now Moira had all my attention.

"What a dynamic speaker. He's like, well, Martin Luther King or something. So eloquent and passionate."

She sucked in a breath and I hoped she wouldn't go on. Of course, she did.

"Such a tragedy. Honestly. But there can't be much mystery who did it. I mean, it was so obvious."

Amber and Jasmine looked a little more interested than before. Jasmine said, "I read the article in the paper this morning. They said there are no suspects."

Amber added, "If the cops don't know who did it, how come you do?"

Moira folded her arms. "They have to say that while they gather enough evidence to make the case stick when they bring him in."

I knew what she was going to say before she said it.

"It's obviously that guy, oh, what's his name? You know, the Border Patrol guy, that super-hot handsome one who was in all the media last year defending the guy who shot the kid. You know. I followed that case really closely." She paused to laugh in a girlish way. "Probably because, hello, that guy is so hot. I can't believe I forgot his name."

You followed the story because of the hot guy, not because there might be serious issues on the border. As you do, of course.

Jasmine and Amber both flicked their eyes to me and then down at the ground as if synchronized in awkwardness.

"So last year, I thought that kid might not have had a gun but he was up to no good, you know, like they said. What was he doing at night on the border if it wasn't to cause trouble? Maybe create a diversion for drug smugglers."

Big breath and she leaned in as if imparting a confidence. "But the Border Patrol guy was there at Manuel Ortiz's speech. Just as bold as you please. And when Manuel was calling for people to take a stand for the immigrants crossing the desert, this guy, he gets all aggressive."

Chris hadn't been nearly as aggressive as Ortiz. I clenched my teeth to keep from defending my brother, knowing it would only escalate the situation.

Amber and Jasmine shifted and looked toward the field. Jasmine said, "Oh look, the girls are taking the field. It's been good to see you." Her smile at Moira looked painful.

Moira lifted her head to the diamond but apparently wasn't ready to give up. "This guy, he gets all up in Manuel's face and he says the immigrants have no right to be here. I mean, he looked like he could kill Manuel right there. It was really scary."

Amber took a step back as if ready to climb the bleachers.

"What was his name? Come on, you remember, don't you? It's going to drive me crazy." She snapped her fingers. "Oh yeah. Chris Wright."

Finally, Moira looked at Jasmine, then Amber, then me. She must have seen something unusual. "What?"

I waited a moment and Jasmine cleared her throat. "Chris Wright is Michaela's brother."

Moira's mouth dropped open. "Really? He's such a racist, though."

I had to unclench my jaw to answer, but I kept it tight to hold back what I really wanted to say. "Protecting the border doesn't automatically equal racist."

Moira studied me a moment. "I know you, though. I've seen you around the ball field for a couple of years. You've got that drop-dead gorgeous husband and those two pretty little girls. They're dark, like their daddy."

I glared at her, warning her to stop.

Clueless. "So how does that work, with your brother being Border Patrol and your Latino husband?"

"It works fine."

She didn't seem satisfied with that. "I know you want to defend your brother and all that, but you weren't there. You didn't see the unbridled hatred in his face."

Okay. That was enough. Jasmine and Amber disappeared and my vision narrowed to the pious face in front of me. "As it happens, I was there. What I saw was a man on his bully pulpit calling for violence against people who uphold the law. I heard him say in plain words that people should get their guns and hunt down Border Patrol while they're doing their jobs." I lifted my hand and pointed at her, taking a step forward. My voice rose in anger. "Do you know how often my brother and the other agents save the lives of people who don't have enough water to survive? He helps people who brought their children on this journey without food or clothing or good shoes. Do you know how often he's saved groups of people abandoned by coyotes who stole their money and left them to die?"

Amber put a hand on my shoulder. "The game's starting."

The ump shouted, "Play ball."

I blinked. Looked around. Most of the parents in our vicinity stared at us. Cheers across the field went up. I looked at Jasmine and swallowed, my throat raw, as if I'd been yelling. "Sorry. Yeah, the game."

Moira stood before me, her complexion pasty and her mouth slightly open. I gave her one last look full of daggers. *Aggressive this, bitch.* I turned my back and stomped down the foul line, my eyes catching Sami, now sitting in a circle with several other children.

"Michaela." God, I'd forgotten about Jared.

I changed directions and met him a few feet away from Amber and Jasmine. Moira's retreating back scurried to her own sidelines. "You shouldn't be here," I spit out.

He nodded. "I know. But you won't return my calls and we need to talk."

I shook my head. "Not here. I'll call you."

Behind me, Deon's voice was far too close. "Hey, I made it."

I spun away from Jared to see Deon grinning like he'd just discovered fire.

I swallowed and tried to get my systems back to normal. Moira and Jared had me all stirred up. "That's great."

Deon turned his attention to Jared and stuck out his hand. "Hi. I'm Deon. Do you have a daughter on the field?"

I tried to sound relaxed and easy. "This is Jared Hanson. We used to work together."

Jared shook his hand. "We sure miss Michaela on the force."

Deon watched the game for a second, then quickly glanced at Jared. "It's a tough job to do when you're a mother."

I might have argued with him at another time. But not today. I put an arm around Deon's waist and drew him toward the bleachers. "Nice seeing you." I didn't look back.

Only a few minutes into the second inning, Ann showed up, Efrain pushing her wheelchair. Deon and I descended to the lowest bench and Efrain positioned Ann next to us. She immediately started cheering for Josie's team.

"Thanks for bringing her," I said to Efrain.

He watched the game. "Watching them play makes her happy."

In another few minutes, Chris arrived. He patted Ann's head, messing her hair.

"You brat," she said and swatted at him, but her voice held a hint of laughter, their spat yesterday forgotten.

He stood behind her chair, resting a hand on her shoulder. "What'd I miss?"

Chris didn't look at me. What had I done wrong? He couldn't really believe I had told anyone about his partner taking bribes. I needed to get him alone and see what was going on with him.

Deon winked at me before he answered. "Josie scored a run."

"Of course, she did." Chris grinned as if he were solely responsible.

He'd barely finished speaking before Sami threw her arms around his waist. "Uncle Chris!"

He ruffled her hair. "Hi, squirt."

Deon shook his head. "I get a wave from across the field. He gets a hug."

"Familiarity breeds contempt," I said. I sought out Moira on the other side of the bleachers. No surprise she'd narrowed her focus to us.

Sami ran off to play with her buddies. Our family made the biggest ruckus of the whole game. Not only did we cheer for Josie, but her teammates and even the girls on the other team when they made a good play. We could afford to be generous, even though we would have supported all of the girls anyway, because we held a firm lead all the way through, with Josie going on to score another run.

After the final out I trotted over to retrieve Sami from her own game. Josie was accepting hugs and congratulations when I returned.

"How about pizza at Oregano's to celebrate?" Deon offered to everyone.

Ann looked tired and begged off. Chris mumbled, "Not tonight," and strode toward the parking lot.

"That's the best idea I've heard all day." I tried to sound enthusiastic, but my eyes tracked Chris's progress to the parking lot. "I'm going to talk to Chris for second. We'll meet you at Oregano's," I said to Deon.

Sami pulled away from me. "I want to go with Dad." Josie had already staked her claim by standing with him. They'd always loved Deon, but Josie had grown to that stage where Dad held all the allure and I was yesterday's garbage. Only natural that Mom lost favor at some point, but it still stung a little.

"Okay. I'll be right behind you."

They stopped to talk to another family before going to Deon's Audi in the other direction. I hurried after Chris, afraid he'd already taken off. Angry voices struck me before I shot from behind the park sign. Chris stood at the tailgate of his pickup, his face red and eyes fiery.

Another man faced him, leaning forward, his chest thrust at Chris. A Latino, he spoke with a mild accent. "It wasn't me, man. I was standing here. Didn't see a thing."

Chris's hands formed fists at his side. "I saw your kid get out of your car and whack his door into my truck. I was right here."

The guy shrugged with fake indifference. "I didn't see anything."

I inserted myself between the two and put a hand on Chris's hard chest. "Hey, I don't see a dent or even a scratch. Come on, let it go."

Chris shifted his attention to me. He shot anger and recrimination at me but only said, "Leave me alone." He spun around and lurched into the driver's seat. The engine roared and the man and I scurried out of the way as Chris backed up.

I shot the man an apologetic smile and hurried to my Pilot to join the exodus from the parking lot. It didn't take long to get to Chris's apartment complex, and I pulled into an empty slot a few spaces away from Chris's pickup.

He had already walked to his apartment door but glanced at me when I pulled up. He turned away.

I jumped out of the car. "Chris, wait!"

He stopped with his back to me on the walkway in front of his dumpy apartment complex. It was one of those two-story stucco complexes built around a tiny pool with a couple of grills and picnic tables cemented in a hardpacked dirt courtyard. Temporary housing for singles and young families hoping for better circumstances. Or people like Chris, who rarely stayed home and didn't care to spend his money on housing.

I stomped to Chris. "What is going on with you? You won't talk to me. You're losing your temper everywhere. What did I do?"

He slowly faced me. "It's not always about you."

"Okay. So, what's it about?"

The anger roiled off him. "Okay. It is about you."

"What?"

"I told you about Andy Bentley in confidence. How did Manuel Ortiz know to throw that name out? It had to be because you told someone."

I stepped back. "Chris. I swear. I didn't tell anyone."

He swatted my words away and started to turn his back but stopped to watch as a faded blue sedan eased into the parking lot and pulled into a place a few spots down from us. Two people unfolded into the fading sunlight.

A middle-aged man with a suit that might have looked good five years ago but now sagged at the knees and elbows joined a woman in an equally unattractive navy pants suit. They looked up at the apartment building, probably noting the numbers attached to the side.

I'm not a psychic, but I knew these people didn't bear good news.

The man caught sight of us and tapped the woman on her arm, nodding in our direction. She gave a slight dip of her head and changed direction.

Chris watched with wariness.

When they approached us, the woman lifted her eyes to his 63frame. "Christopher Wright?"

He narrowed his eyes. "That's right. Who are you?"

The man pulled a badge from his pocket. "Hal Collins, Tucson Police Detective."

She opened her suit jacket and rummaged in the inside breast pocket and pulled out a matching badge. "Maureen Todd."

On a normal day Chris could deal with this and more. But he hadn't been normal for a while. I needed to stand in for him. "What's going on?"

Maureen Todd ignored me and focused on Chris. "We'd like you to come with us."

Chris's face looked dangerous. "What's this about?"

Hal Collins kept his eyes on Chris. "We need to ask you a few questions."

Chris didn't move for a second and then said, "About what?"

Todd's voice sounded firm. "The murder of Manuel Ortiz."

Chris stood motionless for a beat. "What do you think I can tell you about that?"

Todd stared hard at him. "We'd rather talk at the station."

I opened my mouth to protest and Chris held an arm out like a railroad crossing barrier. He hadn't taken his eyes off Todd. "I've got nothing to say."

Collins stepped forward. "Then you won't mind saying it on the record, at the station."

Todd reached out and placed a hand on Chris's arm.

They were not going to take him away. This was insane. Before I thought about it, I grabbed Todd's arm and yanked it from her hold on Chris.

She spun around and reached behind her back for what could only be her weapon. We exchanged one look, the split second it took for me to rethink and withdraw my hand, step back, and raise both my hands in surrender.

Chris lowered his head. "Okay." He stalked toward their sedan and they hurried to keep up.

I resisted the urge to wring Collins's and Todd's necks. "I'll fix this," I shouted before Chris climbed into the backseat

The dark look he shot me over the car's hood chilled me. "You've done too much already."

12

The sunset brightened to flashing oranges and pinks, with the clouds providing a deep indigo before dusk dropped into darkness. I spoke on the car's speaker as I drove across town.

"He got a lawyer, right?" Deon asked.

Deon wasn't making me feel any better. Chris wasn't stupid. He knew what he needed. "I don't know. They didn't arrest him, just wanted to interview him."

"There's nothing you can do at the station. All you can do is wait for them to finish. And that might take a long time."

I whipped off the street into the drive-through of a sandwich place, hoping to get something with a little nutrition to keep my blood sugar balanced. "I can't leave him there alone."

I didn't need to be with Deon to see the small wrinkle of irritation form between his eyebrows. "I'll get the girls to bed and see you when you get home."

Traffic thinned downtown and I had time to wolf down my sandwich before I pulled into the police station parking lot. I entered into heavy air conditioning and walked up to the desk, separated from the small waiting room by thick safety glass.

The officer looked up. I didn't recognize the young man but hadn't expected to. It had been six years since I'd worn a Tucson Police Department uniform. "Is Detective Maureen Todd or Detective Hal Collins around?"

The officer frowned. "They're both busy."

"Do you know when they'll be free?"

He eyed me closer. "Can someone else help you? Are you having an emergency?"

This wasn't getting me anywhere. Those steel safety doors used to be open to me. I knew what it was like to be buzzed through and enter the catacombs of cubicles behind this sentry. I hated not being part of the brotherhood.

While I contemplated my next move, someone crossed the corridor behind the desk. I couldn't be this lucky. Without thinking I reached out and slapped the safety glass and shouted, "Jared! Hey, Jared."

The officer behind the glass jumped to his feet. He put a hand on his gun belt. "Ma'am. Step back from the glass."

He must not have heard me, and I tried once more. "Jared!"

"Ma'am. Please." The young guy looked nervous.

"Page him. Officer Hanson." I pointed behind the desk officer. "He just walked by."

The guy gave me a skeptical look. "I don't ..."

"Do it. Please." I resisted banging on the glass or the stainless-steel counter.

I didn't need to. A foot and leg, then whole body backed from the corridor and with a slight arch to his back, all of Jared slid into view. "Michaela?"

I let out a deep breath. No way should I be engaging with Jared. But I had to do it. "Let me in. I need to talk to you."

Jared made eye contact with the other officer. He nodded his head in an okay to let me in. "She's ex-cop. She only looks crazy."

The guy looked from me to Jared and then hit the buzzer that indicated the door's latch release. Jared held it open and I rushed inside.

Without saying much, he put an arm around my shoulder and gave me a quick squeeze before ushering me through a door to the rows of cubicles.

I cringed at his touch and pulled away. He didn't take it any further. I glanced at my old cubicle in the middle of the room and fought the urge to step inside.

We made it to Jared's space, and I sat in a chair in front of his desk. He said, "You're probably here because you miss the coffee, huh?"

The whole shop smelled the same—stale coffee, fast food lunches and suppers eaten at desks piled with paperwork no one wanted to do, and the underlying odor of people who worked in the desert sun, even though a lot of that time was spent in air-conditioned cars. It gave rise to a flood of memories and nostalgia.

I had loved being a cop. Every time I'd put on that uniform and heavy belt, load myself into a cruiser and set out on a shift, my heart beat a little stronger, the colors seemed brighter. I never knew what the next several hours would bring. A domestic with some asshole wanting to eke out justice on his girlfriend. A drug deal gone bad. A car wreck. Disturbing the peace. Stolen goods. Interviewing victims and slime balls. People needed help, and I could do something about it.

I sat in a chair next to Jared's desk and tried to gather my wits.

Jared leaned back in his plastic office chair that ought to be a larger model. He lost his grin. "So, they've got Chris in for questioning for Manuel Ortiz's case."

I leaned forward. "What do you know?"

He spoke with a fake admonition. "You know I can't tell you confidential information."

"Do you know anything?"

"Nope." He let that sit. "But if I did, I wouldn't be able to tell you, for instance, that someone saw Chris and Ortiz exchange words right after he spoke at the festival."

"Everyone saw that."

"Apparently, it didn't stop with the blow-up at the tent."

At Koffler? Did someone see him enter? "I wonder where they might have been seen doing that?"

Jared folded his hands and rested them on his flat belly. "At the doorway to Koffler building."

So, no one saw Chris enter. "I can't imagine they had anything more to say to each other."

Jared raised an eyebrow. "Chris Wright is known to have an opinion or two on people crossing the border without papers. By all accounts, Ortiz's speech contained plenty of references to the evil nature of the Border Patrol, not to mention a call to arms and maybe some violence directed at said Patrol."

Now I leaned back. A public verbal boxing match wouldn't be enough to peg Chris as a suspect. "Is that all?"

"As far as I know, there are no charges against him. It's a friendly questioning in an ongoing case."

"Will they be in there a long time?"

"Now that I can't tell you." He sat forward and tapped his desk. "My shift is over and I'm just finishing up some paperwork. Why don't you let me take you for a beer?"

If it had been anyone else, I might have taken him up on it. I stood. "Thanks, but I want to hang out here and wait for Chris."

"It might be a long wait."

I nodded. "Yep. But he'd do the same for me."

Jared joined me and placed his hand on shoulder. "I could wait with you."

I ducked from his touch. "Jared." I hoped he heard the warning in my voice. I wanted to growl at him to stay away from my daughter's softball game, but he'd helped me get into the station. Still, he had to stop touching me.

He sighed and sounded frustrated. "Okay."

Three feet separated us as we walked down the corridor and I wished it could have been thirty. I waited for the officer to buzz the door again. "Thanks."

I paced the lobby. Read articles and social media on my phone. Paced more. Played Angry Birds, which didn't help my mood. Finally, around eleven o'clock, the door buzzed and Chris walked through.

He hesitated when he saw me jumping from the hard plastic bench. "What are you doing here?"

I hurried over to him. "Thought you'd need a ride."

"I'll take an Uber."

"I didn't know if you'd have your wallet."

He glared at me. "And you wanted to know what's going on."

I felt like we held two ends of rope in a tug-of-war and I didn't want to give in. "I didn't want you to be alone."

We exited the building with relief. The evening still carried warmth from the day but not enough to cause a sweat.

"Go home," he said. "I can take care of myself."

His rejection punched me. "Whatever you think, I didn't tell anyone about Andy."

He pulled his head up and stared at me. "Since you're the only living soul I confessed to, I can't think of another way he found out."

"I swear it." My voice didn't crack but my insides felt as though they might.

"You were the one person I trusted." He sounded as broken as I felt.

"You can—"

He stopped and pulled out his phone. "I don't need you in this."

"In what?"

"Nothing."

"Chris. Don't shut me out."

He turned his back on me and punched his phone, calling for a car.

13

Deon snored slightly.

I slipped into bed next to him and curled around him as gently as possible. Deon.

I burrowed closer to him, taking in that Deon smell of deodorant, soap, and warm skin. Thank god I hadn't done anything more with Jared. From now on I would have nothing to do with him. No phone calls. No contact. I shouldn't have turned to him for information tonight. Did that mean I owed him? It didn't matter. Jared was not part of my life.

Deon rolled away. "How'd it go?"

"We can talk in the morning," I whispered and snuggled close again, kissing his bare shoulder.

He edged away, leaving a cold space where our skin had touched. Late on a Monday night and he had to work in the morning, it made sense he'd need to sleep. But I remembered a time when making love wasn't contingent on convenience.

I lay awake a long time, fighting an urge to drive to Chris's apartment. I had to fix whatever stood between us. Fate had taken Mom and Dad away from us; I refused to let Chris disappear, too. The only way to win back Chris's trust was to let him know I'd always be here for him. That meant clearing him from any suspicion.

* * *

When I opened my eyes, morning sunlight from the half-open blinds striped the comforter and the wood floor. Mourning doves cooed and the *whirr!* of quail filtered through the window. This wasn't right. I blinked and focused on the bedside clock. Yikes!

The covers flew back and I sat up, grabbing the blood sugar monitor from the bedside table. I punched it, noted that it was slightly low, and raced from the bedroom. I stopped only long enough to grab my bathrobe from the hook on the back of the door and wrap it around my naked body.

"Everyone up. We're late," I shouted as I ran down the hall and took the stairs two at a time. We had ten minutes to get ourselves together and launched down the driveway. And I needed to get some juice down my throat.

My feet slapped the cool tile of the downstairs hallway as I rounded into the kitchen.

Deon stood at the counter facing a fully dressed Josie and Sami as they sat in stools finishing bowls of cereal. They looked at me with a mixture of surprise and humor.

"Good morning, sunshine," Deon said.

I stopped to catch my breath. "Why didn't you wake me?"

He shrugged. "I was about to. I can't get the rugrats to school because I'm meeting Angela and Lupe."

Sami gave me an appraisal. "You ought to brush your hair and put on clothes first."

Josie slid off the stool and walked away. "I'll be in the car."

I turned to Sami. "Have you brushed your teeth?"

She gave me that put-upon look kids do so well. "Oh, man."

I pointed toward the stairs and watched her go.

Deon leaned in automatically and I gave him a closed-mouth kiss to save him from my morning breath. "I'll probably work late tonight," he said.

I nodded. "I might need to leave the kids with Ann. I'll let you know."

He picked up the bowls and put them in the sink. "No problem. What have you got going on?"

I poured a glass of orange juice and took a long drink before saying as casually as possible, "I need to figure out who killed Manuel Ortiz."

He stopped as if mentally doing a double take. Then he laughed. "Single-handedly you're going to find the killer. Even though police are investigating with a team of professionals."

I gulped the rest of my juice. "They think Chris did it or they wouldn't have taken him in for an interview. They aren't going to keep looking when they think they've got their man."

Deon inhaled slowly. "There are so many things wrong with this. And I don't have time to list them all for you. If there's no proof Chris shot Ortiz, then he won't have to worry. Just don't get involved. It's not your fight."

I kept a lid on my temper. "It is my fight. Chris is my brother."

"Okay. I used the wrong word. We can support Chris. Find him a good attorney, help him out with bills or whatever he needs. But you can't go poking your nose into an active investigation."

The *you can't* made me want to punch him in the throat. "Why not? I'm trained. I've got to make sure they don't pin this on Chris."

Deon checked the clock on the microwave. "Are you so sure Chris is innocent? He's been pretty vocal, and Ortiz did try to discredit him in a pretty public way."

His words slammed into my brain and I pulled in an unbelieving breath. "What? Chris had nothing to do with Ortiz's murder. Absolutely nothing."

Deon held his hand up. "I'm sorry. I didn't mean that. You know I didn't. It's just that I've seen Chris's temper. I know how he feels about Latinos."

My hold on my temper was slipping fast. "What do you mean, how he feels about Latinos?"

His glance went to the clock again. "I can't get into this. I've got to be at the office in ten minutes."

"You can't accuse my brother of murder and walk away." I stepped between him and the door to the garage.

"I didn't accuse him of anything. Just do me a favor and don't go getting into trouble on his behalf."

I felt Deon's impatience, but the condescension struck me like a blow.

"Helping him out and finding out who really did this isn't getting into trouble."

"Come on, Michaela. You go too far defending your brother. You always have."

Ann said the same thing yesterday. "What's wrong with loyalty?"

He put a gentle hand on my arm to nudge me aside. "Nothing, except when it jeopardizes your family."

I didn't budge. "How is doing a little checking around into Manuel Ortiz's life putting my family in jeopardy?"

He started to push past me. "What if someone else did kill Ortiz?"

"What if?" I put a hand on Deon's chest and shoved. "*What if* someone else? You asshole."

Deon raised both hands. "Okay. Look, we can talk about this later. I've got to go. Hardworking people are counting on me to help them get justice enough so they can work at minimum-wage jobs."

"Well, don't let me stop you, Mr. Noble. Go save the whole world. I'll look out for my family."

"*Our* family includes Josie, Sami, and me. Don't forget us in your family tree."

"Mommy?"

Deon and I both spun around to see Sami with a look of horror on her face. Her eyes glistened with tears.

"Oh, Sami. It's okay." I hurried to her and knelt.

"Are you and Daddy getting a divorce?"

It might be funny if she weren't so upset. Deon knelt beside me and put an arm around both of us. "Of course not. We were discussing something."

"You were yelling at each other." A tear spilled down her cheek and then another.

This showed how often Deon and I disagreed if it could cause this kind of alarm. I patted her back. "You fight with Josie all the time. This isn't much different. Dad and I are still friends. We still love each other."

Deon hugged her tight, then hugged me, giving me a kiss. "I love Mom and I love you and Josie. Sorry we scared you, but we're good."

I looked him in the eye. "We're good."

He couldn't blame me if he took that to mean I wouldn't look for Manuel Ortiz's killer. It did mean, however, I would be here to look after the girls when they got home from school.

14

The first stop had to be Ortiz's house. It wasn't hard to find his address and it took me to a small adobe bungalow in a historic part of town, several blocks from the university. The house didn't look like much, especially for a lawyer with family money who'd done well for himself. But Manuel Ortiz liked to say he was a man of the people, so this moderate home would reflect that.

Like Chris, Ortiz hadn't been married and he lived alone. My vague plan to get inside involved me donning my uniform and relying heavily on luck.

I pulled up in front of the house and sat for a while, checking the neighborhood. Mid-morning on a weekday in a neighborhood where most homes hid behind adobe walls gave the whole place an abandoned feel.

Deon and Chris—the two most important men in my life, who usually sat on opposite sides in most things—would both agree that I had no business doing what I was about to do. If TPD caught wind of it, I'd be the one sitting in a jail cell.

I got out of my Pilot and sauntered up the sidewalk in front Ortiz's house as if I were any uniformed cop doing what needed to be done to investigate a murder. No matter I wore the Arizona Rangers uniform and not one from TPD. Without looking around to see if anyone watched, I kept the same confident stride around the house to the ornate metal gate into the yard. If it was locked, I'd be screwed, since hurdling over the six-foot adobe fence might not look professional.

Luck was on my side and the gate swung open. The front yard, though small, looked like paradise. A gurgling water feature cascaded over rocks, and leafy citrus trees shaded the patio. French doors guarded the small house. Patios with honeysuckle vines covered in a profusion of salmon-colored blossoms hung over trellises to create a lush, cool space. I wandered around the house, noting the nooks with comfortable outdoor furniture, a clay chimenea in one spot, a built-in tiled fireplace in another, and everywhere citrus trees and flowers, green plants, water fountains. The perfumed smell of orange blossoms hovered everywhere. If I had a million dollars and all the time in the world to plan outdoor living space to tuck an old desert home into, I'd never create something so beautiful. What an awful thought that Ortiz would never spend time here again.

I followed the pathway around the house to another set of French doors that opened into a galley kitchen. These were locked, but with only a little manipulation, they easily popped opened. The cops or Ortiz, or whoever left here last, hadn't secured the doors with the bolt at the bottom. Good for me.

I stood on the stone steps and looked into the Mexican tiled kitchen and waited for an alarm. Nothing. Apparently, Ortiz wasn't a paranoid type. He should have been.

The house probably sat empty most days when Ortiz was alive. He'd be gone to work for long stretches, not to mention speeches and travel. Yet, knowing he was dead, the place felt bereft somehow. Eerie in its silence. I hesitated to even think the word *haunted*.

I had no business being there.

Certainly, the detectives had already searched the place and carted away anything of value in the investigation. I didn't know what I expected to find. But I had to start somewhere. My rubber-soled uniform shoes made no sound on the Saltillo tile as I padded through the kitchen with its fancy espresso machine and new mesquite cabinets with glass fronts. Did Ortiz cook here often, with the outside doors opened to the fragrant blooms? Small but with an efficient layout, the soft oranges and golds blended with accents of turquoise and sunburnt reds. Beautiful and peaceful. Undeniably expensive.

A living room opened toward the front of the house. Cool, with natural light from the doors whose panes showed the fantastic outdoor living space on two sides. It contained an overstuffed couch and chair upholstered with the same desert-bright colors of the kitchen. I pulled latex gloves from my pocket and fitted my hands into them.

With someone so vocal, it seemed Ortiz would have no dearth of enemies. I knew very little about him aside from him targeting Chris as a poster boy for racism. He'd done interviews on cable news, even scoring a few Sunday-morning shows. Always painting Chris as the evil apologist for a racist agency out to destroy lives.

Chris had remained dignified in the face of these attacks, but it took its toll. His days at the Border Patrol might be coming to an end because he'd become a target for protesters. Maybe that's why he seemed to carry so much anger lately.

An authentic Navajo rug accented the living room. Floor-to-ceiling bookshelves of rich dark wood filled one wall. He may pretend to live simply and be an advocate of the downtrodden, but this home—its furnishings, décor, and patios—was a testament to elegance and expense. Sure, this house would fit into the ground floor of my suburban cookie-cutter place, with some room to spare. But living this well was something I could only dream about. And after seeing its existence, I would probably dream about it.

I leaned in to study the pictures on the shelves.

Manuel Ortiz with the governor. With civil rights big cheeses. Cap and gown outside UA School of Law. Nothing out of the ordinary. Heavy law tomes filled most of the shelves, with a couple of bronzes of desert animals and some pottery. All so tasteful and rich.

No computer, of course. If there had been one, the investigators would have taken it. I made my way to the bedrooms. Only two. One looked like a generic guest room. More nice belongings that told me nothing. The bed in the master room was made. The bathroom spotless. My guess is that Ortiz had a very good cleaning person who serviced his home daily. Maybe even cooked for him. Rich people could afford that kind of indulgence. Weird that I could feel that little bite of jealousy when, for all this beauty and perfection, Ortiz would never spend another night here.

I wasn't truly envious. I loved my roomy house with the confusion of four busy lives, the noise and clutter. I didn't have to deal with antique plumbing and wiring and a cramped kitchen and bathroom with no counters. I didn't have to hide behind a curtain of foliage and high walls to keep the street noise at bay. It might be Stepford-ish, but I loved sitting on my deck with its view of the Catalinas.

More built-in shelves in his bedroom contained the same eclectic mix of pottery, photos, and books. I gave them a quick glance. Then stopped and peered closer. My blue-gloved hand reached out and fingers closed around the frame of an old snapshot.

Two grinning young men in Levi's and T-shirts stood on either side of an older man with a well-trimmed beard. I held my breath, my heart thudding. Ortiz looked confident and happy, his grin bright. The older man's picture had been on the front page of today's paper as he stood outside Manuel Ortiz's office, where an informal protest had formed. Dr. Regis Bartholomew.

The same man I'd helped on the day Chris's recruitment presentation was tear gassed.

The newspaper article said Bartholomew had been advocating for a peaceful demonstration, trying to quell the violence he feared would erupt from Ortiz's death. As a law professor at UA, he'd taught Ortiz and served as an advisor and friend since. I hadn't read the whole interview, but the face on Ortiz's shelf jumped out at me, even if this picture was twenty-five years old. The date wasn't a guess. I knew when this picture had been taken, almost to the day.

My eyes bored into the face of the third person in the picture. I remembered that shirt, the one with the cactus and the green lettering that said, *Can't touch this.* At twelve years old, it had seemed hilarious to me and exactly what Chris would like for his twenty-second birthday.

And here he stood with Dr. Bartholomew and Manuel Ortiz, sometime between his birthday on May sixteenth and the accident on June fifth, when he'd ripped that shirt off to use it to staunch the blood oozing from Mom's temple.

The awful scene played out and I couldn't stop it.

Ann, at seventeen, home on a Friday night to babysit, even though I was twelve years old and could take care of myself. But I'd been mad because she wouldn't pay attention to me. I'd done something so stupid. How much of the chocolate had I eaten before I felt dizzy? Before I lurched up the stairs and banged on the bedroom door for Ann to let me in? Before the world swam in front of me and I slipped to the floor?

After that, everything drifted in and out of my memory. It was all bathed in deep blues and shadow. Dad lifting me in his arms. Mom's and Ann's concerned voices. The car door slamming closed and my head resting in Ann's lap. She kept telling me she was sorry, but I didn't know why.

A lurching and rumbling as Dad drove down the dirt road from our house north of Tucson. The isolated desert that suited Mom and Dad was the cause of their three children's endless complaints about being so far away from friends and school and everything worth doing.

I didn't want to take the memory any further, but I had no power over it. Seeing that shirt ... I felt as though my skin was ripped from me, leaving raw and ravaged bone and muscle, exposing my heart to a tearing wind that would race across it like metal on a tooth filling. Every time I remembered, every dream that disturbed my sleep, every breath I took, I longed to stop what happened next. I never could. No matter how much I begged the universe to take it back, the devastation remained.

The horrible crunch of metal on metal, the jolt of movement changing from forward to sideways. Screams, glass, shrieks that might have been human or mechanical. Light that couldn't have been shining but seemed to explode. So much chaos. Everything good ripping from my grasp, my life. Even in that split second, even as a child, I knew. I'd ruined it all.

I remember red strobing light. Ann on a stretcher disappearing into the back of an ambulance. Chris. Holding me. Crying. Clutching me to him, rocking, nearly smothering me. He was bare-chest and only afterward, much later, did he tell me about Mom and Dad and the blood.

I clutched Chris's neck because I didn't know what else to do. Over Chris's shoulder I saw the boy.

No one ever believed me about him. Maybe my traumatized brain concocted him from thin air. But I saw him as clearly as I saw Ann's hand drop from the side of the stretcher. As sharp as the blue and red strobes over the crumpled steel that was our Impala.

His eyes were round and liquid in the glow of the emergency lights. He was staring at me, clenching some stuffed toy to his chest, then he looked to the right. I followed his gaze and saw the man in jeans that hung on narrow hips, a torn Western shirt, his hair ragged and unkempt. His hands were behind him and I realized they were handcuffed.

When I looked back, the boy was gone. I asked Chris about him. I asked Ann. No one saw him.

* * *

I don't know how long I stood in the middle of Ortiz's bedroom holding the photograph. When the ornate mesquite headboard and polished dresser and the full shelves, came into focus I felt tears on my cheeks. This memory blindsided me more than I'd think it would after so many years. I missed Mom and Dad. I hated that Ann spent most of her time in a wheelchair. I ached for Chris that he'd never fulfilled his dream of being a lawyer.

All my fault.

I set the photo back on the shelf. Then picked it up again.

Chris had known Ortiz for a long time. If this picture meant anything, Ortiz and Chris had been friends. Close enough that Ortiz kept a framed picture of them in his bedroom. What did that mean? Chris had never mentioned Ortiz to me in all the years we'd lived together. Even when Ortiz went after him, Chris hadn't said they'd known each other in law school.

I turned to leave the bedroom and glanced at the bedside table, to the books Ortiz had stacked beside the leather-shaded lamp. A thick hardcover on military history. A biography of Martin Luther King Jr., and on top, a paperback thriller. That's what caught my eye. It was a book Chris recommended to me.

A closer look made me approach the bed and pick up the book. A slip of paper marked Ortiz's place. I snatched it from the novel, not like he would need to know what page he'd left off.

The garish yellow that caught my eye turned out to be exactly what I'd thought. A familiar sticky note with *World's Greatest Dad* taking up most of the space. Deon had acted pleased with the gift from the girls but told me they didn't work well for notes because of the colorful slogan. Apparently, he'd found a use for them after all.

I stared at the paper with writing in Deon's distinctive script. The name leapt out at me and I tried several ways to make sense of what I saw. *Andy Bentley*.

The fellow agent Chris had been concerned about. The one taking kick-backs from coyotes carting people across the desert. I hadn't told Deon about Andy. But Ortiz had known, and Chris suspected me. Deon must have heard Chris telling me about Andy while we were on the patio. Why would he have told Ortiz? He wouldn't betray me like that.

Would he?

My stomach lurched and whirled. This couldn't be happening. Deon and I were a team. Together. We always had each other's backs.

Except when you're sneaking off to a hotel room with Jared.

But I hadn't done anything. I'd stopped because of Deon. Because of what we have together.

He'd never betray me. He wouldn't.

But in my hand I held the evidence that he had. I stuffed the paper into my pocket and squeezed the frame of Chris's photo, regretting I'd ever set foot in Ortiz's house.

* * *

I didn't remember walking from the bedroom through the living room and out the kitchen door. I probably closed the French doors on the way out. The iron gate in the front wall seemed firmly closed as I gazed at it from behind the wheel of my Pilot.

Chris's photo with Manuel Ortiz and the note from Deon swirled round and round my head in a confused stew so thick I'd lost track of time. In a jolt of panic, I glanced at the clock and drew in a breath. Still plenty of time before I needed to pick up the girls from school.

My phone buzzed in the shirt pocket of my uniform and I realized it wasn't the first ring. An earlier ring must have jolted me out of my thoughts. Without looking at the ID, I punched it on.

"Michaela." Jared's voice punctured the haze in my brain.

"I thought I told you not to call me."

He didn't hesitate. "Yeah. You did. And I'm not calling you to talk about us. I found out some information about your brother and I thought you might want to know."

I sat up and blinked away the last of my clouds. "I do. What is it?"

"I don't want to tell you on the phone."

I didn't trust him. "I'm not meeting you at a hotel."

"Of course not. I think you want to hear this in person, that's all."

I didn't know where I stood with Chris, and my whole foundation with Deon seemed shaky. The only thing I knew to do was find Ortiz's killer. "Meet me at the McDonald's on Grant and First."

"I'm on my way." He sounded pleased with himself.

I had about an hour before picking up the kids, and this was on the way to their schools.

It only took me a couple of minutes to get there and after checking my blood sugar, I ordered a fruit smoothie and sat in my car under a Palo Verde tree with its yellow blooms.

In a couple of minutes Jared pulled up beside me in his TPD Bronco. He stepped into my Pilot and settled himself in the passenger seat. He eyed my drink. "Did you get me one?"

"You can get your own after I leave."

He looked disappointed. "How have you been?"

I tilted my head and flashed him a warning look. "What do you know about Chris?"

"There's no reason we can't be friends, is there?"

I'd been crazy to hope he'd stick to the bargain. "If I thought you'd be content with that, I'd say sure. But you're pressuring me for more."

He held up his hand. "I'm sorry, okay? I like you. Obviously. I thought maybe we could take it further, but I respect that you want to stay happily married."

"You do?"

He smiled. "Yeah. But that doesn't mean I wasn't frustrated at the hotel.

You have to admit it wasn't cool. I mean, I've known you for years and I've thought about you a lot. To get all the way there and have you stop, well, you can't blame me for being upset."

I hated feeling like a jerk, even when I deserved it. "Let's just forget it happened, okay?"

He nodded. "Sure. Forgotten already. And now, we can be friends again, right?"

I doubted it. "Okay." I gave it as long a moment as I could, then said, "What do you have to tell me?"

He picked up my smoothie and took a sip, as if being friends meant sharing. "I heard they got some numbers off Ortiz's phone."

"I imagine they did. Are you going to tell me what?" I couldn't keep the annoyance out of my voice.

"Jeez. You're testy."

"My brother might be accused of murder. I'm not feeling patient." And Chris has known the dead guy for a lot longer than I realized. And it looked like my husband has betrayed me.

Jared held up his hand. "Okay. So, he got two calls after the demonstration at the festival. One was to this number." He held out a slip of paper. "Do you recognize it?"

I took it. A Tucson area code and digits ending in 2004. "Nope. Didn't they trace it?"

"Burner. No record of the owner."

"Who was the other call?"

"Your brother."

"Chris called Ortiz?" Why?

"It looks like it. Not long after the call, Ortiz sent a text asking Chris to meet him in Koffler. The same room where Ortiz was found."

Shit. "And they're sure Ortiz sent the text? Someone could have used his phone."

"Of course. They know that's a possibility. But it doesn't look good for Chris."

If they knew Chris had been in Koffler, it would look even worse. "Did they question Chris about it?"

Jared shrugged. "I don't know. I'm not supposed to know this much. And you're definitely not supposed to know."

I stared out the windshield. The sun had shifted to send shards of sunlight into the Pilot, letting the heat filter in. The breeze from the open window didn't offer much relief. What would Ortiz want to talk to Chris about?

Jared tapped my shoulder. In a sing-song voice he said, "Thank you, Jared. This is great of you to risk so much by giving me this super-secret information."

"Yes. Thank you. I'm sorry." I tried to give him a grateful smile, but it didn't go very far. "I hate to boot you out, but I've got to get my kids from school."

He frowned at me. "That's it?"

Nothing's free. "I thought we agreed to be friends. Friends do things for each other."

He frowned, clearly not hearing what he wanted to hear. "Yeah. Okay. Guess I'll see you around."

He climbed out and shut the door. I shouted through the open window and he leaned in to hear me. "Thank you. Really. I do appreciate this," I said.

He brightened and I regretted calling him back. "If I hear anything else, I'll let you know."

I pulled out before he'd shut his car door.

15

If Ortiz and Chris had been friends when they were younger, Fritz would know about it. He'd probably be at Mi Casa, doing whatever chore Ann had assigned for him. I might be able to catch him there before he left to open the bar.

Josie was not happy to make a stop at the center on the way home from school. She balked when I told her to find a quiet place and do her homework. Sami, however, loved to hang out at the center. Sometimes she helped Efrain or Fritz with whatever they were working on. She often played with children staying there. If nothing else, she was young enough to enjoy coloring with the markers and crayons always kept there.

When I pulled up in front of the old stucco office building, the girls took off in separate directions—Josie to Ann's office to do her homework, Sami to check out everything at a full run.

A small white Honda, probably twice the age of Josie, puttered into the parking lot and pulled up beside me. A Latina in her fifties smiled at me as she got out.

Efrain appeared around the side of Mi Casa. He paused when he saw me, a look of panic sweeping across his face. He glanced behind him, as if contemplating running away.

The woman squealed and jogged toward him. "Efrain. *Sobrino.*"

He held something wrapped in a tattered towel and with one worried glance at me, turned his attention to the short, round woman throwing her arms around his neck. His face relaxed a little and a rare smile formed. "Tia Alma."

Tia? Aunt. Ann told me Efrain was an orphan and had no family. This painted a different picture. I realized I'd been staring and stirred, heading toward the back of my car.

Efrain thrust the package he'd been holding into the woman's hands.

She gave him a curious look and whipped the towel off to reveal a bright blue javalina about two feet high, sculpted from sheet metal. Her delight was obvious. She thanked him in a string of Spanish I couldn't hang on to and kissed his cheek.

Efrain blushed and looked at the ground, but he seemed genuinely pleased. It didn't seem right for me to watch them, so I opened the tailgate of the Pilot and stacked a case of bottled water onto a flat of juice. I'd had just enough time to buy some supplies as cover for my unannounced visit.

Efrain spoke quietly to her and they enjoyed a quick conversation. She glanced at me and smiled. In a moment, she kissed him again and walked back to her car. She turned to him and held up the javalina. "*Gracias, Efrain*."

He seemed embarrassed and waved at her while she drove away.

I kept gathering supplies and felt Efrain join me. "I can take those into the kitchen," he said.

"Thanks." I stood back so he could lift the stack. "Is that your aunt?"

Efrain jerked his head to look down the street, as if surprised a car had been there. "Yes."

"Oh. Does she live in Tucson?"

He shrugged. "South of Marana. Down Molina Road. She has been there for twenty years."

I roughly knew the area. Desert that hadn't felt the encroachment of Tucson yet. "Did you make that javalina?"

He shook his head. "No. I saw it from a vendor on the roadside. Tia Alma loves the animals. Puts them in her yard. She has many."

"She seemed really happy to get it. And to see you."

He lifted the drinks. "Please. Do not tell Miss Ann. She does not know about Tia Alma."

"Sure." I watched as he lumbered into the building with his head low. Why did Efrain keep his aunt a secret from Ann? Another niggling bit to add to the strangeness of Efrain. But who was I to pry into other's secrets? I had plenty of my own.

I reached into the back for a wrapped package, glad I didn't have to explain it to Sami and Josie. The blaring afternoon sunshine hit my back as I opened the glass door and stepped into Mi Casa. A young woman in ragged jeans and shirt sorted through a box of donated clothes at the long table. A toddler and slightly older child played with blocks on the floor. Sami had joined them and paid me no attention.

Ann's door was open and Josie sat in front of the desk while Ann spoke on the phone behind it. The back doors were propped wide where sounds of hammers and a radio blared.

I walked up to the woman at the table and she turned to me, wary and cautious. "*Perdón.*" I stumbled through Spanish asking her if she knew a new arrival by the name of Sophia.

She said yes, Sophia was in her room. I asked about Tomás, and she said he was probably with Sophia.

"*Gracias.*" I headed down the hall. The corridor ran the entire length of the building. A stub wall with windows on the upper area ringed the inside, giving a view of the courtyard. Offices, now converted to dorm rooms, lined the other wall. I'm sure there was some kind of regulation about housing people like this with communal bathrooms and I had no idea how Ann got around it all, but she managed to move immigrants in and out, helping desperate people find jobs and more permanent homes. I was proud of the good work Ann accomplished here.

The door to Sophia's room was open. Tomás giggled as the two of them sat on the narrow bed they shared in the sparsely furnished room. He had the Batman figure in his fist and was waving it in the air, dive bombing his mother. I knocked on the door. "*Hola.*"

She jerked as if shot and whirled around, keeping Tomás behind her on the bed. When she saw me, she relaxed and her face split into a grin. "*Hola!*"

She jumped up from the bed and hurried over to me. "Please, come in." She spoke in Spanish, and I concentrated to catch what she said. "I am very thankful for you giving me this chance. Ann is so kind and she helped me to find a job. I am going to share an apartment with another woman and her children."

Her enthusiasm made me smile. With halting Spanish, I told her how happy I was for her and Tomás. Then I pulled the wrapped package from the Target bag. "May I give Tomás a gift?"

Her eyes grew wide and she started to shake her head. "You've done so much for us already. A gift is not necessary."

In halting Spanish, I said, "It's not much and it would make me happy."

She must have seen it mattered to me because she spoke to him. "Tomás, this nice lady would like to give you something."

Tomás, his dark eyes big and shy, slid off the bed and took slow steps toward me. He focused on the brightly wrapped box in my hands.

I held it out to him. "For you."

He seemed unbelieving. "Another present?"

"You've had others?" That surprised me.

Sophia pointed to a sock monkey sitting on the desk. "From a new friend."

Tomás seemed to be using x-ray vision to see through the wrapping paper of the package I held.

With a wince, I said quietly to Sophia, "Those always seemed kind of creepy to me." Something kicked at the back of my brain, a memory I didn't want to see.

She nodded toward her son. "To him, too. I'm afraid he hurt our friend's feelings."

I held the package out to Tomás. "I hope he likes this."

He gave his mother a questioning glance and she nodded. With eyes on me, he extended his hands and let me place the box in them. I urged him. "You can open it."

Again, he looked to his mother for assurance, then sat on the floor and gently tugged at the tape on first one end, then the other. With care, he slid his finger under the center tape and the paper ripped. He gasped and looked up to us.

"It's okay," I said. My kids were paper rippers, confident there would always be more presents in their lives. They'd have shredded the paper getting to the good stuff inside. I wished Tomás could rely on the assurances of more gifts.

When he finally had the paper loose, Sophia leaned over and lifted it off the box.

Tomás gasped. He squealed and jumped up, the box in his hands. He yelled now, his excitement too much for him to contain. "Batmobile! Mamá! A car!"

He shoved the box at me, leaving me little doubt that I was supposed to extract the car from the plastic chains that held it firmly in the box. I ended up having to pull a pair of travel scissors from my purse to saw through the impossible restraints. All the while he jumped and chattered, almost not believing his good fortune.

Sophia thanked me over and over and I exited as soon as I could to leave them to themselves, happy I'd brightened Tomás's day and, by association, Sophia's. Still, an old weight tugged in my chest.

I looked through the window into the courtyard and located Fritz in the shade of a mesquite tree hammering on some kind of scaffolding.

The thump/squeak of Ann's crutches made me turn to her approach. "What have you got Frtiz doing?"

She glanced out the window. "Building a frame for beans. He's been at it all day. Thank you for the drinks. We were getting low."

"Give me a heads up next time." I wanted to talk to Fritz before he took off for the Hot Spot and took a few steps down the corridor.

She started to move with me. "You brought something for Tomás, didn't you?"

I shouldn't feel as if I'd done something wrong. "Just a Batmobile. Not a big deal."

"Maybe."

I slowed my pace so she could keep up and she clumped along beside me. Using her wheelchair was more efficient, but she struggled with her crutches often to try to keep herself as strong as possible. I hoped the new pool would help.

Two chairs snuggled in a bright alcove on the inside wall of the corridor. Ann paused and braced herself to sit. I guessed that meant we were going to talk. I peeked at Fritz with the hope he'd still be there after Ann finished with me.

She lowered herself and propped the crutches against a round glass-top coffee table, while I thought of the best ways to answer her inevitable questions about Chris. Somehow, she must have found out he'd been questioned.

The afternoon sun left this sitting area in shade, so it felt comfortable. "Should I get us a soda?" I asked.

She shook her head. "I'm worried about you."

Oh boy. At least I wouldn't have to dodge questions about Chris. "Me? I'm okay. Nothing to worry about."

She eyed me. "Really? Because you just brought a gift for little boy you don't know. Or, maybe you do know him?"

Busted. As usual. I could do a dance around it, but there didn't seem to be much point to that. "Yes. It was me at the hotel who told Sophia about the center."

"I knew it was. We'll get to that, but I want to talk about why you brought the toy."

Suddenly defensive, I shot back. "Why not? He doesn't have much. It seemed like a nice thing to do."

"It is a nice thing."

There.

She wasn't done, of course. "But I think there's more to it."

"What more could there be?"

"Guilt."

I folded my arms. I had other things on my mind. Such as Deon's betrayal and Chris's friendship with Ortiz. "Right, Dr. Ann. What am I so guilty about?"

"The same old story. You think the accident was your fault."

I forced a laugh. "My god. That was so long ago. I hardly even think about it."

Her look told me I hadn't convinced her. "You can't lie to me. You've never been able to get away with it. So, I'm here to tell you once again, that accident was not your fault."

Most of the time I didn't argue since it did no good. Today I fought back. "It was."

She sighed. "You were twelve. You have diabetes and went into insulin shock. We took you to the hospital and there was a traffic accident. None of that is your fault."

"But the chocolate ..."

"Yes, the chocolate. We've been over that. You were twelve. Mom shouldn't have left something so dangerous in your way. But I'm more worried about this obsession you have with the little boy. Your guilt over someone who doesn't exist."

I didn't argue about seeing the little boy the night of the accident. I'd fought that battle and given up. They wouldn't believe me.

She put a cool hand on my wrist. "You can't go around giving every little boy a present because you think you're responsible for the pain of a boy you see in your dreams. Even the therapist said it's likely you conjured him up as a symbol of your guilt."

She meant the therapist they'd made me see once a week for a year after the accident. Even Chris and Ann didn't think she helped me much and eventually let me quit going. Whatever they said, the boy wasn't a phantom. I know the man he saw, the one driving the car that killed Mom and Dad, was that little boy's father. I know it. And because of everything I'd done that night, the boy's father hit a car and killed two people.

The United States government wasn't about to forgive that kind of mistake. Even twenty-five years ago, before the vitriol of the current border situation. They'd deported that driver. Sent him back to Mexico. But they hadn't found a little boy.

Because of me, that boy had grown up without a father. I knew better than anyone what a hole losing a parent leaves in your life.

Ann waited and I didn't say anything. "Okay, you aren't going to talk to me about that. So, let's talk about what you were doing at a hotel in the middle of the morning."

This was even worse. "Let's not."

Ann leaned forward, squeezing my wrist. "Something is bothering you. I've seen if for a long time. You need to talk to someone."

I jerked my arm away. "You're imagining things."

She raised her eyebrows. "I am? Let me start with the man watching you from the ballpark parking lot last night."

How did she know?

"Remember that field day for Sami last month? I sat in the stands while you were at the sidelines. The same man was there that day and I could tell by your body language he was not just a coworker from your cop days."

That day Deon had to be in court. I'd "accidentally" mentioned it to Jared when we'd crossed paths while I was working security at the courthouse a day earlier. I had been flirting with Jared. Seeing how close I could get to the fire without getting burned.

Ann sounded like a stern mother. "And now I find out you were at a hotel in the middle of the day."

I stared at the tiled floor.

"Look, I'm not judging you. I'm trying to help you."

I finally looked up at her. "You can't." I thought a second. "And you are always judging me."

She reached for my hand again and I let her take it. "Okay, maybe I am. I think you're being stupid and selfish, and I think I can help you. You're trying to destroy your life. Somehow, you think you don't deserve to be happy and you're going to do everything you can to make sure you aren't."

"That's crazy."

"No, Mike. It's not."

Tremors started from inside of me and radiated outward. Great heaving sobs rolled in my stomach and I shoved them down. "I love Deon and the girls. I don't want to ruin our lives."

"Of course you love them. But this thing with this other man. What are you doing?"

"Nothing," I whispered.

She sat back, clearly frustrated. "If I can figure this out, don't you think Deon knows something isn't right?"

Is that why he betrayed me by telling Manuel Ortiz about Andy Bentley? Retaliation?

She sighed. "You've been given so many gifts, Mike. So much in life has gone well for you. You have a wonderful husband, two bright and healthy children. A beautiful home. And yet, you seem determined to throw it all away."

"I'm not." I mumbled the words, but my thoughts turned to what Ann didn't say. That she wasn't given those gifts. She married Fritz, a man who would rather drink beer and watch baseball than do anything else. She pushed and prodded him constantly. The Hot Spot barely paid their bills. It was no secret Ann had wanted children, but the accident that destroyed her legs damaged her so she couldn't bear children. She never complained; at least, not that I heard. But she must harbor resentment for what she thought I took for granted.

She leaned in, her voice one of concern. "What about being a cop? Huh? You can say what you will about helping people and wanting to be the good guy, but you and I both know you thrived on the danger. You keep wanting to tempt fate, maybe hoping you'll finally get what you feel you deserve."

I leaned back in my chair and folded my arms, keeping my mouth tightly closed.

"And Deon. Does he deserve this game you're playing? Do you understand how lucky you are to have a man who adores you so much?"

And yet, he betrays me and my family.

"He not only makes a great living, he's an involved father. I know you always say he's not perfect, but, honey, he's as good as they come. And you're going to fool around and throw it all away."

I stood up. This had gone on too long. "I need to get the kids home and start dinner."

She stared at me a moment. "Are you walking away from me?"

I shifted my gaze down the hall. "Yeah. I think you're spending too much time worrying about me. You're off base about all of it. I'm not having an affair. I'm not trying to sabotage my life." What I was trying to do was help Chris. But I didn't need to drag her into that.

She reached for her crutches. One thing about Ann, she wouldn't give up on trying to make me talk it out. It seemed impossible she'd put the clues together and figured out about Jared, but she'd always had a preternatural sense about me and trouble.

After the accident, when Chris and I visited her every Sunday, she'd read our faces as we walked into her room and knew immediately if we'd had a good or bad week. She always voiced an opinion on how we should proceed. We listened to her advice, then did whatever we planned to do anyway. If we failed, she'd be the first to tell us she had known better. If we succeeded, she might just take credit for that, as well.

She seemed to know she wasn't going to get anywhere with me now, but I wasn't fooled that she wouldn't come after this again. She lurched to her feet. "I need to get back to work. See you later."

Fritz stood back to survey his work and I worried he was about to quit for the day. I took off in one direction as Ann lumbered the other way.

I poked my head into Ann's office to check on Josie.

She looked up from her algebra book. "Can we go now?"

"Just a few more minutes." I left to the sound of her supremely annoyed sighing.

Sami had two tots playing leapfrog in the lounge room while their mother looked on.

I sped into the courtyard. When Ann bought the office building, the courtyard had been a landscaped center with cactus, succulents, and stone benches. She'd been transforming it into a vegetable garden. Over the course of the years she'd had volunteers—as well as Efrain, Fritz, Chris, even Deon and me and the kids—hauling out pea gravel, shoveling in dirt, hoeing, raking, fertilizing, planting, and doing it all again until now the soil was rich. Her garden supplied fresh produce to many grateful people.

I found Fritz at the back of the garden amid a tumble of lumber and rope, creating a trellis for Ann's climbing beans and peas.

"This is going to be great," I said, hoping to sound encouraging when really I thought the whole thing would collapse in the first big wind.

Fritz looked up from where he knelt on the ground, packing dirt around a post. "It's a good thing beans aren't heavy."

I edged closer to Fritz. "Can I talk to you a minute?"

He jerked his head up. "That sounds serious."

I waved it away. "Not really. Just have a question to ask."

He pushed himself to his feet with a chorus of grunts. "Maybe when it falls over, Ann will believe I'm not a carpenter and will never make me build something again."

I laughed. "Doesn't work that way. Wish it did."

Fritz grabbed a half-full water bottle from a bench and followed me to the shade of a grapefruit tree. The branches hung heavy with fruit Ann gave to anyone who asked.

Fritz dropped to the ground and I squatted close to him. "What's up?" He tipped his head back to let the water drain down his throat.

There didn't seem to be much reason to draw this out. "Did Chris and Manuel Ortiz used to be friends?"

Fritz coughed on his water. He didn't look at me as he slowly set the bottle on the ground and placed the cap on top. "Why are you asking?"

"Detectives took Chris in for questioning last night. I'm afraid they suspect him in Ortiz's murder."

Fritz's jaw dropped open. "Oh, shit. That's not right."

"I'm trying to head them off by finding them another suspect. Chris and Manuel used to be friends, right?"

"What makes you think that?"

It didn't seem like a good idea to tell him I'd been rummaging around Ortiz's house. It might technically be breaking and entering. "How long were they friends?"

Fritz seemed to be mulling over his answer. "I'm not sure I'd call them friends, exactly."

That's exactly what they'd looked like in that photo. "What would you call them?"

He took his time. "Don't know. Classmates, maybe? I don't think they knew each other long."

"Why did they quit being friends?"

The back of Fritz's throat clicked as if he swallowed in a dry mouth. "I don't know. Maybe because Chris dropped out of law school."

"But before that, they'd been tight?"

Fritz brought his eyes to mine. "Who knows? I was working at the bar then. I hardly saw Chris. He had a lot of new friends. Seems like they were always having study group and staying up all night talking about case studies or whatever. I hung out with them sometimes after the bar closed. They were always up late studying or arguing about boring stuff."

It sounded like maybe he'd felt abandoned. "All that ended after the accident?"

Fritz dragged a hand over his face, wiping the sweat that had accumulated. "Everything changed. You know that. Chris dropped out of school to take care of you."

He caught himself and looked me in the eye. "I mean, he was glad to do it. You were, are, really important to him. He never regretted it for a single day."

Right. That's what everyone took great pains to tell me. The accident wasn't my fault. Chris made the decision not to let me be placed in foster care. Ann didn't miss having two strong legs. They could lie to themselves; I didn't believe them.

"If they'd been such good friends when they were in school, why did they end up such bitter enemies?"

Fritz picked up the water bottle and toyed with the lid. "Manuel wanted to make a name for himself. Like all those civil rights leaders. Martin Luther King Jr. or Cesar Chavez. Chris happened to be a means to that end."

That didn't seem enough. "What about you? Did you know Manuel back then?"

Fritz shook his head. "Maybe he'd been at some of those study things when I showed up late. I couldn't say."

I watched him for a minute. This hadn't got me any further along. "Okay. I'm trying to come up with something to help Chris. I thought you could help me."

He stood. "Wish I could. Sorry, but I've got to shower off and get to the Hot Spot." He didn't walk away, though. Instead, he shifted from one foot to another. "One thing."

I'd bet anything he'd been debating telling me this *one thing* the whole time. On alert, I waited.

He banged the empty water bottle against his leg. "Manuel came into the Hot Spot last week when Chris was there. Manuel hardly got a word out when Chris all but threw him out. That's when Chris started acting weird. Mad all the time."

Chris and Manuel spoke last week?

"I've really got to go," he said. As he hurried off through the back gate to his house, I turned to gather up the girls, trying to think why Manuel would have sought Chris out at the Hot Spot. A rustle near the newly constructed trellis caught my attention.

Efrain stood staring at me, his face striped with shadows from the trellis.

16

Deon sent me a text on our way home saying he'd be working late again on the cleaners' case. His pro bono work usually came after hours. My heart already pounded in my chest and sharp pangs stabbed my stomach. The last thing I wanted was to face Deon with the evidence he'd betrayed me. What would I say? What did I expect to happen?

I had to confront him, of course. I couldn't let this go. With thoughts sticking and bunching in my head, the foundation I relied on felt shaky. I tried to keep from showing the girls my distress. My blood sugar level showed I needed to eat, but cooking seemed too difficult.

"How about In-N-Out?"

Even Josie got excited about that. I didn't have to give any thought, just ordered my usual animal style and the girls didn't notice when I wrapped up most of it and tossed it along with the rest of the trash.

The hours after we got home were filled with the usual homework, TV, permission slip signings, and discussions about upcoming ball games and schedules. Because of a teacher training, the girls had the next day off school, so getting them to wind down and drift off to their own rooms took a long time. Eventually the house quieted as the girls settled in and presumably went to sleep.

I paced. Dreading what was coming and yet hoping he'd Deon would get home soon. I finally shut off the lights, turned on the night light above the stove, and sat upright on the couch in the family room off the kitchen.

Close to midnight the garage door sounded on its track and Deon's car purred into place. The kitchen door opened, and Deon entered the dark house. He quietly set his briefcase on the wide granite breakfast bar and slipped off his shoes to leave by the door.

He made his way to the refrigerator and when he swung open the door, the light shone on me. He startled, then laughed. "You look like a ghost. What are you doing up so late?"

I stood up. I ached from sitting motionless for so long, grinding away on everything. "We need to talk."

His face showed concern. He closed the refrigerator door, leaving us in the gloom of the night light. "The girls? Josie flunked her algebra test?"

I shook my head.

"Sami? What's going on?"

"It's not the kids." Even to my ears, my voice sounded strained.

Now his eyes zeroed in on me, something deep and afraid in their depths. "What's going on? Are you …?"

Whatever he wanted to ask, his throat stopped him from saying. Maybe Ann was right. He knew about me and Jared. Or knew me well enough to suspect something.

"Why did you tell Manuel Ortiz about Andy Bentley?"

He might have been worried I'd say any number of things, but this didn't seem to be one of them. He seemed knocked off-guard. "Andy Bentley? I don't know an Andy—"

He stopped, his face registering the name. I waited.

"Oh. The Border Patrol agent."

Now I advanced on him. "Yeah. The man who is taking bribes. The one Chris was having a moral dilemma about. The same man Chris spoke to me about confidentially, in the privacy of my own home."

Deon looked more defiant than regretful.

I took another step, my voice hard. "How could you do this to me?"

He took a moment, as I'd seen him do when arguing in court. "I didn't do anything wrong. In fact, I did Chris a favor."

My jaw dropped open. "What?"

He leaned a hand on the counter. "Think about it. Chris was agonizing over what to do about Andy Bentley. What Bentley was doing killed him, but he also had a duty to the brotherhood. He felt trapped."

I heard him but couldn't believe him.

"What I did was take the matter out of his hands. I gave Manuel the information so he could stop it."

"That is some messed up logic."

Deon closed the gap between us. "It's perfectly reasonable."

"You betrayed me."

"No. You know what Bentley's doing is wrong. He's hurting people and he needs to be stopped."

"But it wasn't up to you. And your meddling made everything worse for Chris. You should have known Manuel couldn't be trusted not to drag Chris into this."

"I didn't mean to overhear you and Chris. I happened to open the window when you were talking. But once I knew, how could I do nothing?"

I slapped the counter. "Because I'm your wife and Chris is my brother, and now you've given the cops a reason to suspect Chris."

"Bentley's actions don't reflect on Chris."

"Manuel Ortiz sure made it seem like they did. It triggered Chris to lose his temper in front of a bunch of witnesses."

"It wasn't me who made it bad for Chris. How well do you really know Chris? You have an illusion of a big brother who took care of you. A hero who is out helping those in trouble in the desert. But what do you really know? This man, this noble person, was letting his friend make money on human trafficking. He was allowing people to suffer to protect a friend."

"He would have turned Bentley in. You know he would have."

"No, I don't know that, and neither do you."

We stared at each other, both of us breathing hard. His eyes found mine and a question formed in them. "How did you find out?"

"It should have been because you told me."

He didn't let that distract him. "Where did you find out?"

I pulled the note from my back pocket and laid it on the counter in front of him.

He looked at it, then back at me. "That's the note I gave Manuel. How did you get it?"

"This isn't about me. It's about you and why you decided to destroy our marriage."

He narrowed his eyes. "You were at Manuel's house."

"You sabotaged Chris and now he's under suspicion for murder. If he's arrested, I'm dropping it at your feet."

He reached out and grabbed my arm, a move that shocked me into silence. I'd never seen Deon strike anything or anyone, not even smack a golf club on the ground after a slice. But his fingers closed tight around my wrist. "Why were you at his house?"

I yanked away from him. "I'm trying to help Chris. I need to figure out who killed Manuel Ortiz so my brother won't end up in prison."

"Damn it, Michaela. Do you realize a man was murdered? Manuel Ortiz didn't die in his sleep. Leave this alone or you could end up the same way."

"I'm not in any danger. Whoever killed Manuel is not coming after me."

"If Chris is the killer, then no, you're right. You're safe."

"I can't believe you said that. You bastard."

"I'm sorry. But if you're right and it isn't Chris, then someone else is out there and if they find out you're poking around, it could be bad for you."

"Quit being so paranoid."

Deon's voice rose. "Manuel was pressuring people on both sides of the border. You have no idea the danger you're in."

"That's stupid."

"Or the kids."

I looked at the note, my stomach a broil of acid. I'd hoped he'd be contrite and apologize. I never expected him to act like this. My heart shattered and the shards ripped through me. "I want you out of here."

He clenched his fists. "This is my home. My family. I need to be here to protect you."

"You're the one we need protecting from. You betrayed us."

He huffed. "That's over the top."

"I don't think so."

"You can't kick me out of my own home."

"That's exactly what I'm doing."

"I'll sleep in the guest room."

"I don't give a shit where you sleep, but it won't be under my roof."

We stood in the half light of the kitchen. I couldn't say how long we faced each other, neither of us speaking. Deon's face sifted through emotions: wrath, defiance, frustration, concentration, resolve. I loved that face.

Everything about it. The way he suddenly broke into a grin at an unexpected sight of me. The concentration while he figured out how to take apart my broken toaster oven and put it back together. I love the way his eyes got a wicked gleam when he wanted to take me upstairs. And the way those same eyes grew dark with passion. I loved the way he rubbed his whiskers on the girls' faces on Sunday mornings, making them squeal and swat at him. His was the face that greeted me when I came out of an insulin coma in the hospital. The face I woke to every morning.

How could I be sending this face from me? If he left, would he ever come back? Would I want him back? I held on to my resolve by gripping the edge of the granite.

Finally, Deon let out a breath. "I'm going to a hotel. Just for tonight. We'll talk about this tomorrow."

I stood silent. If he'd have held out two seconds longer, I would have caved. I watched him slip his feet into his shoes and pick up his briefcase from the counter. I thought about rushing upstairs to get him a clean shirt and underwear. How absurd to even consider it. Let him figure it out on his own.

* * *

I washed my face and climbed between the sheets. But I didn't sleep. After tossing and turning, I gave up and tried to busy myself to keep from going crazy. By the time the eastern sky lightened, I had cleaned the refrigerator and sorted the pantry. My hands were occupied, but my brain jumped and pivoted with no straight line.

What had I done? Did I want to find some excuse to send him away before he could find out about Jared and blame me? Was our marriage always destined to end in failure? Maybe turning Bentley in to Ortiz had been the right thing.

Deon hadn't turned Chris in to Ortiz, though. Couldn't, because Chris hadn't been guilty. But by turning in Bentley, he'd exposed Chris to Manuel Ortiz and tossed him back into the storm.

I couldn't help wonder about the phone call from Chris on Ortiz's phone, the meeting between them at the Hot Spot, and why Chris had fought with Frtiz. Always, my mind kept seeing Chris's back rushing away from Koffler. What did this all mean?

My phone buzzed across the granite of the breakfast bar. It was barely dawn. The only person up now would be Deon. Was it too late to apologize?

I'd overreacted. We could talk about this. I'd tell him he might not have been right to do it, but I was relieved he'd stopped Bentley. I eagerly reached for the phone and flipped it over.

But it wasn't Deon's ID shining from the face. I punched it on. "Ann?"

She sounded scared. "It's Chris. He's been arrested."

My heart slammed into my ribs and I propped myself on the counter.

"They picked him up last night and are taking him to the jail soon. We have to go there. We have to help him."

"Arrested? How do you know?"

"His attorney called me. She said the cops went to his house and took him."

I gulped, trying to get my air.

"Come and get me now. We have to be there," she said.

If there was a crowd, Ann couldn't hold her own in her wheelchair or crutches. "It's not safe for you to go. And I can't leave the girls alone."

"Deon can get them to school this once."

"No. He's not here. It's a day off of school so they'll be home."

"Where's Deon?" She paused. "Okay, well. He's not there." Maybe she thought Deon had found out about Jared and left me. She didn't ask. "Drop them off here. I'm sure we can find something for them to do."

That seemed like the best solution since I didn't have time to call their friends' parents and make other arrangements. I had to get to the courthouse. Hoping my Ranger uniform would give me the illusion of authority, I chose to wear it instead of civilian clothes.

I woke Josie and Sami, standing in the hallway outside their open doors so both of them could see and hear me. We needed to get moving, so I spoke while they woke up. I tried to explain—in a factual but not scary way —that Chris had been arrested. I told them Deon was at work and I needed to go help Chris. Sami popped out of bed and chattered about helping Efrain plant pole beans.

Josie rose slower and seemed worried. "They arrested Uncle Chris? But he didn't do it."

I stood in the doorway urging them to hurry. "Of course not. We're going to fix this and that's why I have to go."

She pushed herself up, her dark hair tumbled, full of tangles. Her face was so much like Deon's it ripped at me. "What can you do?"

Good question. "I don't know. But he's got to see me there. Know that we're here for him."

She considered that. "Tell him we love him."

I hugged her, took the stairs two at a time to pack them juice and cereal bars to eat on the way to Ann's, and rushed out to the garage. The Pilot moved through traffic as I wove in and out of lanes to cut seconds from the commute. When we reached Mi Casa, I flew from the car, held the door open for the girls, and gave them a quick kiss, not ushering them inside.

I made another flying trip across town. Word of Chris's arrest had circulated quickly. There had to be more than a hundred people gathered outside the downtown police station. They seemed to know the officers would bring Chris out the back to the parking lot to drive him to jail. A mass of about a hundred people bunched around the gate arm that kept them from the lot.

They chanted "Murder patrol" and shouted the same lines about Border Patrol as an extension of the KKK they'd used at the recruitment event. With someone as skilled as Manuel Ortiz at their lead, they might have been more cohesive. This felt like a roil of anger and frustration surging like lava inside a volcano.

I fought my way through the throng. The jostling and shoving didn't stop me. My Ranger uniform didn't seem to give me any priority and no one made room for me. Two of the local network affiliate news crews held positions just inside the gate arm. The cops and protestors left them alone. I worked my way nearly to the barrier and wedged myself against a wall of bodies, hoping to slip through so Chris would see me when they escorted him into the parking lot.

Twenty minutes later the station door swung open and three uniformed cops filed out close on each others' heels. Next, Maureen Todd squeezed through, maybe wearing the same navy blue suit she'd had on when she'd showed up at Chris's apartment to take him for questioning two days ago. Only now it looked even more wrinkled. Her partner, Hal Collins, eased out sideways, his left arm wrapped around Chris's handcuffed arm. He pulled Chris through the door and Maureen Todd grabbed Chris's other arm. Three more cops exited the station behind Chris. The entourage made their way toward a marked SUV.

The crowd erupted in shouts so loud the words blended into a wave of vitriol. A surge from behind welded me to the first line of people and my feet left the ground for several seconds as we all billowed forward, leaving me scrambling for a foothold. The man in front of me stumbled and I finally slipped to the front with people pressing me against the guard arm.

This must be what Christians heard when they reached the Coliseum arena and the lions were let out. "Chris!" I shouted, sure he'd never be able to hear me above the roar.

Miraculously, Chris's head snapped toward me.

"Chris!" I screamed again. I couldn't tell him how much I loved him and believed in him. There was no time or space to say anything, I only hoped he'd be able to hear it all when I said his name.

Someone burst through to the front line, as I had done. I wanted to create a link with Chris so he could feel my love. I searched for his face, but the man who'd broken through raised his arm.

The movement triggered all my training and instincts. Without waiting for the action to register, I lunged on legs more like springs. Airborne, flying toward the man, my arm outstretched and already swinging in a downward arc to intercept with his hand holding a gun.

Pointing at Chris.

It all happened without my conscious thought, in a millisecond stretched over a decade. No sound, no plan, just my overpowering need to protect my brother.

My forearm connected with the shooter's, bone on bone, driving his arm down as the shot exploded, bringing back the sounds of the crowd, the sudden screams, the clatter of the gun as it fell from his grasp. I didn't know the bullet's exact path, but it was aimed at the pavement. A ricochet could injure someone. I'd done the best I could.

Hands closed around my arms, dragging me back, lifting me from the ground as I fought. I needed to get to Chris. Touch him, make sure he was safe. Bodies, some in uniform, some in plainclothes, men and women, pulled and dragged. The same kind of group crowded around the shooter and he was lost in a bustle of people moving away and through the door of the station.

Noise and confusion and a clatter of voices and feet on the hard-surfaced floor rattled as the other bunch hustled down the corridor and out of sight. I assumed they were taking the shooter to a holding cell.

My captors shunted me into an interview room without closing the door. When they released their hold, I realized only four people had held me and dragged me inside the building. They circled me like a wall of protection.

"He had a gun," I managed to say. "He was going to shoot Chris."

One of the women, this one in a TDP uniform with a name tag identifying her as J. Lourey, spoke quietly to me. "Do you know who he is?"

A sudden urge to maim made me clench my fists. "He wanted to kill Chris. Is he the only shooter? Is Chris okay? Where is he? I need to see him." I tried to wheel away from the four people around me.

Lourey stood in front of me, legs spread, arms at her sides and ready to react. "Do you know Christopher Wright?"

I looked over her shoulder. In the station there was no sound from the crowd outside. "He's my brother. Is he okay?"

J. Lourey seemed to be the unofficial spokesperson for the group. "He's fine. He's protected and safe."

"Safe? Like he supposedly was when you let someone open fire on him?" I wanted to take a swing at anyone and everyone. Chris could have been killed. And these jerks wouldn't get out of my way.

"Am I under arrest? And why? You can't keep me here." I put a hand on the shoulder of a man in chinos and a polo shirt. He might have been Johnny Citizen or a clerk or intern. He looked uncertain as I tried to shove him out of my way.

"Hey." We all turned our heads at the authority in the one word.

Jared strode into the room. "What's going on?"

Lourey said, "There was an active shooter. This woman disrupted the shot."

Jared cast a worried look at me. "Are you okay?"

I raised my arm and pointed out the door. "He fired on Chris." I started to shake, the concept of how close Chris had come to death loading onto my back. "He could have died."

Jared eyed Lourey, dismissing the others. "So, she's done nothing wrong. Wasn't armed, didn't cause the danger. I know her and we can be in contact if she's needed for questioning."

Lourey watched me for a moment. "We were holding her for her own safety. Just wanted to keep her here until she relaxed a little."

Jared nodded as if he approved. "This is Michalea Sanchez. She's former TPD, now Arizona Ranger." As if my uniform hadn't informed them of that last bit.

After a moment of silence, Lourey offered me a tense smile. "You did good work."

I waited for them to walk away. Lourey and the other three seemed slightly cowed by Jared and somewhat respectful of me. They inched away from us and stepped outside the room together. They'd probably walk around the corner out of view and talk to each other for a while. It's not every day a shooter goes wild in front of you.

My trembling intensified, the incident catching up to me. "Is Chris really okay?"

Jared watched me. "Of course. Thanks to you."

I'd shot a man in the line of duty once. I had been trained to handle the rush of danger. Acting and reacting in the face of an accident or attack was something that also came naturally to me. Deon would be beside himself if he'd witnessed what I'd done. He would smother me with protection and concern.

Jared held a chair for me. "Sit."

It's not that I fell apart or couldn't function, but there's an inevitable fallout. I often shook and my teeth clattered as adrenaline dissipated.

I dropped into the metal government-issued chair.

Jared sank down close to me, our thighs touching. He draped an arm around my shoulder. "Take your time. I'm right here."

I shrugged his arm off me. "No. This isn't me needing comfort. It's just a reaction. It'll be over it in a minute, then I need to get to the jail and see Chris. He'll need me to arrange bail—"

Jared interrupted. "They aren't going to let him out. Someone just shot at him. They'll keep him in jail for his own protection."

I jumped to my feet and started for the front door. "I've got to be there."

Jared followed me. "You can't do anything to help him."

I knew Chris better than anyone. He'd wither and die locked up.

17

The crowd outside the police station had drifted away by the time I recovered from the shooting and made a new plan. Ann would be beside herself if she knew about the shooting. The fact I had no messages on my phone only meant she hadn't seen or heard the news yet. I dialed her cell.

After three rings the chirpy voice of Sami said, "Hello? Aunt Ann's phone."

"What are you doing answering?"

"Mommy!" She sounded delighted. "Efrain let me put bedding plants in the ground. Do you know what those are? They call them bedding plants because someone else planted them in their pots and you buy them and put them in your flower beds. Or vegetable beds. And we had peppers and some tomatoes, but Efrain says it's really too late to plant them, but if they live it will be—"

Obviously Sami didn't mind hanging out at Mi Casa. "That's great. Where is your Aunt Ann?"

She sounded distracted. "Uncle Fritz took them to the Goodwill to find some sheets for the center."

Seemed like everything was chugging along fine at Mi Casa. "Will you have Aunt Ann call me when she gets back?"

"Okay. Can we plant beans at our house?"

"You never like beans when I cook them."

"I promise I'll eat the beans we grow."

"Sounds like a good plan to me." Sami didn't say goodbye, but the call ended and I supposed that was good enough.

If Ann couldn't get my phone call, she wouldn't be receiving any others. I checked the time. Maybe I had another couple of hours before I needed to get the kids. I started the Pilot and drove across town.

From my car I called Dr. Bartholomew's office with the flimsy excuse of checking up on him after the tear gas incident on campus. I told the assistant on the phone I'd helped Dr. Bartholomew that day and wondered if I could see him today. She returned my call in less than ten minutes saying yes, he'd love to see me anytime.

I kept a box of protein bars in the car as an emergency stash in case my blood sugar took a dive. My fingers closed around a bar, then I opted for another drive-through, this time a burrito. I probably wouldn't die from malnutrition or become obese in a few days, but my diet had taken a bad turn the last couple of days. I finally found a place to park by campus and the walk in the sun from an outlying parking garage to campus took longer than the drive from downtown.

I clambered up the stairs in James E. Rogers College of Law building on the UA campus, the clanks of equipment in my utility belt louder than the soft pad of the rubber soles of my uniform shoes. Dr. Bartholomew's office boasted a premier location. A local legal rock star, he even had an administrative assistant who looked up from her desk when I entered the office.

"I'm Michaela Sanchez. I called earlier to see Dr. Bartholomew."

Pleasant and efficient, she greeted me, rose from her desk, and disappeared behind a door. Moments later she emerged and ushered me inside.

Dr. Bartholomew had already made his way around his desk, hand outstretched to shake mine. "Ranger Sanchez. Glad to see you so I can thank you again."

I let his warm hand, covered in age spots, briefly clasp mine. "No need. Just wanted to drop by and make sure you're okay."

He indicated a chair opposite his desk. "Still, it was brave of you." He made his way around his desk and waited until I sat before sinking to his own chair. "So, can I do something else for you?"

I wondered again how to begin. Wouldn't he question why I wanted information about Manuel Ortiz? I eased in. "I read in today's paper how close you were to Manuel Ortiz and I wanted to give you my condolences."

Bartholomew's smile dribbled from his face. "Tragic. That young man had so much going for him. He was on the brink of something great."

I suppose to Bartholomew's octogenarian status, Manuel in his forties would seem young. "So many people admired him and were loyal followers."

"Oh yes, he was always like that, even as a student."

Asking Bartholomew who would want to kill Ortiz would be too abrupt. "You said he was on the verge of something. What was that?"

Bartholomew didn't seem to be at all curious about my line of questioning. Maybe he was used to being the center of attention with everyone slavering for his views. "We'd discussed him running for office. I'm not talking about starting small. He had the current Democratic representative's endorsement to run for Congress when she retires in two years."

I tried to look admiring. "He'd have been brilliant at that."

"I agree. He'd worked very hard toward this goal. Honestly—and this is between you and me—I might have questioned his motives from time to time. But never his results. As you said, Manuel inspired people. Who cares if his goal was politics? He did good things for a disenfranchised population, and I think he could have gone all the way."

I doubted Bartholomew's coy statement of confidentiality. "So, he was planning a Congressional campaign. Were there rivals who might not have wanted him to run? Maybe one of them shot him?"

Bartholomew looked confused. "They've arrested Chris Wright. As far as I'm concerned, he's the culprit."

I wanted to jump out of my chair and close my hands around his throat. He was a lawyer, supposedly someone wise and not prone to unfounded conclusions. I struggled to maintain a casual tone. "Maybe the cops just needed a quick scapegoat. Probably don't have evidence to support the arrest. That guy might be out of jail before the end of the day."

The wrinkles in his face seemed to deepen. "Maybe they don't have conclusive evidence now, but I won't be at all surprised if they find the smoking gun. Chris Wright is full of the kind of rage that could translate into murder. I don't have to tell you; you witnessed him at the campus recruitment event."

I fought to keep from clutching the arms of my chair. I couldn't let myself react or Bartholomew wouldn't tell me anything else. "You know Chris Wright?"

"I've known him for years. He started law school the same year as Manuel. They were in the same study group. Law school is a small world and the professors see more than the students think. I knew Manuel and Chris had hit it off almost from day one."

I gave an appropriate murmur to show general interest while my heart hammered for more.

Bartholomew obviously liked having an audience. "I thought the two of them would go on to be lifelong friends and colleagues. Perhaps an epic relationship, such as Alito and Bader-Ginsberg. Chris was every bit as intelligent and engaging as Manuel."

"But Chris Wright didn't finish law school?"

He spoke with deliberation, as if writing an essay. "Sadly, no. It's one of those tales of two roads taking different turns. Chris's family was involved in a tragic accident. His parents were killed by an illegal immigrant in a terrible car crash. Chris dropped out of school to care for a younger sibling. To say I was disappointed would be an understatement. He had such potential."

I swallowed a thick glob of guilt. "Did he and Manuel stay in touch?"

"Not that I'm aware. Chris eventually trained for the Border Patrol and pursued a career there. Honestly, I lost track of him until he hit the news last year. It's unfortunate he is in the position of spokesperson for the Border Patrol at this time. That kerfuffle about the shooting of the young man at the border put Chris in a precarious position."

I cringed at the word *kerfuffle* to describe a sixteen-year-old being shot, no matter the circumstances surrounding it. "I remember a little about it."

"I never understood how those two men, who had been so close at one time, ended up such bitter enemies. But I place that blame firmly at Chris's feet."

Keep calm. "How so?"

Bartholomew leaned forward as if imparting gossip. "Jealousy, pure and simple. Right after the accident that changed Chris's life, Manuel did all he could to help Chris out. He spent all his free time—and I don't know if you're aware how little free time a law student has, most of which is needed for sleep —helping the legal team prosecute the driver of the car that caused the crash."

"Manuel was responsible for that man being deported?" I blurted it out and immediately regretted it.

No question Dr. Bartholomew had a sharp mind at one time, but a collection of brain cells might have gone to fertilize a prize-winning crop of ear hair. His thought process must have dulled, because he didn't pause to wonder how I knew the man had been deported. "Yes. Manuel Ortiz is known as a defender of the immigrant and supporter of free borders. What is not so well known is that he started his career deporting a Mexican man. Separating him from his young son."

Son? I nearly choked. "There was a child?"

"Well, the man claimed to have a child, a five-year-old boy, but the authorities could never find him. Whether the man was lying to gain sympathy or if he told the truth isn't clear. My opinion is that there was a son, but he was taken in by other illegals and raised as their own. Probably one of our DACA recipients now."

All these years no one believed me about the little boy. It was there in the court records the whole time. He was real. And he'd grown up without his father. Because of me.

"The point is," Bartholomew said, drawing me back, "Chris Wright turned on Manuel. I can't tell you if they'd been in contact over the years, but I do know when Chris was thrust into the spotlight last year, Manuel agonized over confronting him in such a public way."

"You know this?"

Bartholomew shifted in his chair and I thought he might be restless and wanting to end this conversation. "I've mentored Manuel since his first year of law school. I've watched his career take off and seen his carefully planned progress. He knew going after Chris in the media would get him the national platform he needed to launch a political career. Yet, I think he felt loyalty for his classmate. It tore him up."

I'll bet. If it bothered him at all, you couldn't tell. He seemed to eat up all the attention.

Bartholomew glanced above my head, maybe at a clock on the wall. "I thought perhaps they were putting their differences behind them."

"What made you think that?"

"Not long ago, I stopped by Manuel's house to drop off some tamales one of my colleagues had given me. Whenever his family gets together to make tamales, he brings me some. He's been doing it for years and I don't have the heart to tell him I don't care for them. So I usually give them to Manuel."

I couldn't care less about that old man's food preferences.

"To my surprise, Chris Wright and Manuel were having a heated discussion on the patio outside the kitchen."

"What were they arguing about?" I couldn't help myself from blurting out.

"I didn't say they were arguing. I got the distinct impression they discussed the solution to a problem. I'd seen them with that intense concentration before. Albeit, over twenty years ago. Focused and serious, but not antagonistic."

"What do you think it was?"

He shrugged. "Who knows? They dropped it when they saw me, and Chris made a quick excuse to leave."

It didn't track for me. "If they didn't seem to be fighting then, why would you think Chris Wright would kill him later?"

"As Manuel walked him to the gate, I heard Chris threaten. He said, 'This isn't over.'"

"But that could have meant anything."

It didn't seem to disturb Bartholomew to form an unfounded opinion. "I suppose, but coupled with the obvious jealousy a man with a failed career and a life of disappointment would have for someone as successful as Manuel, and with Manuel using Chris as a platform to further his own career, I'm not surprised Chris snapped at Manuel's provocation at the festival."

I gave no credence to Bartholomew's jealousy theory. Chris never gave any indication he was jealous of Deon's law career. Chris might feel loss at not being a lawyer, but he never acted as if he held it against anyone else. Not even me.

I had more questions, but before I could speak the office door opened and the efficient admin assistant announced an important phone call. It didn't take a trained lawyer to figure out the fake phone call was a prearranged cue from a man who often rattled on without ceasing.

I thanked the professor and left, walking slowly from the law building. The sharp sunshine of late afternoon beat on the top of my head as I walked the several blocks to my car.

Manuel and Chris. A long history. So much I didn't know.

And, there was a little boy.

18

I checked my phone. No missed call from Ann. No messages from the girls. I still had another hour and half before I needed to pick them up to get Josie to ball practice. Since Ann had them busy and under her watchful eye, it gave me a little more time.

Jail kept Chris safe for the time being, but he'd be miserable. Chris spent his days patrolling the vast expanse of desert, the sky overhead as open as a timeless universe. Locking him up would be torture. The only time I'd seen Chris content to stay still was when he studied for law school. He'd given that up for me. If I could find the real murderer and save Chris an hour of that agony, I owed him that much.

Bartholomew said everything between Manuel and Chris had changed the night of the accident.

I sat in the Pilot with the AC running, staring out the windshield, focusing on the night that for twenty-five years I'd tried so hard to forget. The awful reel that ran beneath my every breath and surfaced in my nightmares.

Twelve years old, the youngest and often dismissed as a pest. Ann was seventeen that year. Her clothes and make-up drew me like a hummingbird to honeysuckle. Every song she loved, every movie she watched, all her idols and preferences became mine. To me, Ann was the epitome of cool. I wanted nothing more than to be Ann.

Mom and Dad had parent/teacher conferences that Friday night at my middle school. There had been arguing and slamming doors when they told Ann she couldn't go with the rest of her friends to a movie but had to stay home with me. Even though I felt bad about Ann missing her fun, I looked forward to spending time with just the two of us. Maybe she'd experiment on me with make-up and hair styles. Maybe we'd watch one of her favorite movies. It didn't matter, as long as we did it together.

I'd wandered into her room while she talked on the cordless house phone. She hollered at me to leave her alone. But I hung around, listening to her deep conversation with her best friend about the boys they hoped would ask them to prom. After the third or fourth squeal from her to get out, she finally rose with the phone still attached to her ear and stomped to the kitchen.

I followed of course. It wasn't so much that I wanted to torture her, but since she wouldn't do anything fun with me, it was the only way I could get her attention.

She opened the pantry door and rummaged on the snack shelf. Because of my diabetes, this shelf was strictly out of bounds for me.

"Hold on," Ann said into the phone. She pulled down something and tore off the wrapper before I got a look at it. The she broke off a thin square and I saw it was chocolate. She held it out to me. "Here."

I stepped back. "I'm not supposed to have that."

She rolled her eyes. "It's your special one."

"It is?" I was hopeful for a second, then backed away. "Yeah. But Mom will find out I had some 'cause no one else would eat it. I'll get in trouble."

A tinny voice filtered from the phone. She snatched it. "Wait. Start over. I didn't hear you." She shoved the candy at me again.

I shook my head.

She pulled the receiver from her ear. "I'll buy another one tomorrow and replace it. Mom will never know."

That sounded like a good plan. I took the square and watched as she headed back upstairs. "If you don't leave me alone, I won't replace the candy bar."

Dang it. She tricked me again. Now she owned me. If she didn't get more chocolate, Mom might ground me or maybe never let me have any candy again. She watched my blood sugar pretty closely and kept watch on the sugar-free treats she let me eat. She said she didn't want me to develop a habit for sweets.

As the evening wore on, Ann kept talking to her friends. Bored, the idea of the chocolate nagged at me. If she was going to replace it anyway, there was no reason I couldn't have another little taste. And another. Before Mom and Dad got home, I'd eaten nearly the whole bar.

I didn't feel good. It only got worse.

✳ ✳ ✳

I brought myself back to the car. At only twelve and so sick, my memories were little more than a dream's perspective. I needed to find out what really happened that night.

My phone showed no calls. The kids would be okay for a little while longer while I followed one more trail. I drove from the university to downtown and parked along the street. Trees shaded the courtyard of the main branch of the library and the sweet smell of the orange blossoms and mesquite swirled in the air as I hurried to the building that was all angles, glass, and metal.

Even though I charged the front desk and probably looked frantic, the young man sitting there looked up with a smile. "Can I help you?"

"I need to see an article from the daily paper on June 6th, 1997. How would I do that?"

He considered. "What paper is that?"

"I don't know."

"Okay, let's find that out and then I can get the microfiche for you. You'll have to take it to the readers downstairs."

I had no experience researching in a public library, so his willingness to find the paper and how fast he worked impressed me. In no time I sat in front of a reader, scrolling through the *Tucson Daily Star*.

It didn't take long to find the article on the front page of the local news section. I sucked in a breath. The photo blindsided me. I don't know what I expected and hadn't thought about there being a picture. I didn't want to see it but couldn't look away.

Our Impala was centered within the glow of the camera's flash. The other car, an old sedan, was nosed into the front passenger side. That was where Mom sat. The bodies of Mom and Dad were gone by the time the photographer snapped the image. An ambulance sat at the edge of the picture, the back doors open.

I forced my eyes to travel to the article. The journalist wrote about the tragic accident that took the lives of three people. The number startled me. Three? I knew about Mom and Dad, but as I read on, I realized there had been another woman. The man who hit us, someone identified as Carlos Rodriguez, had lost his wife. A young woman listed as twenty-four years old.

I sat back, too confused and horrified to continue reading. Of course I knew my parents had died in that wreck. But reading their names, seeing the mangled metal, finding out another person has lost her life overwhelmed me. I pressed my hands to my temples and closed my eyes, forcing myself away from the sorrow.

A little boy no one knew about. His mother died that night. And his father was taken away in handcuffs and eventually sent to Mexico. Had the little boy made his way back to his father or had he stayed here, as Bartholomew thought? Either way, his life had been as wrecked as mine. As Ann's, who would only walk with pain. As Chris's, who gave up his dream of being a lawyer.

I leaned in again. The article said the cops had discovered an immigrant camp on the desert outside of Marana. In those days, Marana was a small town several miles from Tucson. It was where we lived in a house surrounded by cactus, mesquite, and creosote bushes. Now, Marana and Tucson bled together.

The spokesman said they thought the camp accommodated a dozen or more immigrants who were in the area working for local farmers. Rodriquez didn't give any names or information, no doubt frustrating law enforcement. That probably hadn't helped him in his deportation trial.

The picture drew me again. I didn't want to see that image or think of my parents in their last moments. The guilt clogged my throat and I couldn't swallow, the sickening taste of chocolate coating my tongue.

People stood at the corner of the ambulance. At night, the camera's flash illuminated the wreck and everything else faded into the background, but I pushed my face toward the reader, my nose practically touching the screen. I made out Manuel Ortiz. At least, I could imagine the man I'd seen at the festival as being this young man. But the person next to him is what made my heart bang against my ribs.

I knew the tilt of that head.

Fritz.

19

I asked the librarian to scan and print the article, and he was as accommodating as he'd been earlier. It had taken me longer than I'd expected. Josie was going to be late for practice and the only challenge now was to keep the delay as short as possible.

I hit all the usual rush hour traffic in Tucson. Maybe it's like that everywhere, but today, I cursed the city planners who hadn't had the foresight to create a sane traffic flow. I drummed my fingers on the wheel. After an eternity, the congestion eased and the streets widened, and I sped in and out of lanes, making the turns on autopilot. I screeched to a stop in front of Mi Casa and jumped out, trotting toward the door, the late-afternoon sun drilling into my neck.

Ann jerked her head from her computer and stared at me. "About time you showed up."

I waved at her. "I know. I'm late. Josie's probably throwing a fit. Where are they?"

She sat back, clearly annoyed. "Not here."

My heart clawed up my throat but before I could ask any more, Ann continued. "Josie forgot her iPad and she said she had an assignment due. Sami wanted to swim and I wouldn't let her into that death trap Fritz constructed, so Fritz took them over to your house and Efrain's staying with them until you get home."

Efrain. Alone with the girls. Ann trusted him and Sami and Josie seemed loyal to him, but Efrain kept secrets, at least the one about his aunt, and that made me nervous. "You couldn't have called me?"

She let out a huff of air. "You couldn't have called me?"

"I did!"

"I never got a call."

Damn it, Sami. No, damn it, *me*. I should have followed up. "I'm sorry. Sami took a message, but I guess it stopped with her. Thanks for keeping the kids today."

"So what happened? Is Chris okay?"

A good sister would stop and give Ann all the information. Clearly she didn't know about the shooting or my phone would have blown up with calls and she'd have met me at the door with a thousand questions. I should tell her about Dr. Bartholomew and ask her about Fritz and the night of the accident.

But my children were with Efrain. "Chris is okay. They didn't bond him out." I hurried on before she'd ask why. "I've got to get Josie to practice. I'll call you later."

"Hey. You can't leave it like that."

I was already out the door. Feeling guilty, as usual, but stampeding away as fast as I could.

All through the drive from the eastside to the north, I tried to convince myself Efrain was a decent person. I couldn't come up with any evidence to doubt that, but I still felt jumpy.

I roared into our quiet neighborhood and actually squealed in the driveway. The garage door slid up and I was half-surprised Josie didn't pop out in her practice clothes.

I raced into the kitchen, already hollering. "Let's get going. We'll be late."

It took only a second for the silence to hit me. No one was home. "Josie."

Nothing.

Where could they be? I walked through the kitchen and down the hall, looking into the family room and office on my way to the stairs. Nothing jumped out at me as a clue to where they were. I bounded up the stairs and peeked into their bedrooms.

The phone in my hand vibrated and Ann's name showed on the screen. I punched it on. "Did Efrain call? Where are they?"

She fired back without answering my questions. "A shooting? Where have you been since then? The kids aren't there?"

She said it with such urgency I immediately went on guard. "I just got home. No one is here."

No answers, just more questions hitting me. "Were you with Chris? How is he? Did either of you get hurt?"

"No. We're fine. I was going to tell you. How did you find out?"

She sounded frantic. "It's all over TV. We saw it on the news at five. It probably aired at noon, but we didn't have it on. I can't believe you haven't been with your girls."

"They were safe with you. The shooting has nothing to do with the girls."

"It has everything to do with the girls. Especially after the death threats Chris gets. The news showed someone shooting at Chris and you jumping on him. Then they mentioned your name and that you are Chris's sister. Don't you think if someone is crazy enough to try to kill Chris they might come after you? Or your kids?"

Oh my god. I hadn't thought about the news crews or that I'd be identified. "You haven't heard from Efrain?"

"He's not here. Fritz is at the bar."

I stared at the kitchen, frantic to see some sign of where they might be. "I've got to go." I ran to the garage. The door was already up since I thought I'd be leaving with the girls right away. I swung open the door of my car as Deon's Audi pulled into the driveway.

He jumped out and ran to me. "Are you all right? I just saw the news. You and Chris—" He stopped and looked at the open door of the Pilot. Panic must have been all over my face. "Where are you going? Where are the girls?"

"I don't know." My voice sounded as scared as I felt.

"What?" His eyes flew to the door into the house as if they might appear. "You were at the courthouse. Where were they? How could you leave them?"

"When Ann called and said they arrested Chris, I took them to Ann's. But Fritz brought them back here with Efrain."

"Where are they now?"

"I don't know," I repeated, but now my voice rose along with my growing fear.

"Where were you?" I'd never seen this anger and fear in him. It looked as if he wanted to grab me and shake it out of me.

"Trying to help Chris."

"You said Fritz brought Efrain here, so they don't have a car. Ann doesn't know where they are?"

I shook my head.

Despite the fire that lasered me with blame, he tried to walk through it logically. "Josie was supposed to have ball practice. Maybe she called someone to give her a ride and Sami and Efrain went to the ballpark with her."

Deon spun around and ran back to his car. I sprinted after him, but he was backing up before I got to the passenger side. The only choice I had was to drive my own car. He squeezed through a red light on the way, but I had to stop for it. The two-mile drive to the ballpark took a decade and by the time I got there, Deon was running across the field.

I jumped out to follow, already locating Sami in her usual place among the younger siblings at the edge of the field. Efrain stood like a sentinel to the side of the diamond, positioned between Josie and Sami. I caught up to Deon behind the fence to the right of home plate, fingers wound in the chain link. His face was drained of color and lines deepened around his eyes. I knew, like me, he'd be fighting the urge to run out onto the field and grab Josie. He didn't look at me.

I stood beside him while I fought tears of relief. After a moment, I said, "I'm going to go see Sami." I walked over to where she played with her friends.

"Mom!" She ran over and hugged around my waist. I held tight to her and didn't let go immediately when she released me.

She tugged out of my embrace. "Can we eat at In-N-Out tonight?"

I cleared the lump from my throat. "We ate there last night."

"So? Can we?"

Such a small thing to make her happy. "Why not?"

"Yay!" She ran off, shouting to her friends. "We're gonna get In-N-Out!"

I watched her for several minutes, feeling love for her burn in my chest. On my way back to the field, I stopped to talk to Efrain. "Thank you for watching the girls today. How did you get to the park?"

Efrain pointed to Jasmine and she waved at me. "Josie said she had practice so we thought to ask one of her friends for a ride."

Exactly as Deon had deduced. I'd let myself get caught up with Ann and Deon and their paranoia. No one was after me and my family. But I'd be keeping a close eye on my girls from now on, anyway. "Thank you for coming over today."

He looked at the anemic grass under his feet. "You have a nice family."

I put a hand on his arm. "You're part of our family, you know."

He flinched and I dropped my hand. "Ann and Fritz have been good to me. But family is different. You include me, but I'm not your family."

Now seemed like a good time to find out more about him. "Besides your Aunt Alma, do you have any other family?"

He looked away from the field toward the Catalina mountains. "Tia Alma raised me until I came to Mi Casa. My mother and father didn't make it to the United States. My aunt did the best she could, but she has no papers."

"Do you have contact with your parents?"

He swallowed. "No. Tia Alma lost her job and had hard times, so I came to live with Ann and Fritz when I was young."

"But you stay close to Alma."

He made brief eye contact. "Ann and Fritz think Tia Alma is not good for me. I try not to upset them, so they don't know I see her."

"They don't own you. If you want to spend time with your aunt, you should."

He brought his attention back to me. "Fritz met me when I was a little boy. He's always been around to help me out. Ann sort of took over when I started middle school. She didn't like the school I was attending, so she enrolled me in the Catholic school and they paid for it. I am grateful to them."

I hadn't known any of this. Ann and Fritz didn't have much to spare, and yet they'd found a way to help Efrain as if he was the child they never had. That didn't give them the right to rule him. "Is it okay to wait until practice is over to give you a ride home?"

A flush crept to his face. "Thank you. But someone is going to pick me up."

Was he too shy to accept a ride and was planning to walk the several miles back to the center? "Sure you don't need a ride? How about some dinner with us at In-N-Out? It's the least I can do."

He looked at the ground and mumbled his answer. "No, thank you."

Of course Efrain would have friends other than Fritz and Ann. It shouldn't surprise me he might call someone else. But it did.

I went back to stand by Deon. "I promised Sami we'd eat at In-N-Out tonight."

Deon didn't say anything.

"You were right. They got a ride to the park with Jasmine."

He still didn't answer.

"I'm sorry." I let it out, like a balloon with a pin prick. "I shouldn't have left the girls alone all day. I was trying to follow some leads about who would want Manuel Ortiz dead."

Deon stiffened.

"He was going to run for office. See? That could open him up for anyone to come after him."

Deon's jaw tightened as if he clamped his teeth.

"The cops have some evidence that Chris and Ortiz had contact recently because of a call from Chris on Ortiz's phone, but I found out they were friends in law school and—"

"Stop it," Deon hissed low. He kept his gaze on the field. "Just stop it. I don't care about Chris and what the cops say. I care about our children. I care about you." His voice was quiet, keeping it between us.

I tried to speak under my breath. "Nothing happened. I won't leave them alone again."

"Do you have any idea what it felt like to turn on the news—in a hotel, by the way—and see your wife fighting with a gunman? Do you know what it's like to imagine you dead?"

I touched his arm and he jerked it away. "I'm sorry. I didn't realize—"

"Exactly. You didn't realize. That you were in danger. That you put our children at risk. You didn't realize because you're so focused on your brother. You don't hear yourself talk about 'your family' meaning you and Chris and Ann. Don't you know your family is me, Josie, and Sami?"

"Are ... are you jealous?"

"It isn't about being jealous. It's about safety. You can't go around investigating the murder of someone to help your brother at the cost of putting our children at risk."

"Of course you're my family. But so are they. The three Ta-mutals. They're a part of me. You can't ask me to choose."

He clenched his jaw again, still not making eye contact.

"I truly am sorry for scaring you. I promise not to do that again."

"You won't get the chance."

I faced him, even if he wouldn't look at me. "What do you mean?"

"I gave you the choice between your brother and your children. You chose Chris. I won't allow you to expose our children to such risk. I'm taking them to my parents' house. We'll leave tomorrow. I need to come back for work, but they can visit my family for a week or so. Tonight I'll stay at home to protect my family."

I grabbed his arm and forced him to look at me. I'd throw myself in front of bullet to save my kids. "You don't know anything about protecting people. It's a job I'm trained for."

"And yet you think nothing of putting them in danger." He finally looked at me. "We were planning on going down to Mexico in a couple of days anyway. I'll take them early."

I fought to keep from screaming in front of the entire ballpark of parents and children. "No. You can't."

He searched my face, dark eyes digging deeply into me. "At least for now. You refuse to abandon this chase of yours. You might get yourself killed. I won't stay around to watch it. I refuse to leave our children in harm's way."

20

I stood next to Deon for the next hour, neither of us speaking. After practice I gathered up Josie and Sami and gave them uncharacteristic public hugs. They accepted the affection without seeming to notice how hard and long I held on to them. Deon didn't look at me, and the girls didn't seem to notice. If I stuck around for In-N-Out and all the evening settling in, the girls would feel the tension between me and Deon.

I ruffled Sami's brown hair, something she hated. "You all go get your burgers. I want to change out of this uniform and then I promised Jamie I'd help her out at the center."

Sami grabbed my arm. "Oh, man. You'll miss your animal style."

I smiled at her. "I'll survive." I eyed Josie. "Make sure you get that algebra done. I probably won't be home until after you go to bed."

Josie rolled her eyes.

Deon relaxed visibly. "Okay, girls, I'm thinking a double-double with a chocolate shake."

Josie's face became animated. "An old guy like you should watch what you eat. You probably ought to have protein style."

"I'm not that old and I like buns."

"Gross."

The two of them walked away without looking back at me. Sami gave me a short hug and ran after them.

Dads and daughters. I loved their devotion to each other, even if I felt left out.

I walked to my Pilot with my stomach a mass of acid. Maybe Ann and Deon were right. I'd put the girls at risk for my mission to save Chris. I shouldn't have to choose one over the other.

No, I didn't agree with them about the danger to Sami and Josie. Tucson wasn't Chicago or Detroit. It seemed unlikely that more than one deranged shooter would act in a city this size. It wasn't likely someone else was angry and crazy enough to come after Chris's family. But the people at the festival had been ready for blood. And at the courthouse earlier, they'd been only short of a mob.

I'd be home soon to keep them safe. Until then, they'd be fine with Deon. While I had a couple of hours, I'd do what I could to help Chris. I slid behind the wheel of the Pilot and thought about what to do next.

Even after my lousy day, I almost smiled at what I saw out the windshield. Now I understood why Efrain blushed when I asked about his ride. He walked across the grass of the field toward the playground at the far side. Hand in hand with a little boy. He smiled at the woman walking next to him.

Sophia and Tomás. Deon and I might be falling apart, but here a new relationship sparked. Maybe Sophia and Efrain would grow together, make a safe place for Tomás. The possibility lifted my load a tiny bit.

I spared a few minutes to rush home and change into a skort and T-shirt. The traffic had thinned from full force rush hour and dusk dropped over the desert, cooling the heat of the day. I turned on NPR, hoping to hear local news of the events at the courthouse. All I got was another story about the president's war on the border, commentators' interjections on how unfair and inhumane border policies were, and comments from people who didn't live and work close to the border. The tangled mess wouldn't be straightened out with politicians fighting for votes and skirting real understanding of the issues.

I shut off the racket. My life was pushed and pulled because of that damned border. My husband couldn't spend time with his parents without passports and plans. Ann dealt with border fallout in the form of broken lives. Chris faced danger from despicable drug smugglers and coyotes and witnessed the horrible deaths the desert could deal out. Who entered, who was locked out, and why? I didn't have answers and the questions grew larger every day.

I pulled the Pilot next to Fritz's new pickup in the sparsely populated gravel parking lot of the Hot Spot. At this time of day, the trendy bars downtown and in the tony sections of Tucson would be packed with people buying signature cocktails and craft beers. Fritz's bar didn't look any different than I'd ever remembered, probably the same since his father opened it in the 1970s, though more rundown, as would happen to a business not cared for.

The old-school neon beer signs glowed in the deepening darkness. I pulled open the heavy wooden door and stepped into an overly air-conditioned room. The splintered wooden bar took up one end of the area with a TV mounted in the corner above. A few tables with a smattering of customers filled the dark room. It smelled of stale beer and the lingering ghost of cigarettes smoked there decades earlier, before they banned smoking in public places.

Fritz stood behind the bar. He'd cut back the bar's hours over the years. Now it opened somewhere around five and closed before nine. It wasn't the kind of place people met for happy hour or sought out for after-dinner drinks. It serviced a few regulars who stopped for a quick one on their way home from low-paying jobs before going to an empty home or a complaining family. I didn't spot many women. Fritz served a lot of beer and some inexpensive drinks with well alcohol. I didn't think he'd be able to stay open even these few hours for much longer.

His jaw actually dropped for a second when he saw me. He recovered and let out a laugh. "What in the Wide Wide World of Sports are you doing here?"

I pulled myself up on a tattered vinyl-topped bar stool. The stuffing had long since quit providing comfort. "I wanted to talk to you."

He gave me a puzzled look. "Okay. Can I get you a beer? Dos Equis, right?"

I nodded and he reached under the bar into the cooler and pulled out a green bottle. He popped the top and set it in front of me. "Ann was pretty worried about you today. She couldn't find out about Chris's situation. She was frustrated you didn't call but thought maybe you were busy with Chris."

Yeah, so worried she left her phone at home when she ran errands.

"Then they showed that whole scene at the courthouse on TV." He left it there, reeking of blame.

I should have called Ann. It must have been hell not knowing anything. "We're all okay. But because of that damned shooter, they aren't going to set any bond for Chris."

Fritz shook his head. "Man, that's harsh."

"It's got to kill him being locked up like that."

Fritz grabbed a glass of what appeared to be ice water and took a drink. "He's always hated to be inside. He almost didn't graduate from high school because he couldn't stay still."

Fritz exaggerated. Chris needed the right motivation, one he found in law school, not high school. I let the beer roll down my throat. Cold and wet, but I didn't enjoy it. Too much worry and stress.

Fritz watched me. "You got me curious. What's this about?"

I set the bottle down. "I went to see Regis Bartholomew today."

He drew his head back and threw me a confused look. "Who's that?"

"He was a professor when Chris went to law school."

Fritz frowned. "Why would you go see him?"

"He was a close advisor to Manuel Ortiz, and I thought he might have some insight on who killed Ortiz."

Fritz gave me an intense glare. "Did he?"

I peeled the label on the beer bottle. "No. He's convinced Chris did it."

"Why would he think that?"

"Because he thinks Chris is jealous." I wanted to roll my eyes as Josie would. "He said they were good friends in school."

Fritz shook his head. "Like I said yesterday, I really don't think so."

I pulled the article out of my purse and handed it to Fritz.

He kept his eyes on me when he took the pages and slowly lowered them to the bar. His face froze. "What are you doing with this?"

"After I talked to Bartholomew, I wanted to know what happened that could have come between Ortiz and Chris. I don't buy the jealousy angle either."

Fritz didn't answer, as if waiting for me to clarify.

I pointed to the pages. "You're in this picture, Fritz. You were there."

He picked up the paper and studied the picture again. "I wish I wasn't."

"What happened that night? Why were you and Manuel Ortiz at the wreck?"

Fritz closed his eyes. When he opened them, tears caught the dim light of the tavern. "That was the worse night of my life." He let out a rough chuckle. "That sounds bad. I mean, you lost your parents. And Ann and Chris ..." He shook his head. "Man."

A guy sitting at the end of the bar hollered. "Hey, Fritzy. I'm dry."

Fritz swiped at his eyes, even though the tears hadn't dropped. He held up a finger to me and spun away. With practiced efficiency, he scooped the man's glass from in front of him and angled it under a tap. The beer spilled into the glass and at the last moment, Fritz tipped it upright to give it a half-inch head. He set it back in front of the round-bellied man wearing a shirt stained with dried sweat and dirt.

I took another unwanted sip of my own beer while I waited for Fritz to pass a few comments back and forth.

A handful of patrons approached the bar and spoke briefly. Fritz filled another man's beer, pulled a couple of bottles from the cooler for others, and poured two shots of Wild Turkey before returning to me. Maybe the patrons had seen he was busy with me and had been waiting for a break to get their refills.

"What do you remember from that night?" I asked.

He looked above my head, as if seeing it all again. "You don't want to hear this. It can't help Chris."

"I don't know what will help Chris, but I have to follow up on anything. Something broke between them that night and I need to know what it was."

Fritz rubbed his beard. "Okay. We'd been out together and were bringing Chris home because he drank too much. We were almost to your house when we came up on the wreck. That's about it."

I glared at him. "There's more."

He sighed. "You know, that night was the first time I ever really saw

Ann. I mean, I'd been around your family all my life practically. I knew you all. But she was always just Chris's little sister. That night, Chris was busy with your parents and with you. I pulled Ann from the car." He blinked a few times. "I swear, we thought it was going to blow up, like they do on TV. We didn't know any better."

He stopped and swallowed, his Adam's apple traveling up and down his throat. I waited.

He looked me in the eye as if begging forgiveness. "I did so many things wrong that night. So many."

I wanted to reach out and put my hand over his. But I let him gather himself.

"The car wasn't going to blow up. They hardly ever do that. But, you know, we only reacted." He swallowed again. "They said moving Ann might have damaged her spine even more." Another pause. "If it wasn't for me pulling her out, she might have recovered fully."

How could I have never heard this? No one told me Fritz had been there. They didn't say he saved Ann or that maybe he hadn't saved her but damaged her more. "You don't know that."

He blinked and turned around to grab another customer's empty glass from the bar without asking. He filled the beer and set it in front of the guy, who grunted his thanks.

Fritz came back to me. "So, yeah. It was a bad night. I stayed with Ann on the way to the hospital and then spent a lot of time with her while she was stuck there. I guess by the time she got out, we were pretty much a pair. Been together since."

Did that sound like love? Duty? After twenty-five years, maybe he didn't remember what it felt like at the beginning. I wasn't sure Deon and I would have twenty-five years together. The memory of the hike down the mountain with my buddy hanging between us burned in my mind. That first giddy rush of attraction that turned into love, represented by a collection of St. Christophers on our mantel. I knew what love felt like. It felt like Deon's arms around me. How could I screw up a relationship with a man so wonderful? I'd been careless with the love that wound through my days and nights, that wrapped itself into my plans, my thoughts, my decisions.

The love that stayed with me, even when I did everything I could to destroy it.

I would go home, tell Deon how stupid I'd been. How sorry I was. Give up this crazy search for Manuel Ortiz's killer. Do anything I could to repair our life.

I pushed my warm beer aside. "So, why do you think Manuel Ortiz and Chris had a falling out?"

Fritz frowned at me again, an expression I found foreign on his face. "You keep talking about them like they were buddies. I was Chris's best friend since third grade. I think I'd know who he hung out with."

"Yeah, but Chris went to UA and you were working. Then law school. I'm sure you both had other friends."

Fritz furrowed his forehead. "Friends are friends for life."

"If he wasn't friends with Manuel, then why were you all together that night?"

Fritz leaned on the bar and tapped his fingers. "I don't remember. Maybe they were done with a test or something. Chris and I were getting together, and Manuel tagged along."

"Did that happen often?"

Fritz fidgeted some more. "I never liked Manuel, you know? He was always hanging around us and trying to act smarter than me. Like he'd make a joke with Chris about something they learned or some *case.*" The emphasis he put on it made it sound like a curse word.

I watched him.

He tapped his fingers. "So, that night it was going to be me and Chris, like old times. But Manuel was there."

"And you were partying?"

Fritz shrugged. "Not like we used to. But yeah, I s'pose we'd had some beers."

He'd said earlier they were taking Chris home because he'd drank too much. "And you came up on the wreck. Chris was helping me and you were with Ann. Where was Manuel?"

Fritz's fingers tapped faster. "See? That's the thing. Manuel ran after that guy. Rodriguez. He didn't help anyone. Then, afterward, he used that guy as an opportunity to join the legal team and get Rodriguez deported. That started his career."

Bitterness tinged Fritz's words and he needed little encouragement to keep talking. "So yeah, while Chris dropped out and spent years struggling to get by and I married Ann and took care of her, Manuel got this huge reputation for being a good lawyer. And then, like people can't remember anything, he jumps sides and becomes this big talker for the immigrants. And the kicker is, Manuel probably wasn't that good at any of it because he always had his rich daddy to pay for everything."

A man in painter's whites stepped up to the bar and held up a hand. "Can I get two Coors?"

Fritz tossed off, "In a sec." He didn't take his eyes from me. "And even though I'm the one who stayed by Ann's side all these years and I'm the one who took care of everything else from that night, even though it was Manuel's fault, too, he comes swooping in and gives Ann a donation for the center and she's all grateful and saying what a generous man he is."

"Manuel is the big donor?"

"Sure. He writes a check from his family's foundation, not even from his own account. I get the first new pickup I've ever had and I'm supposed to be kiss his feet. I guess I ought to be more grateful."

With that, he whipped away from me and grabbed the two Coors from the fridge under the bar and handed them to the customer.

No wonder Ann loved Ortiz so much if he'd supplied funding for Mi Casa.

He came back to me, contrite. "I'm sorry. I shouldn't have downloaded on you. That guy, though, he's always been an asshole. He did some good for Ann's center. I know I shouldn't say anything bad about the dead, but I'm glad he's gone. And I'm glad someone killed him, that he didn't get to die of old age."

"You sound like you think everything that happened that night was his fault." Pushing his buttons didn't seem fair, but I felt like I'd scratched something and I wanted to know more.

Fritz rubbed his beard again. "He screwed Chris over. All his life. Even last year, when he went after Chris in the media. It nearly cost Chris his job. I know there was bad blood between them. And it hurts me, you know?

Chris is my best friend and to see Ortiz fuck him over and over. I think him going after Chris at the festival was the last straw."

He couldn't have meant what it seemed he hinted at. I had to be wrong.

"What I'm saying is I don't blame Chris."

I sat back, the air nearly knocked out of me. My eyes must have popped wide and I finally drew in a breath, staring at Fritz. "You think Chris did it."

Fritz stared at me for a moment then looked down at his tapping fingers.

21

I didn't know what to do with Fritz's monologue. Was I the only person who thought Chris was innocent? I sat in the Pilot, my heart racing. I needed to talk to Ann.

Fritz had said Manuel helped out at the center. Ann hadn't told me that. When Manuel's murder hit the news, wouldn't she have mentioned it? She'd surely have said something when Chris was arrested for it. I couldn't imagine why she'd keep his involvement in the center a secret.

Everyone had turned against Chris. It was down to me and Ann now. The three Ta-mutals, as always.

I drove through the dark streets. Not even eight o'clock, it felt like midnight. Lights shone from the windows of Mi Casa, but the front blinds were closed. I drove around to the back and parked on the street, leaving the driveway open for Fritz, though I hoped to be gone before he returned.

A dog barked down the street and a chorus of crickets kept up an early evening concert. The rush of cars on the busy street in front of the center sounded muffled back here. TVs cast moving blue shadows behind barred windows in the houses along the dark block.

I knocked on the screen door and tried the latch. It opened easily. "Ann," I hollered as I walked in and turned to lock the door after me. She sat at the dining room table, a laptop in front of her and piles of receipts and documents scattered on the table.

"How many times do I need to tell you to lock that front door?" I said.

She swiped a hand over her forehead, pushing her bangs up and letting them drop down. "Fritz will be home soon. I hate to make him rummage for his keys."

The sliding door stood open to the night air and the pool filter bubbled behind her. "You get the pool fixed?"

She looked up from her screen and twisted her head around, as if remembering the pool for the first time. "Oh, yeah. Deon dropped the parts off and fixed it yesterday."

When I was breaking into Ortiz's house or meeting Jared at McDonald's? Guess Deon and I weren't the best communicators, especially when we were fighting. I tried not to focus on Deon having time to fix Ann's pool and do pro bono work for her, yet he'd been working late nights and weekends. "Good." Beyond the back fence, sounds of Mexican music floated softly into the night. "Have a full house at the center?"

She sighed and shifted her attention to me. "What is it, Mike? I'm knee-deep in bills tonight. If you're only here to say hi, can we do it some other time?"

Just a couple of hours ago she'd practically begged me to talk to her. Now I was in Ann's full passive-aggressive kingdom. To get along here, I needed to let her be in charge. "I want to talk to you."

She gazed into my face as if assessing my earnestness and shut the lid on her laptop. "Okay, but first you need to eat something. There's leftover pasta salad in the fridge."

I loved Ann's pasta salad and something that didn't come wrapped in paper and delivered through a window sounded good. I served myself and sat at the table.

"What's bothering you?" The way she said it made it sound as if she made a huge sacrifice to indulge me.

I was too tired to play her game. "Chris is in real trouble. I thought you might be more worried."

She bristled. "You don't think I haven't been upset? I called you this morning and told you about the arrest and asked you to take me. But you wouldn't. Instead, you dropped everything and ran over to the courthouse. And then I get nothing. All day long. Nothing. Do you know how that made me feel?"

God, what an insensitive jerk I'd been. "I'm sorry. I should have talked to you."

"Oh, you think? And now you come over here and wonder why I'm not wringing my hands?"

"Okay. That was really bad of me."

"And then, I see you on the news and when you finally call it's to tell me your kids are missing. And then when you find them, still nothing."

"Oh my god, Ann. I'm so sorry."

"If it hadn't been for Efrain telling me you were all at softball practice, I still wouldn't know everyone is safe."

I put my hand over hers. "I can't believe I forgot. I'm really, really sorry."

She stared at me for a moment, then covered our hands with her free one and squeezed. "I know. It's okay. You were taking care of Chris and then you were worried about your kids. I'm sure you were relieved and just didn't think about me. I get it."

There was that tolerance and forgiveness. It's what made her a great director of the center. It's what made her a great sister. "I'm trying to help Chris. But doors keep getting shut. It's not looking good for him and I need help."

Ann didn't meet my eyes. "No, it's not looking good."

"I just came from talking to Fritz."

Her head jerked up. "What? Why?"

"I found out he was at the wreck that night with Chris and Manuel."

She sighed. "Why is this coming up? What has this got to do with anything?"

I stood up, too agitated to stay still. "I don't know. Chris and Manuel were friends and then something happened that night and they became enemies. Fritz was there. I thought he might know."

She propped an elbow on the table and rested her cheek on her hand as if too tired to hold her head up. "That night was horrible. The accident. Mom and Dad. But no one talks much about Carlos Rodriguez. He lost his wife, too."

"And the little boy."

Ann closed her eyes. "There was no little boy, Mike."

"Regis Bartholomew knows there was."

Her eyes flew open. "Regis Bartholomew?"

"He thinks the boy was raised by family or someone in the immigrant community."

Ann frowned. "Are you kidding me? All this time I thought you made him up. From guilt."

"I can see where that would make sense. But he was there. It's strange that not you or Fritz or Chris saw him. Only me."

She looked sad. "I wonder what happened to him."

"Bartholomew says Chris and Manuel were friends, but Fritz says they hardly knew each other. He says that night they were all together was unusual. Do you think that's true?"

She thought about it. "I don't know. We were all doing our own thing then. I was in high school with my friends and couldn't care less about Chris. He was barely at home anyway. I know law school is rough and I think he probably studied most of the time on campus. Could be they were friends."

"But Manuel came after him so hard last year. Do friends act that way?"

Her eyes fell to an invoice beside the computer. It was hard to say if she even saw it. "I'm sure Manuel had reasons for what he did."

I watched her closely. "You got some big donations lately."

She didn't move. Then slowly raised her eyes to mine. "Fritz told you."

"That Manuel Ortiz was the anonymous donor? Yes."

She pursed her lips. "He wasn't anonymous. You can see his name on the donor list or even see a copy of the check I deposited. I wish Fritz hadn't told you."

"Why?"

Her eyes found mine. "Because I thought you'd react exactly like you are."

"And how is that?"

"Outraged. Judgmental."

I folded my arms. "Why aren't you? Ortiz went after Chris. He got himself killed and because of his public fight with Chris, now Chris is in jail. How could you take money from him?"

Ann sighed. "Will you sit down? You're making me nervous."

I didn't want to sit but forced myself to a chair at the table.

"You always jump in the fight to save Chris. Can you listen to someone else for a change?" she said.

Deon's words knocked against my skull.

She softened her voice. "Your blind devotion to our family is admirable. But sometimes you don't think things through."

"Such as?"

"Maybe Chris shouldn't be a Border Patrol agent." Ann paused while I fought my disbelief that she would side with Ortiz. She forced me to look at her. "He's got a lot of anger. You must see that."

"What does that have to do with anything? He's good at his job. He helps people. He protects the border."

She turned her head away as if trying to think of words to say. "I love Chris. You know I do. But I see him clearer than you do."

"I don't know what you're talking about."

She kept her eyes on me. "Fritz told me things about Chris you don't know."

"Like what?"

She gave me that sympathetic Ann voice she used when talking to her clients at the center. "You see him as this superhero, swooping in to save undocumented people crossing the border, helping them get to safety. Giving them food and water and shelter."

"That's his job. Remember? He also is willing to stand in harm's way to keep drugs out and stop human trafficking. To keep terrorists from entering."

She narrowed her lips again, to show me she disagreed with me. She wasn't a big Border Patrol fan. Her perspective rested firmly with the people in her center. Those people she helped to remain in this country, whether legally or under the radar. "Chris talks to Fritz with language even you would hate."

"Even me? You do know I'm married to a Mexican man. It's not like I'm out spouting hate speech."

Her small smile didn't relax her face. "Deon is Mexican, yes. But he's done all he can to distance himself from his people."

"His people?"

She frowned in annoyance. "He doesn't claim his heritage. He denies it."

"As far as I can tell, he's proud of being Mexican."

"If he were, he'd be in the trenches. He's a lawyer. He could be doing so much for immigrants. He could be fighting for his people."

"Like your hero Manuel Ortiz did?"

She slapped the table. "Manuel created awareness of the issues. He put himself on the line for his people. And now he's dead. He wasn't afraid to fight for those less fortunate than himself. Deon should be doing the same."

I ground my teeth for a second. "Less fortunate than himself. Interesting choice of words. Deon's family crossed here illegally in the seventies. Mama and Papa Sanchez and their three children. Papa worked in the fields, Mama cleaned houses. Not a great living, but they survived. And they conceived their fourth child. Deon, the only one born in the United States. The only citizen."

She glared at me. "You don't need to—"

"And he grew up smart and ambitious. Meanwhile, one of their other sons, Paco, didn't have the same work ethic. He thought it might be better to rob convenience stores than work for a wage. And when Paco got caught, the whole family saw their American dream go up in smoke. They were deported."

Ann frowned. "I know this—"

"All except the legal one, Deon. Barely eighteen and just about to graduate from high school. As valedictorian. Can you imagine how *unfortunate* you might feel to be alone that young and have to earn a living, but still make it through college and then law school?"

"This is not—"

I leaned forward. "Do. Not. Tell me how Deon should be working for those less fortunate than himself. And especially don't compare him to Manuel Ortiz, who grew up with a silver spoon full of honey placed in his open mouth. He never had to worry or scrimp. And if you think he was doing everything he did out of human kindness, you should talk to Dr. Bartholomew, who isn't suffering from your rose-glasses syndrome. He believes it was all a political ploy."

I sucked in a breath. "You should be down on your knees kissing Deon's feet for working on your case pro bono. Not to mention fixing your damned pool."

Ann sat back, her face full of disdain. "Are you finished?"

I nodded.

"We were talking about Chris. And you wanted to know why I think he shouldn't be working for the Border Patrol."

I stood up and walked to the kitchen and found a water glass in the cupboard. I filled it and set it in front of Ann, then did the same for me. "Ranting makes me thirsty."

She thanked me. "Fritz told me Chris talks about the border crossers with hatred. He has stories of cruelty."

"How does Fritz know any of this?"

"Chris stops into the Hot Spot with his friends and Fritz hears the way they laugh and curse the people they find."

"I don't believe this."

"You think Fritz would lie? Why? Chris is his best friend. Fritz may not be an activist or as involved as I am, but he is kind and this hurts him deeply."

"I've never heard Chris talk like that."

She drank from her glass. "He's never gotten over the accident. He blames all undocumented people for the act of one lone driver."

"That doesn't make sense."

"A driver who hit a car turning left onto the highway in front of him. He lost his wife, his home, and if you're right, his son. And it probably wasn't even his fault. Dad wasn't paying attention and pulled out in front of him."

Because he was worried about his daughter's insulin shock. Because of me.

I shoved the thought aside. "I think I'd know if my brother was that kind of racist."

She laughed without humor. "You don't know as much about everything as you think you do."

A creaking of old hinges, followed by the giggle of child sounded from the backyard. I looked through the open sliding door to see Tomás running and looking over his shoulder at the gate. He swiveled his head forward and jetted through the sliding door into Ann's open arms.

"Gotcha," she said in English. "Who are you hiding from?"

He wriggled free and ran to me, his fingers wrapped around Batman in one hand and the Batmobile in the other. He threw himself into my lap and in Spanish yelled, "Save me, save me."

The words might be startling, but he was laughing so hard it didn't seem like a real threat. I answered in English, as much so he'd get used to the language as because it would take me some time to find the right words. "I won't let them get you."

Sophia strode through the gate. She didn't have the delighted expression of her son. In Spanish she said, "Tomás. You are not allowed into the yard. You know that. Now come over here this instant."

He pressed into me, still playing the game. "You won't take me alive."

Ann smiled as Sophia stopped outside the door. Ann spoke slow Spanish. "Please don't worry. I love seeing Tomás laugh and play like a five-year-old should."

Sophia lowered her eyes to the ground. "*Gracias*. But he still needs to follow the rules and to obey his mother."

I gave him a hug and pulled him off my lap. "She's right, partner. You need to listen to your *mamá*."

His eyes still twinkled but his laughter ended. He trudged to the door. "I'm sorry. I wanted to see Señora Ann."

Sophia took him by the wrist allowing him to keep hold of his toys. "Señora Ann is a nice lady. But we cannot run to her house whenever we want."

"*Sí, mamá*."

Tomás took off running for the gate then turned around and held up the hand with the Batmobile. Sophia's doting gaze rested on Tomás. "He loves his Batmobile." She lowered her voice. "I'm afraid maybe too much."

Ann said, "Why is that?"

I knew. That creepy sock monkey he'd tossed aside while loving my gift. Again, something rattled at my brain, but I pushed it aside.

Sophia's face filled with the love of a mother sharing about her son. "Efrain bought him a toy. I think it meant a lot to Efrain because he said it was like a toy he'd loved as a child but had lost when they came to the United States. But Tomás loves his Batman and Batmobile and hardly looks at Efrain's gift."

Ah. Efrain was the origin of the sock monkey. It wasn't right for me to find that fitting.

Ann dismissed it. "I'm sure Efrain understands." She hesitated, then added, "You and Efrain seem to be getting along well. He likes Tomás."

Sophia colored and looked away. "He is very nice to us."

"*Mamá*," Tomás called from the gate. "I'm getting away."

Sophia laughed. "I must go," she said to us.

Tomás slipped through the gate, then popped back into the opening. He waved vigorously. "Good night," he said in English.

Ann and I both replied in the same way.

Sophia closed the gate and I lowered my eyebrows at Ann. "Front door unlocked. Back gate unlatched. Have I taught you nothing?"

She waved her hand. "I see no reason to lock the gate. I trust the people at Mi Casa."

"I'm sure Lizzy Borden's parents thought she was sunshine on a stick. You never know."

"Being a cop has made you suspicious."

Good thing I didn't get whiplash when Ann and I switched positions. She'd been mad I wasn't taking proper safety precautions with my kids. And now I was going after her for lax security. "Okay, if you won't do it for your own safety, how about for the children at Mi Casa?"

"What do you mean?"

"The pool. One of the little ones could crawl in and drown."

She laughed. "You really do look on the dark side. I don't keep the ladder in the pool. They'd have to drag it from under the eaves of the house. None of our children could do that. I need Efrain to do it for me."

"I can see I'm not going to win the fight to keep you safe."

She agreed. "You can save your energy for Chris's battle. That's an uphill one, as far as I can see."

Maybe I should have been gentler, but I blurted out, "Fritz thinks Chris killed Manuel."

I expected Ann to gasp. To protest. At the very least to laugh off my suspicion. But she didn't. She looked at me and waited with expectation.

I stared at her for several seconds. "Oh my god."

She hurried to defend herself. "Look at the facts."

"What facts? That Manuel attacked him in the media last year and he led a similar attack at the festival? You honestly think that's enough for Chris to murder him? Maybe Chris has some anger and maybe he does blame undocumented people for Mom and Dad's death, but come on, he wouldn't kill someone for that. He wouldn't kill anyone."

She stared at the invoice again. "He's been at that job for a long time. We don't know what he's seen and done. Maybe he's got PTSD. The point is, we don't know. And Chris is so angry. He lashes out without provocation."

Chris's face at the recruitment presentation had scared me. He'd overreacted in the parking lot after Josie's game. "Okay, sure. Chris can lose his temper. But murder is something different. He'd never kill anyone."

Ann leaned in, her voice gentle. "He's been trained to do that. He's been Border Patrol for years. You can't tell me he hasn't killed people out there."

"We don't know that. He's never been accused of it."

"Does it matter? He flat out defended the murder of a sixteen-year-old boy at the border."

Everything she said was true. But I'd been through law enforcement training, too. I wouldn't shoot a kid. I wouldn't murder anyone in cold blood. I would only shoot if someone else or I was in immediate danger. I knew Chris was the same.

Didn't I?

22

I walked out of Ann's house, reminding her to lock the screen after me. Her reply that Fritz would be home very soon didn't cajole me, but the sight of Fritz's pickup in the driveway convinced me she'd be safe. He must have driven up while we were talking. That I didn't hear the rumble of his new engine told me how intense our conversation had been. I was relieved he hadn't come in until we were done.

He stepped out of the garage before I got to my car. "Making the rounds tonight, huh?"

I walked back to him. "Wanted to see what Ann remembered from that night."

"Did she tell you anything new?"

I shook my head. "Would you put some pressure on her to keep the doors locked when she's home alone?"

He laughed. "How much good do you think I can do?"

"Well, it's worth a try anyway."

Fritz's head jerked to the side and he lunged, yelling, "Hey, what the hell?"

I reacted automatically when I saw a dark figure by the side of the house and reached for my weapon. Of course, I didn't have it on me, but that didn't stop my hand from moving. "Who's there?"

A quiet voice said, "It is Efrain." He stepped from the shadows. "I did not mean to scare you."

Fritz clenched his fists. "What are you doing out here?"

Efrain lowered his eyes. "I wanted to talk to you."

"Oh." Fritz stayed tense, but at least he didn't look like he'd punch Efrain. "Don't lurk in the dark."

"I am sorry," Efrain said.

"Okay, well. Guess that's good for tonight." I climbed into the Pilot and drove away.

I wanted to get home to Deon and the girls. With little sleep the night before and everything that had happened, the day wore down on me. My weariness made everything seem hopeless.

No matter what, I couldn't give up on Deon and me. Somehow, I needed to let him know how sorry I was for not putting him and the girls above anything else. Part of me argued with him, though, about the importance of the rest of our families. I had Chris and Ann, the three Ta-mutals. But Deon was equally devoted to his family in Mexico.

We traveled to see them at least twice every year, for Easter and at Christmas time. Most years we also spent our summer vacation with them. The girls loved their cousins, and both Deon and I felt that connection to family was vital.

I understood Deon's worry that I'd put the children at risk. None of my protests about my duty to Chris would alleviate his concern. I owed it to him to respect that.

My phone rang and when I saw Jared's number on the ID, I cancelled the call. The phone immediately rang again. We played that cat-and-mouse game three more times and when he called a fourth time, I got the picture that he wasn't going to quit. I hit accept. "What?"

He hesitated. "Hi. How are you?"

I watched the headlights of other cars and the colorful signs of businesses as I drove along the still-busy street. "I asked you not to call me anymore. This isn't happening."

"You're still trying to help your brother, right?"

My resolve to honor Deon and reject everything connected to Jared warred with my need to protect Chris. "Is there anything new?"

"Can you meet me somewhere and I'll tell you? I'm at the Tap Room, north of your place."

He was crazy if he thought I'd meet him anywhere, especially a bar. I didn't hear any noise in the background so he must be sitting in his car. "You tried that before. If you don't want to tell me, fine. I'll go down to the station and try to find out myself. But I'm not going to meet you."

He paused, clearly frustrated. "Okay. I only want to help you. I don't want to make your life more difficult."

If he cared at all about making my life easier, he wouldn't contact me. This was all about him. "What do you have?"

He sighed. "I did a little snooping around where I shouldn't have been, and I found out the investigators discovered something suspicious in Ortiz's bank accounts."

God, I wanted him to quit playing coy. "And that would be ...?"

"There are two really big withdrawals in the last two months."

"He's a rich guy. He can afford nice things."

"Yeah, maybe. But the investigators are trying to find out where the money went."

Mi Casa. A healthy donation to please Ann and somehow stick it to Chris. "He can do whatever he wants with the money. It doesn't make it a crime."

"I'm not sure what the investigators are working on, maybe eliminating purchases and trying to determine what happened. They found out he took the money in cash. Their guess is that someone was blackmailing him."

I let that sit for a while. Blackmail? With the big money coming from Ortiz into Mi Casa, it couldn't be blackmail or Ann wouldn't have been so open about it. But she'd kept it quiet until Fritz popped off with the information. "How could blackmail money lead to Manuel Ortiz's death? Wouldn't it have been the other way around, with Ortiz killing the person blackmailing him?"

Jared chuckled. "You'd think so. But it sort of points to bad business going on. Maybe Ortiz refused the next payment and they let him have it."

It wasn't unheard of for a man with political aspirations to be the subject of blackmail. Old lovers, bad business. Extortion. Desperate if they'd resort to murder. "Okay, well, thanks."

"Wait." Jared sounded desperate.

I held my finger over the disconnect while I made a right-hand turn toward our neighborhood. My stomach tightened but I stayed silent.

"I saw you and Deon at the ballpark today."

His tone and words made my blood cold. "You're stalking me?"

"No. God, no. I wanted to see you. Talk. That's all. I care so much for you."

"Isn't that the definition of stalking?"

"I need to see you. Just meet me here at the Tap Room."

I didn't want to ask what it was he felt he needed to tell me. "You wanted to talk to me in front of my kids? My family? In case I didn't make myself clear the last two times I told you, let me say it again. We had nothing to begin with, and it's over now. I appreciate you keeping me informed of Chris's situation. I really do. But that doesn't mean I'm going to pick up where we left off. It was a mistake, one I stopped before it went too far."

"It's already too late. I love you. I want us to be together."

I should punch off. Engaging him further wasn't smart. "Stop it. You don't love me. We're never going to be together. I'm married and I love Deon."

"But does he love you?"

A well-aimed punch to the gut. Did Deon still love me? Had I already destroyed it?

"He didn't ooze love for you at the ballpark. He looked done with you. I think you should tell him about us."

"There is no us." I repeated, "NO US."

He whispered. "I could tell him."

No. It took a second for me to get my breath. "There's nothing to tell. Leave me and my family alone."

I hit off and kept hitting end call the next five times he tried. I pulled over and messed with the settings on my phone until I figured out how to block his calls. Why hadn't I done that long ago?

My nerves in a jangled heap, my brain jumpy, my whole future up in the air, along with Chris having to spend his first full night in jail, I pulled the car into the garage and shut off the engine. I closed my eyes and concentrated on sipping one breath into my lungs, until my diaphragm expanded, then letting it out slowly between pursed lips. Three more times as slowly as possible and I thought I might actually have control.

I stepped into the kitchen. The night light above the stove cast the room in the comforting shadows of home. Banging overhead told me at least one person was still up. I dropped my purse on the counter by the back door and climbed the stairs.

Music thudded from Josie's closed door. Sami's singing erupted from her room. I opened the door and poked my head in to catch Sami dancing in front of the full-length mirror on her closet door, hair brush microphone held to her mouth. Her brown hair was piled on top of her head and her sleep shirt yanked up with the end tied at her back to expose her belly. She wore her favorite skirt, which I'd made her add to the Goodwill bag a couple of months ago. Her coltish legs had grown too long for it, and now it barely covered her little behind.

She jumped and yelled, "Moooooom! Privacy please," her embarrassment coming out as indignation.

I tried to keep the grin from my face. "It's time to for bed."

Some protests and grumbling, but she knew she'd already beat her regular time by a half hour. We talked about school the next day and how she never thought I'd let her eat at In-N-Out two days in a row. She didn't know how far my life spun out of orbit that something so unthinkable could happen. She pulled off her skirt, untied the knot at the back of her sleep shirt, and slipped between the sheets. I kissed her and turned off the light.

I didn't mention the pilfered skirt. As long as she didn't wear it out of the house, it wouldn't hurt for her to keep it.

Down the hall, light filtered from under the master suite door. Deon wasn't in the guest room. Maybe he figured first come, first served and I'd get the other room.

I wanted to talk to Deon and make everything right. But I needed to get the girls settled first. Josie had turned down her tunes and was already in bed with her English book propped on her knees.

She looked up at me when I peeked in her door. "How's Jamie?" she asked.

It sounded so grown up it startled me. I'd forgotten I'd used Jamie as an excuse. "Good. She's got some projects going to build self-esteem in the girls she's helping."

Josie nodded in a sage way. "Maybe they ought to play sports. Softball helps my self-esteem."

In its own way, her words—probably taken from a speaker she'd heard at school or maybe from her coach—were as cute and naïve as Sami's rock star fantasy. But she was growing and thinking and turning into a wise kid.

Much of motherhood is a series of skirmishes, frustrations, second guessing, and a test of wills. But there are precious moments when your heart swells until it closes your throat with tears, moments when you touch the mystical thread that reveals your children as human beings with a future of their own that you can't imagine. Then every battle over dirty faces, homework, or uneaten vegetables fades away. You are gifted with the realization that these helpless beings you brought into the world are living their unique experience.

I could go on trying to analyze my amazing children forever. I wanted to live in this exact point in eternity. Mom and Dad had so few years to know this inexpressible feeling.

"Except," Josie said, "I'll never have great self-esteem if I don't get that new mitt like Lily Anderson has. So, can we go shopping on Saturday and get it? Please?"

So much for youthful wisdom. I crossed the room and leaned over to kiss her on the head. She tolerated it. "'Night, Josie-bun." I used the old nickname.

She kept her eyes on her book. "I'm taking it that means no. Like usual."

I smiled and didn't correct her grammar. "Don't stay up too late."

I stepped into hallway and stared at our bedroom door. I should figure out the right words to begin. I could stand outside forever and never conjure the magic combination. So, I'd do what I always do, barrel in and hope for the best. I approached, closed my fingers around the latch, and pushed it open.

Deon stood by the big window looking out at the Catalinas. It was the money-shot that sold us the house. The mountains couldn't be seen in the darkness now. He pulled the shade and turned to me.

What to say? I opened my mouth. "I—"

At the same time, he said, "I—"

We both stopped. I tried to read his dark eyes. He didn't hold my gaze. Whatever that meant, it probably wasn't good.

I stepped closer, keeping my voice low so the girls wouldn't hear our tone and worry. "I'm sorry."

He snapped his head up. "Sorry? For what?" It sounded like a test.

That old defensiveness crept up my back, but I pushed it down. "I know I didn't take your concern seriously. You'd asked me not to investigate Ortiz's death and I ignored you."

He considered that. "Thank you."

We stood in silence for a moment. I didn't know how to direct him to my point of view and was trying to pick out the right words when he started again. "I had decided to take the girls down to my parents' tomorrow after school. I thought it would be best for them to be away from the house and, frankly, I wanted to get as far away from you as I could."

Wow. I expected him to be mad at me and he'd already said he was taking the girls away, but this felt like a blow to the gut and I took a step back.

"But what you said just now. 'I'm sorry.' It sounded true. Like you meant it."

I swallowed. "I did. We're a team."

He held up his hand to stop me. "No. Don't ruin the beginning. I'm not happy with you. I think you selfishly put our daughters at risk."

I strangled on the word *selfish*. I was trying to help Chris. I wasn't investigating for me.

"I've been thinking of leaving you for some time."

Blood roared through my ears. "You didn't think to talk to me about it?"

With the tilt of his head he acknowledged my point. "I've been trying to get your attention for so long. But you aren't here."

"So you decided to leave without giving us the chance to work it out?"

He sighed. "I've been trying. At first I asked you to take a long weekend away and you took on a Rangers assignment. I did everything I could to let you know how important you are to me."

I could hardly get a breath. "But you didn't talk to me about it."

He frowned. "I won't beg you to love me. When you didn't seem inter-ested, I started working longer and longer hours."

"You were testing me? Playing games?" I wanted to turn this around, blame Deon for everything. But he spoke the truth. I had backed away.

"Maybe it wasn't the right way. I don't know. What I do know is that we are only going through the motions. Taking care of Josie and Sami. Talking about house and schedules. But nothing else. You're growing away from me. Taking more assignments with the Rangers, volunteering more for Mi Casa and helping Jamie. You don't seem interested in me or our life together. And I've heard ..."

Oh god. Jared had told him. He knew. I felt the blood drain from my face and my body go cold. I couldn't move.

He waved his hand. "I didn't believe what I heard. But tonight, after we got home, I looked at our beautiful girls. At our home and our life together. I stood in front of the mantel and the St. Christophers and I prayed. I said, 'If Michaela speaks to me. To me. Not at me or by me. If she puts me in front of her brother, then I'll stay. I'll give it another chance.' And your face when you said 'I'm sorry.' That felt like the first real thing you've said to me in a long time."

Ann said he'd know. My sister knew my husband better than I did. I'd started out a self-centered and willful child and I hadn't changed much since then. It was high time I learned how to bend. I whispered, "You are everything to me."

He inhaled. "No. I'm not everything and I shouldn't be. Even the girls. We should be important, but not everything. You love your brother and sister. They deserve to have a piece of you, too."

He understood why I needed to help Chris. I knew he would. "You aren't leaving?"

He frowned. "Yes, I'm leaving."

The air disappeared from the room. If my legs hadn't turned to stone, I would have collapsed. I'd ruined it. Every good thing in my life would walk out the door with Deon.

"I booked three nights at the Bar C. The girls will have to miss school on Friday." He paused when he saw my hopeful expression. "Yes. I prayed you'd say something to change my mind from going to Mexico. To give me a reason to give us a try. I booked the resort, but I could have cancelled if you hadn't said what you did."

We'd talked about taking the girls to the Bar C, a dude ranch north of Tucson. Like little girls everywhere, they loved horses and we thought a weekend of riding would be magical for them. I thought of them in the sunshine, giggles and grins, bouncing in the saddle, eating burgers off the grill at the bunkhouse.

"We'll leave tomorrow after school as I'd planned."

I mentally arranged my schedule and thought about what to pack for the girls.

Deon gave me a sad smile. "I booked it for three. You aren't going."

Again, that frozen air stayed between us.

"You stay here and do what you have to do. Chase the dragons and fight the ghosts. Save your brother or at least try. We're coming back on Sunday afternoon. Either you are done with this by then, or you're done with me."

We spent the night in our bed, but I couldn't say we slept or that we were together. The chasm between us in our queen-sized bed felt wider than Death Valley.

23

I stood in the kitchen cradling my coffee mug. I'd laid out cereal, bowls, and milk for the girls and buttered toast waited on a plate. The brew grew cold as my mind sifted through everything that happened in the last few days. Chris arrested for killing Manuel Ortiz and finding out he had known Ortiz for over twenty years. They'd been friends and rivals, challenging and pushing each other in law school. They'd been bitter enemies, at each other's jugulars for the last year.

What if the investigators were right and Manuel was being black-mailed? They must have some reason for believing that. Maybe the cartels were involved. My heart squeezed when I thought of blackmail and pictured Chris's shiny new pickup.

Or maybe Chris, as Border Patrol, knew about something and had tried to warn Ortiz. That could be why I'd seen him at Koffler. It might be why Dr. Bartholomew thought they'd mended fences. But if the cartels were involved, I'd placed my family in harm's way.

Chris would have warned me of any danger from the cartels. He wouldn't have shut me out. Unless he thought giving me information would put us at greater risk. I needed to talk to him as soon as possible.

Deon had slipped out of bed earlier and drank his portion of our shared pot of coffee before I'd come downstairs. Now he was showering and putting on one of his expensive suits for a day in court or meetings with clients, or maybe laboring on briefs and research in the office. I didn't even know what cases he was working on.

Sami let out a whoop and bounced down the stairs. Deon must have told her about the weekend plans. She galloped through the hallway to the kitchen and stopped in front of me, prancing like a pony, with her hands curled in front of her. "We're going to the Bar C! All weekend!"

I drummed up excitement. "You're going to have a blast."

She trotted around the dining table. "Dad said you have to work so you're going to miss it. But you can come next time."

Josie entered the kitchen with a wide smile and an unabashed giddiness she hadn't shown in a while. She swung her backpack from her shoulders and plopped it on a bar stool and jumped up after it. "Dad said we'd be gone all weekend. I'm supposed to have practice on Saturday morning. Can you call coach and tell her I won't be there?"

Going to the ranch might be the only thing Josie wouldn't mind skipping practice for. And I was going to miss seeing her delight. I had no one but myself to blame for that. "Sure."

Sami hoisted herself onto the stool next to Josie and they filled their cereal bowls and munched on the toast, keeping up an animated conversation about how far and long they'd be allowed to ride every day. It had been too long since they'd shared something that lit them up like this. We should have gone away sooner.

My recklessness had put this wonderful life in jeopardy. I'd never be that stupid again.

Deon didn't look at me when he entered the kitchen. He opened the fridge and pulled out a container of yogurt but didn't open it. He probably meant to take it to work, getting away from me as quickly as possible.

"I'll pick you up from school, so get yourselves out as soon as the bell rings." He pointed a finger at Josie. "That means you. No hanging out with your friends or flirting with the boys."

"Yeah," Sami said, pointing at Josie, too.

Josie's cute smile beamed on Deon. "As if."

"Okay." He walked past me to the garage door. "See you later." The door automatically closed behind him and he never said goodbye to me.

I struggled to paste on a bright face. "Hurry with breakfast. We've got ten minutes."

No resistance as they snarfed down the rest of their cereal, tipped the bowls for the last of the milk, and rushed upstairs to brush their teeth.

I didn't need to contribute much to the conversation on the way to school. They didn't fight over the music and Josie didn't lecture or tease Sami. Instead, they laughed and acted like friends, exactly as I always wanted them to.

I dropped them off and neither thought about kissing me goodbye. I should be glad they were independent enough to not need me. They were growing up in all the best ways. It broke my heart in equal measure to my motherly pride.

I didn't want to waste time. I had to talk to Chris. He needed to know I wasn't giving up and he had to help me. I'd only had a glimpse of him yesterday as he'd been escorted from the building. He'd been pale and his face closed in on itself. He might be afraid and alone, angry, defeated, defiant. I had no way of knowing. Even if he didn't want me, I needed him. Visiting hours at the jail would begin soon and I wanted to get there quickly.

The house felt big and too quiet when I got home. I dashed up the stairs for a shower, realized I needed to change the port in my insulin pump and took care of it. That led to me remembering I needed to eat, heading back downstairs for a cereal bar, and I grabbed bites while heading back upstairs. My heart thumped with impatience while I waited for the water to heat in the shower.

The heat and pressure of the shower felt nice and I'd have loved to stand under the flow for hours, letting the worry and stress wash away. But I didn't have that luxury. I twisted the faucets and stepped out in time to hear the doorbell ring.

I should let it go. This time of day in the quiet suburb, the only people ringing doorbells were pest control salesmen or some religious sect out to save my soul. But it rang again and created just enough curiosity that I grabbed my robe, ignored my wet hair, and took the stairs two at time.

Through the windows at the side of the door I saw a TPD uniformed cop. My heart jumped into my throat. I fumbled with the lock and threw open the door.

"No!" I shouted as soon as I saw his face. "Get the hell out of here."

Jared opened his mouth as if surprised at my reaction.

I stepped outside, my wet hair swinging against the back of my robe. I planted my hand on his chest. "This is it. I'm getting a restraining order."

He held up his hands and spoke above my yells. "I'm only here to bring you news. I swear."

What if he'd showed up when the girls were home? If Deon saw him? "I don't want to hear it from you. Leave me alone."

He talked fast. "It's Chris. They found something."

I pushed him back, striding across our front porch. The neighbors might see, but most of them were at work. "Leave now."

"The ballistics came back on the gun."

I stopped. Jared would bring me the news if the gun proved to be Chris's or not, either way, as an excuse to see me. It didn't mean anything that he drove over here. Except Jared's worried expression told me otherwise.

The pavement under my bare feet felt like shifting sand. I wanted to plug my ears. Slam the door and lock it.

Maybe he could tell I had lost my ability to speak because he said gently, "It's a match with Chris's gun."

"No." That word, more of a moan than anything, had to have come from me. I spun around and ran into the house. Away from what Jared said. It made no sense but it's the only thing I could think to do. I raced to the kitchen behind the island and tried to find a mistake in what Jared said. The St. Christophers on the mantel in the family room drew me. I wished they'd protected Chris.

The front door closed and Jared's footsteps stopped at the kitchen entrance. "I'm sorry."

I blinked. Jared couldn't really be standing in my kitchen telling me ... what? "You're saying Chris's gun was used to kill Manuel Ortiz."

He nodded slowly.

The air hurt my skin. This couldn't be happening. "Are they sure? It's an officially supplied side arm. It could be any number of guns." But I knew better. A matching ballistics test is like matching fingerprints.

Jared took a step into kitchen. "I know you don't want to believe that Chris did it—"

"He didn't," I yelled at him. "There's some mistake."

He tried again. "You love him, I know how that is. But sometimes the people we love are not who we think they are."

My eyes burned as if I'd shoved myself face-first into the desert sand. "Stop talking."

He stood next to me and put a hand on my arm. "It's a shock, I know."

I didn't bother moving away and gave myself over to finding a way out of this for Chris.

The door to the garage opened. Deon stepped in. He froze and time stopped as I stared at him. Slowly, his face melted and he turned the color of spoiled beef.

No one moved or spoke. I doubt anyone breathed.

Then Deon stepped backward into the garage and the door swung shut with a click.

I shook Jared's hand off my arm. "Oh my god. No." I sprinted to the door and wrenched it open. "Deon."

He already had his car door open. He didn't look at me, but he stopped with one foot already in the car. "I didn't believe it."

"I don't know what you're talking about," I said, desperation clear in my voice.

Deon's face went from pasty to a crimson glow. He pointed to the door, where Jared stood inside, holding it open. "You and him."

I spun around. "Get out of my house! Leave!" I screamed, leaving my throat raw. Jared didn't move and I advanced on him. "Now."

He stepped out and walked past me, then Deon, down the driveway and onto the sidewalk. His cruiser was parked down the block on the curb.

Deon and I stood in silence.

"Nothing is going on," I managed to croak out.

He let out a snicker. "Right. You aren't dressed and he's in our house. How stupid do you think I am?"

If I ran to him as I wanted to, he'd shove me away. All I could do was stand in the garage and face him. "He came to tell me ballistics confirmed Chris's gun was the one that killed Ortiz." It sounded as awful as it felt, but now, something even worse was crashing down on me. I grasped for a hold and felt it slipping through my fingers.

Deon's face registered a pang of sympathy for me. "I'm sorry. I'd hoped he hadn't done it."

I couldn't defend Chris, not when my world lay in shards. "I was in the shower when Jared got here."

Deon's face hardened again. "And cops normally park a block away when delivering messages."

Two fluffy bichon frise dogs pranced into view on the sidewalk behind Deon. Attached to their leash, Mrs. Hamilton from down the street appeared. She sang out, "Morning, Sanchezes."

Deon and I both waved and did our best with weak smiles. Deon was able to mutter, "Have a good day."

I waited for her to pass down the street, then said, "It's Jared, I swear. I told him never to contact me again. He's stalking me and I'll take care of it."

"Again. Don't contact me again. How many times was it okay for him to contact you?"

I slumped against the Pilot. "I'm sorry. I made a mistake."

He started to climb into the car.

"Wait." I ran to him and grabbed the door so he couldn't close it. "I didn't do anything. Okay, I did, but not what you think."

He glared at me. "What is it I think?"

"We weren't having an affair."

He folded his arms. "That's not what I heard." He let out a disgusted breath. "She told me. I didn't believe her. I said, 'Michaela wouldn't do that. She doesn't lie.'"

She. He had to mean Ann. I shoved that aside for now. "I didn't have an affair." He needed more. "I thought about it. It's true. I don't know why. My life seemed so ordinary. The same thing every day. Softball, school, Rangers assignments, Mi Casa, dinner, housework, again and again."

He made a point of taking in the house and cars with his eyes. "You poor baby."

I nodded, noticing the tears streaming down my face for the first time. "You're right. Spoiled." Ann would say that. "I was wrong. But I didn't go through with it. Because I love you. Because you're all I ever wanted. Because you are so good to me."

"Didn't go through with it? Just how far did you go?"

"I flirted—"

He held up his hand. "No. Never mind. I don't want to know." He let his gaze shift away. "I came to pack the girls' things for the weekend. I'll give you a half hour, then I'll come back to do that. You won't be here then."

"Deon, I'm sorry. This isn't something we can't—"

He lowered himself into the car. I let go of the door and he slammed it closed.

24

I grabbed the first thing my fingers closed on in my closet. A casual skirt and T-shirt. With my hair damp and no makeup, I flew from the house and across town to Mi Casa. I bounded in the front door.

Efrain held a dust mop and his head jerked up. "Good morning."

"Where is she?" I didn't try to hide my anger.

"Your sister? She is in her office." He took a step toward me. "Is something wrong?"

I tossed my hand up to indicate it wasn't his concern and stomped toward her office.

She sat at her desk, crutches resting against the edge of the desk. She gave a surprised "oh" when I burst into her office.

My voice vibrated against the walls. "Why? You couldn't keep your meddling to yourself or maybe your clients here?"

She sat back and gave it a minute, putting it all together. "Deon confronted you."

Tears pushed up my throat, but I refused to shed them. "My marriage may be over because of what you've done."

She frowned. "No, Mike. I wasn't the one messing around."

"I wasn't messing around," I yelled.

She reached for her crutches. "We're not going to do this here where everyone can hear you."

"You don't want them to know how manipulative and judgmental you are?"

She struggled to slip her arms into the crutches and make her way around her desk. "I don't want the residents to see you like this. They've been through enough trauma without having to relive it through your hysterics."

I didn't care. But if she wanted to take it to her house, that suited me. I didn't offer to help her as she trundled down the hall and awkwardly out the door. She fought with the rickety gate into her backyard and I crossed my arms watching her. I left it open and followed her to the house.

She grunted and pulled open the sticky sliding door and stepped inside. I slammed it closed behind me.

She dropped into a kitchen chair and hung her head, shoulders heaving as she panted. "Can you get me some water?"

I started to tremble. Damn me. "You're right." I sounded like my words sifted through gravel.

Ann gave me a confused look.

"It isn't your fault."

I grabbed a glass and filled it with water from her tap. My hissy fit had cost her energy she didn't need to waste on getting herself from there to here. I shouldn't be dumping my anger and frustration onto her. I set the glass in front of her. Tears threatened, but I stuffed them down. I'd cry later. "It wasn't you risking my family. But why did you tell Deon?"

She sipped her water and pushed damp hair from her forehead. "He's a good man. He doesn't deserve to be treated like that."

"But it was over with Jared before it started. I ended it. I didn't actually do anything."

Her eyebrows dipped. "This is so like you."

"What is like me?"

"You do whatever feels good in the moment. You think only about yourself. But you aren't mean and when you figure out you've done something wrong, you want to say you're sorry. The problem is, you've always been so sincere, so cute, so loved and adored, everyone always forgives you. They go on loving you no matter what you've done."

I wanted to believe I meant well, that I wasn't this awful person Ann described. She knew Deon so well, she must see into me, too. "I'm going to do everything I can to make this up to Deon, to earn his trust again."

Her lip curled a little. "And he'll probably forgive you. Not because you deserve it, but because he's a good man."

My throat ached with tears I held back. "He is."

"Too good for you."

The venom in her voice smacked me and I drew in a breath.

She stretched her neck toward me. "Do you have any idea how many of us would kill for a husband like Deon? He takes the kids, he helps out without having to be asked. He's provided you with a gorgeous home, new car, clothes and things to spare. You don't even *have* to work."

I hated her accuracy. "I always wanted to work. I had a career I gave up because Deon didn't want me working."

"He didn't want you to be a cop. And why? Because he loves you and your daughters so much he doesn't want you to put your life on the line. But that's not good enough for you, is it? You have to do whatever you can to let him know he doesn't own you."

She'd never spoken to me like this before. My voice sounded scratchy as it pushed past the lump in my throat. "Why are you doing this?"

She narrowed her eyes at me. "I've finally had enough. For twenty years I've been trying to hold this family together and for that same time, even before, you've done nothing but try to rip it apart."

"That's not true."

"Oh? Let's see, from the time you were born, you worked your ways on Mom and Dad, making them give you all their attention. Poor little Mikey, with her diabetes. You needed special food and insulin monitoring. Chris and I had to be at the babysitter while she took you to appointments or stayed with you in the hospital."

"That wasn't my fault," I said weakly.

She waved that off. "No, of course not. But you lapped it up. Even when you were home, you learned to cry or whine and make them jump through your hoops."

Mom and Dad died when I was twelve, so much of my life before then was bits and specs of memories, all unreliable. I'd felt loved and part of our family. This side of me wasn't something I recognized.

"I know you didn't mean for the accident to happen. You never wanted to kill them. But the truth is, your selfishness caused it. You knew not to eat too much chocolate and you did anyway. All to get my attention because I might have had something better to do on a Friday night than play with my little sister."

I gripped the side of the counter to keep from sinking to the ground.

"You made sure I'd never have anything better to do than be your sister, though. You walked away from the accident intact. I lost my future. Because of you I couldn't run, dance, even go to school. Because of you I married the only man who would have me, and his love for me is based on pity."

"You and Fritz have a good marriage. You have an amazing career. You're making a real difference." It sounded like a way to justify my actions. Just last night, as I'd listened to Fritz talk about Ann, I'd wondered about their marriage. They might just be better at hiding their dysfunction than me and Deon.

She snorted. "You have no idea what marriage is like for most of us because your husband adores you. He gives you everything your heart desires. The rest of our husbands don't look at us the way Deon looks at you. But you wouldn't notice."

"It's not—"

She held up her hand. "Don't bother. You're the pretty girl. The precocious one. I might not have been everyone's favorite, but before the accident, I had my share of friends and even boyfriends. You robbed me of all of that and I had to work so hard ..." She choked up. "So hard to chisel out this life. No one handed me anything."

The refrigerator, the backyard pool, the weekends spent putting in gardens or renovating the center—none of that made up for what I'd done by indulging in the chocolate. "Deon was going to leave me."

She raised her chin is self-righteousness. "You only have yourself to blame."

"I have a chance to make it right. He's taking the girls to the Bar C this weekend. They're leaving today after school. When he comes home, it's all going to be different."

She shook her head. "It's not going to be different unless you change. Stop trying to manufacture excitement in your life and enjoy the thrill of your husband and children."

"You're right." I would find a way to put my law enforcement career behind me. Quit the Rangers.

Ann's voice took on an edge again. "Look at Chris. You ruined his life, too. He never would have finished law school. We both know he's not that smart. Certainly not as smart as Manuel."

Not what Dr. Bartholomew said. "Chris is—"

"When Rodriguez crashed into our car and killed our parents, it poisoned Chris's heart. For twenty years it's eaten him and now look what he's done. The murder of Manuel Ortiz is on your shoulders."

This I could fight back about. "Chris didn't kill Ortiz. I know that."

"Why?" Her eyes flashed with fury. "Because you know him so well? You should. After he dropped out of school and became your guardian, it was the two of you against the world."

"The three of us. The Ta-mutals."

She sneered. "Well, thank you for including me, but we all know you both wanted nothing to do with me. That was your joke with Chris. You wished I'd died along with Mom and Dad."

A sharp and stinging slap. "No. Never."

"You don't have to lie anymore. I saw it from the first. You and Chris sharing books and jokes and taking care of each other. He gave you away at your wedding, but he wasn't there at mine."

"You and Fritz got married at the courthouse and didn't tell us."

She swallowed as if holding back her own tears. "Because I couldn't walk down the aisle. I couldn't afford a wedding dress, and no one wanted to see Frtiz throw away his life by marrying a cripple." She gasped as if struck. "He's not a Deon, handsome and accomplished. But he's mine. Maybe more than I deserve."

My tears flowed freely. "How could you doubt we wanted to be at your wedding?"

Ann swiped at her eyes. "Don't lie to me." She inhaled. "This situation might be a surprise to you and Chris, but I knew something like this would happen. I thought when it finally came out, Chris would see you for who you are, and you would understand how damaged he is."

"Stop it. We are the Ta-mutals. Like always. You, me, and Chris. Family."

She slapped the table. "But that's not the way it is. Look at Chris. He wants to see *you*. You betrayed his trust, told Manuel Ortiz about Andy Bentley, and ended up giving Manuel fuel to bait Chris. And Chris killed him. Oh sure, Chris was mad at you for a minute. But now, all he wants is to see you and grant you absolution."

"I didn't tell ... Wait, did you talk to Chris?"

"Fritz went to see him earlier today and that was his message: send Michaela."

I jumped up, but Ann grabbed my wrist. "I'm not done talking to you."

"I've got to see Chris."

"Of course you do."

I sighed. "I'll come back. I promise. Then you can tell me every terrible thing you want. Even come up with more while I'm gone."

She dropped her hand and twisted away from me. "Just go."

Fighting with Ann wasn't new. But this time, it felt far worse. I glanced out the sliding door and my eyes focused on the pool. I started to ease around her chair to go outside. "I thought you were going to move that ladder when you aren't using the pool?"

She held her hand up. "Stop. I'm going to swim later."

I glared at her. "You weren't even over here when I drove up. The gate wasn't locked. Anyone could have climbed in. What if Tomás wanted to swim?"

"I know where the residents are all the time."

"Why haven't you drained any of the water? It's too deep for you to stand up in."

She sneered. "Are you worried about me?"

Efrain slipped into the yard from Mi Casa, like a shadow. He watched us through the glass as he approached. Not waiting for us to open the door for him, he slid it and addressed Ann. "Is everyone okay?"

Why would he need to check up? Had he heard us arguing, even through the closed door? His vigilance bothered me.

Ann tipped her chin at him. "Fine. Thanks for checking." She flashed me a self-righteous smirk, as if confirming the pool was well guarded. To Efrain she said, "I'm going to have some lunch and go for a swim before I come back to my office. Everything should be fine for a couple of hours."

Efrain's worried eyes searched her, then turned to me. He gave it a moment before nodding and retreating, closing the gate behind him.

"I'm going to talk to Chris." I hated to say it because it made it real, but I should tell Ann. "The ballistics test confirmed Chris's gun killed Ortiz. I need to find out how that happened."

Ann dropped her forehead to her hand. "For god's sake, Mike. Isn't it obvious?"

I gritted my teeth. "He didn't do it."

"What more proof do you need? Stop trying to create a new reality."

"Our brother isn't a murderer."

25

I stood in a chilled room with ten other people, most of them women. The cinderblock walls painted a cigarette-smoke yellow looked perfectly suited to the industrial tile worn to a dirt-beige by all the people waiting to see prisoners on the other side of the door. We'd been instructed to stand here until the door opened and we were let inside.

None of us wanted to be here. Perhaps one or two of the people waiting with me felt comfortable with the arrangement, their significant other locked away with his anger and violence. But some had to be like me, anxious to be with their loved one. Brothers, sons, fathers, lovers were being herded to tables on the other side of the door and every one of us had a story. None of them happy.

The door buzzed and a loud *clack* signaled a lock being opened. A Latina in a guard uniform swung the door wide and the most anxious of us pushed inside. Amid the eruption of voices, I found Chris sitting at a chipped table by the far wall. I knew better than to touch him when I got close, though I wanted to throw my arms around him.

He was pale after two days of incarceration and seemed to have withered. "Thanks for coming." That vibrant Chris quality was gone from his voice.

The world thought of Chris as a violent man, someone comfortable using force at the border. They might picture him yelling at weathered and desperate people in the darkness of a desert night. Maybe yanking them to load into trucks, being rough with children. I'd seen enough movies and documentaries myself, showing angry men in power. I could imagine how someone might view a Border Patrol agent.

Chris hadn't helped himself by losing his temper in public. Or by being so visible defending someone who had shot a teenager.

Those other people didn't know I'd seen Chris leaving the Koffler building right after Ortiz's murder. The people sipping coffee in front of their TVs on Sunday morning watching Chris and Ortiz spar about immigrants and enforcement had no knowledge that a ballistics test proved Ortiz's murder was committed with Chris's gun. If they did, they'd have no doubt Chris killed Manuel Ortiz.

But this man sitting at the table was no killer. He'd held me when I woke with nightmares. He'd dropped out of school to care for me. He'd worked a part-time job so I had a prom dress and later, so I could buy college textbooks. He'd given up his life to raise me. I couldn't believe he was a murderer.

"Tell me what's going on," I whispered.

"I didn't do it. I didn't kill Manuel."

I believed him. No matter what the evidence said, my gut knew the truth. "I've been doing some digging."

He dropped his hands onto the tabletop. "That's exactly what I didn't want you to do. I didn't care if Manuel knew about Andy. But I wanted to convince you I was mad to give me an excuse to push you away."

"That's stupid. You can't get rid of me." I made my voice firm. "You need me."

He studied me for a moment. "I'm sorry."

I plunged ahead. "I talked to Dr. Bartholomew. He told me you and Ortiz had been friends until the night of the accident. What happened?"

Whatever he'd expected, it wasn't this. His eyes widened and he drew in a breath. "Bartholomew? How the hell did you make that connection?"

"I'm a trained officer of the law. And your freedom is at stake. I found out, okay? So you and Ortiz were friends until that night. Why did you stop being friends?"

He put his elbows on the table and lowered his face to his hands. He massaged his eyes. "It was so long ago. I can't believe it has anything to do with Manuel's murder."

I leaned forward. "It has everything to do with it. That's when the trouble started."

He drew his head back and looked at me. "That was twenty years ago. Manuel has known a lot of people since then, been dabbling in who knows what. It wasn't his family who died that night."

He was going to make this hard. "I know Ortiz and Fritz were with you that night."

"More crack investigating."

I ignored his sarcasm. "Okay, tell me everything you know about Manuel Ortiz."

His eyes wandered over the other tables. I doubt he saw the prisoners or their visitors. He probably didn't hear the murmurs and exclamations, either. He concentrated on his thoughts. "Manuel had this competitive streak. He always wanted to be the most successful. I think it came from his father. Manuel had a ton of money, but it was the typical story of a lonely kid wanting his father's attention."

"Doesn't Ortiz's father own a bunch of restaurants? Seems business or even a big law career would be more impressive. Why did he go into social activism? It's not exactly a path to great fortune."

"If he became the leader in immigration reform, cleaned up the border, was a savior, he would splash onto the national scene. He'd earn the support of a huge block of voters. He wanted to be the first Latino president. I think he might have done it."

"An ambition like that could put him in a few crosshairs."

He shrugged. "The cartels have a vested interest in border chaos, so they probably had their eye on Manuel. Other candidates, maybe. I don't know what Manuel might have been mixed up in."

"The investigators think he was being blackmailed."

Chris let out a long breath. "And my new pickup looks pretty suspicious, huh?"

I nodded.

"Dead people don't pay to keep their secrets quiet. The only way someone would kill him in a blackmail scheme is if he decided not to pay anymore."

"Let's say that is the motive. Why use your gun? Why set you up?"

His face fell. "I'm an easy target. Might take the heat from an investigation if they think the cops have an obvious suspect. Manuel and I were sworn enemies."

Enemies. That's why stacking everything against Chris made sense. I studied Chris as I said, "But you weren't enemies."

He snapped his head to me. He seemed to be deciding whether to argue or come up with some explanation. Finally, his shoulders slumped, and he muttered, "No. We weren't."

He dropped his arms to the table and looked at them. "Manuel wasn't all bad. He had ambition and it rode him harder and faster than I've ever seen it ride anyone. There was no falling out after the accident. We just didn't have anything in common to keep us together. We both loved law school and the competition with each other. When I dropped out, we went different ways. I can't say that I really liked Manuel that much. I always felt that he had an agenda."

I lowered my voice and leaned closer. "I saw you leaving Koffler the day of the festival. What were you talking to Ortiz about?"

He opened his mouth in surprise. Then shut it and looked resigned. "After the shooting at the border, Manuel found out I was still on the Border Patrol. He contacted me. He'd discovered corruption higher up in the Patrol. He wanted me to help him weed it out."

"Are you kidding me? You were spying on other agents? You came to me about the Andy thing, but you are digging deeper. Did you lie to me?"

Chris closed his eyes and opened them again. "I didn't know Andy was in on some of it until recently. And yeah, that is what upset me. I thought we'd uncover the top guys and what happened is that I unmasked someone I cared about. I wanted to wrap up the whole thing, report it, and get out of there."

"But Ortiz was against it?"

He nodded. "I had no proof of anything. We all know guys who were corrupt and those who abused people we find in the desert. But I had no documentation. Besides, stopping the offenders one at a time would take too long. Manuel wanted me to keep my mouth shut until we could build a good case on someone higher up. Once I spoke up, I'd have to quit the agency and we'd lose any chance of getting any more evidence."

"You were willing to add death threats from Border Patrol advocates to those from immigrant rights people. One of them could be successful in killing you. Yesterday's incident proves that."

"That's just it. If I expose the corruption and violence, it would paint everyone on the Border Patrol as bad. And there are good men and women out there doing a damned hard job."

"What did you and Ortiz have planned?"

"I agreed to be a public face. Manuel would engage me in a visible way and we'd try to create drama and conflict enough we'd make good media. We hoped to shine a spotlight on the Border Patrol so others might start to dig into the agency. Maybe find out what was going on. I didn't want to turn anyone in, but we thought if Manuel went after me in public, it would draw attention. Media or other investigators might get in and see what was happening. Or maybe those higher up would get scared of the spotlight and clean things up. In the end, Manuel would take credit for it and spring-board his career."

"You've been so angry lately. Is this why?"

His fists clenched on the table. "I'm not cut out for intrigue. I've never been able to lie. Even as kids, Fritz wouldn't tell me half the stuff he did because he knew I'd never be able to keep it secret. This is killing me."

I hated to hear him use that phrase. "You went to the book festival specifically so Ortiz could draw you into a fight."

"It really pissed me off when he called for violence against agents."

"So you talked to him in Koffler?"

Chris flexed his hand as if his fingers cramped. "I called him and told him I wanted out. Then he texted me. Asked me to meet him there."

"Did you see him?"

"When I got to the room the door was closed, but I heard him shouting at someone. I didn't want to deal with him and whatever he had going on, so I left. He was alive. I swear."

"Whoever he was talking to when you were there killed him. With your gun. You didn't hear the other voice?"

He dropped his head. "I wish to god I'd opened that door. Manuel would be here today."

"Or you'd both be dead." After a pause I said, "Did you know he gave Mi Casa a ton of money?"

He looked shocked. "When?"

"Not sure, but recently."

He found a small smile. "That's how Fritz got that new pickup. Exactly like mine. He said he'd been saving up for it. I knew it had to be something else."

"Ann says it belongs to Mi Casa, from the big donation."

Voices from the others in the room rose and fell, chairs scraped the floor. Drama played out at the tables scattered in the gloomy place. Chris said, "Would the donations to Mi Casa be what the cops think is blackmail?"

"The donation was made with a check, so it's on the up and up."

Chris dropped his head on his hand again. He looked exhausted and defeated. "If the cartels are involved, you need to back off. Stay completely out of it. I'll be better off going to jail and you'll be safe."

I chewed on the little I knew. "Tell me about that night of the accident. Even though you weren't enemies from then on, I feel like something important happened."

Lines around his eyes deepened with sadness. "Maybe not enemies, but we weren't friends after that. Manuel got involved in the case to deport Rodriquez and it pissed me off. I was sure he fought to deport Rodriguez to hide his own involvement in the incident.

"I thought Rodriguez had been punished enough by losing his wife and causing the death of two others. He wasn't a bad guy, just scared. He couldn't speak English, so there's was no way he'd ruin Manuel's bright future. He didn't have to get sent back to Mexico on top of everything else."

"You wanted to help Rodriguez stay in the United States?" I couldn't have been more shocked if he'd donned a gorilla suit and sang "Waltzing Matilda."

Chris's lip lifted at the corner of his mouth. "Yeah. The big, bad Mexican-hating Border Patrol agent wanted to help a poor immigrant find a new life in this country."

"Sorry. It's just that you aren't usually that guy."

His gaze moved to the wall behind me. "You don't know everything you think you do."

First Ann, then Chris. "I'd know if you'd tell me."

"What do you want to know?"

"About you and Manuel."

He seemed irritated by that. "Manuel went after Rodriquez with such fire. I'm not sure he planned it this way, but he impressed the senior prosecutors on the case. From there, he got the prime clerking assignments. He definitely used those contacts to build his career. He sacrificed Rodriguez on the altar of his ambition."

"Did you keep track of Rodriguez after he was deported?"

Chris looked at his hands on the table. "He went back to his village. After I joined the Border Patrol, I used their tools to track him. He either died or was absorbed into rural Mexico. I couldn't find him."

I wanted to ask about the little boy but knew it would be a dead end. "I know Fritz and Manuel were at the accident scene with you. Fritz said they were taking you home because you drank too much, but that didn't seem right. Why were you all there?"

Chris sat still for several beats. "Okay. If you hate me after you hear this, I'll understand."

I put a hand on his arm. "I could never hate you."

He looked doubtful. "That night, Mom and Dad had conferences at the school. They asked Ann to stay with you, but she wanted to go with her friends someplace, so she called me. I could have done it." He stopped and rubbed his eyes again. "You don't know how many times I've wished I had. But we'd had our last final of the semester and Manuel and I planned to blow off a little steam before we started in with the next semester."

He closed his eyes and blinked them open. "We'd had a couple of beers when Fritz called. He was at a party in the desert and he wanted us to come and bring more beer. Manuel and I didn't want to go but Fritz started laying on the guilt about how I never had time for him anymore."

This is a side of Fritz I'd only witnessed in the last couple of days. Until now he'd always been passive, if a little hen-pecked.

"So we picked up a case and headed out to where Fritz told us, a place outside of Marana where we used to party in high school. But when we got there, we discovered it was an immigrant camp. In those days, there weren't many families crossing, mostly single men came over, worked long hours, and lived with other groups of men. They made their money and went back to Mexico. No problem. But this camp had a couple of families."

Chris's eyes lost their focus as memory took over. "Manuel and I were going to drop off the beer and go back to town, but I saw this girl. She was pretty and made it plain she liked me."

He blinked again and said to me, "It was a really bad decision. I hadn't been dating because law school took up all my time. I was so competitive with Manuel and that took focus. For so many stupid reasons, I let that girl take me over a hill and we were there maybe an hour. All of the sudden there was a lot of yelling and a gun shot, maybe two.

"The girl just laughed, said it was how it happened a lot of nights. Too much beer, too many hot heads. They liked to shoot jackrabbits or snakes, or just into the desert."

He rubbed his eyes again. "But Fritz and Manuel started yelling my name. I left the girl and ran over the hill. The whole camp was going wild. People shouting and a woman crying. One dusty old sedan jetted out of the camp, heading toward town. The dirt whirled around in the campfire and I couldn't see anything until Fritz and Manuel pulled up in our car. They slowed enough for me to jump in and took off."

His voice had risen an octave or two and he spoke faster. "I still don't know the details because we never talked about it. Manuel was driving and Fritz sat up front and kept shouting for Manuel to drive faster. I asked what happened and they didn't answer me. Manuel yelled over and over at Fritz, 'Did you see it?' I don't know what happened, but we were chasing that car for some reason. That's all I could figure out."

He swallowed and inhaled deeply. "We came around a bend in the road. You know the one. Right as you get to our driveway."

His voice cracked. "This plays out in my head so often. Mom and Dad's Impala pulling onto the road, making a left-hand turn. The junker that left the camp speeding toward town. The crash. I know I couldn't have heard the metal on metal, the screams, the shrieks. But I do. They fill my head so much, sometimes I think I'm going crazy."

His voice scratched out of his tight throat. "It's my fault. We were chasing a car with Rodriguez and his wife and he killed my family."

I wanted to speak, but it took me several tries. "It's not your fault. If I hadn't eaten the chocolate, we'd never have been on the road in the first place."

This blame Ferris wheel wouldn't get us anywhere. I tried to get my mind back on track. We had to figure out who killed Ortiz and I couldn't see a connection between the accident and the murder. "How could someone get your gun?"

Chris gazed at his hands. "I've been trying to figure it out. I keep that gun with me all the time. I even carry it when I'm not working. The only time I don't have it on my person is when I'm at home. And then it's locked in the gun safe."

"Did you take it off at work and another agent switch them out? There has to be something."

He rubbed his hands down his face again. "It's always on my person when I'm on duty. No one could have stolen it from me. I can't figure it out."

"Ballistics wouldn't match if it wasn't your gun. Think, when do you ever take it off?"

He stared at me with a look of loss.

The fog in my mind parted but I almost wanted to draw it back. There was no way I could think this, let alone say it out loud. Yet, it was the only answer. I sought out Chris's eyes. "Ann."

He stared at me.

"She always makes you take your gun off and put it on the fridge."

He gave me a confused look. "How does that help? It's there while I'm there and then it goes home with me."

"But what if your gun was substituted. They took yours and replaced it with another gun just like it. It's a service weapon so there has to be a ton of them. They used your gun to kill Manuel, and then switched it back."

"This is going nowhere, Mike. Someone would have to know I keep the gun there, which means you, Ann, Fritz, Deon. None of those people had the means or motive."

I couldn't swallow. Couldn't move. After a second I said, "Ann did. She was at Koffler that day."

"That's crazy." He waved me off and leaned back in his chair.

Another piece slid into place. "No. The last incoming call on Ortiz's phone. Jared showed me the number. I didn't put it together at the time, but it's the phone Ann gave to Efrain. She had that phone on the day of the festival. She must have called Ortiz to meet her there."

His face lost whatever color it had left. "This is Ann. Our sister."

I hated to think it, let alone say it. "She's bitter. She thinks you and I cut her out. That we don't love her. She's jealous of our relationship and our lives. It's possible she set you up."

His mouth dropped open. "How can you say that?"

"I don't know." Guilt ate at me, but I continued. "She's always had that unpredictable streak. She can lash out with no warning."

Chris looked at me for a moment. "Like me."

"But you wouldn't kill anyone."

"And you think Ann would?"

God, it felt sticky and hot to let my mind go down this road. "She told me earlier that Manuel's death would be a good thing for immigrants because now they have a martyr."

Disbelief clouded his face. "This can't be."

"I don't know when she could have taken your gun, but she could have put it back on Sunday."

"Stop it," Chris said, raising his voice. "You're wrong."

"You didn't see her face when she was accusing me of ruining her life. She hates me. And probably you, too." I stood up.

"What are you going to do?"

"The only thing I can do."

26

By this time of day, Fritz would probably be at the Hot Spot getting ready to open. I pulled up in Ann's driveway. As expected, the front door was unlocked and I let myself in. Moving quickly and silently to the sliding door, I peered out. The ladder was still in the pool and Ann's head bobbed up and down as she did her exercises. She couldn't tolerate more than a twenty-minute workout and I didn't know how long she'd already been in the water. I didn't have much time.

The most obvious place to start searching was on top of the fridge. Nothing, and I hadn't expected there to be. No gun in the kitchen drawers, the sideboard, or the desk. Nothing but the expected detritus of a home where people had lived for nearly two decades. Papers, pens, pencils, odds and ends. But no gun.

I glanced out the window at Ann's bobbing head. She'd have to be getting out soon.

The run into the bedroom took seconds and I rummaged through their dresser. What kind of person suspected their own sister of murder? But the rage and hatred in her face this morning shocked me. It seemed she might be capable of anything.

The only other suspects were Deon and Fritz. Deon wasn't close enough to the whole situation to risk anything like this. Besides, he was

Deon; he couldn't kill anyone. And Fritz, I'd only glimpsed fire in him a few days ago. Most of the time, he was as passive as a hippie sniffing a sunflower. Ann always complained about his lack of ambition.

But Ann. She had ambition. Fire. Follow-through. She knew how to plan ahead for the long game. And this morning, I'd seen how much resentment and jealousy fueled her. Murder was more extreme than I'd thought possible. But everything pointed toward her.

No gun in the bedside tables. I started for the closet but stopped. Ann should be coming in the house now. No time left.

Maybe I could get Efrain or Sophia to call her to the center and then finish the search. I hurried toward the front door and glanced out the sliding door to check Ann's progress.

The ladder was gone from the side of the pool. Ann's head didn't bob up and down. She must be on her way in. I grabbed the latch on the front door to let myself out when something nagged at the back of my mind.

The ladder. Ann couldn't drag that out. My head whipped back to the pool and I saw a small splash. A hand reached up to the wall of the pool, grabbed the side, and held for a second before slipping off.

Oh my god. She was in the pool! I was out the sliding door and to the poolside without knowing how. With the momentum of my run, I grabbed the wall of the pool and launched myself up, splashing into the water.

Ann struggled meekly. She slipped under, her eyes wide. My feet hit the bottom and I wrapped my arms around her when I pushed up. She clung to me as I grabbed the side of the pool holding around her ribs so her face was above the surface.

She gasped and cried and sputtered and pulled me tighter. "You're here. Mike."

I held her with all my strength, seeing her wide eyes under the water, trying not to think what would have happened if I hadn't been there. "Where's the ladder?"

She closed her arms around my neck. "I don't know. I was doing my exercises and I got tired. The ladder was gone. I couldn't hold on." She broke down and sobbed. "I almost drowned."

"Shhh." I hugged her. She was trembling. "I've got you." I had to figure out how to pull us out of the water.

"Plug your ears." She didn't pay any attention, just held on and kept crying.

I took a deep breath and let out, "Help!" Hoping the always-lurking Efrain would come running. I hollered several more times before the gate to Mi Casa pushed open. Sophia poked her head into the backyard, eyes questioning.

"Oh thank god." I gasped. "The ladder. Bring the ladder." I had to stop and try again, searching for the Spanish word. "*Escalera.*"

Sophia's concerned eyes grazed the backyard until she spotted the ladder halfway between the house and the pool as if someone had flung it aside and dashed off. She ran to it and shoved it toward the pool. With one arm strapped across Ann's back and holding her to me, I tried to get the ladder positioned without going under.

Sophia climbed her side and helped me anchor the legs on the interior so we could help Ann.

Ann shivered with shock and exhaustion. Her legs were too weak to hold her weight as she climbed, so Sophia stood at the ladder's platform and bent over to brace her arms in Ann's armpits. I straddled her and hugged her tight around her hips and together we managed to drag her out of the water and over the ladder to the grass.

Sophia held her up while I ran for a lawn chair. Sophia settled Ann and I dashed inside for a blanket. We swaddled Ann and kept her in the sun. She shivered and closed her eyes. I sat next to her and held her hand, repeating, "It's okay."

Sophia glanced behind her at the open gate. "I don't want to leave, but Tomás is in the playroom with Donita."

I waved her off. "Go, go. Thank you."

She said, "I will be back."

When she left, I hugged Ann again and she let her head rest on my shoulder. "I'm sorry," Ann said. "For what I said to you this morning."

"It's okay." Whatever I thought about Ann, I didn't want to lose her. I loved her. Every bit as much as I loved Chris.

"No," she said. "It's not okay. And it's not true. None of it."

I rocked her. "Don't. It's time I heard all of that."

She sniffed and pulled back from my embrace but grabbed my hand

and tucked it into her lap. "You aren't the first woman to think about having an affair. I knew you didn't sleep with Jared. But I wanted to hurt you. I wanted you to know what it was like to lose."

I shook my head. "You don't have to do this."

She swallowed. "Yes. I do. You always thought the accident was your fault. I let you take the blame. But it wasn't your fault. It was mine."

My face must have shown my confusion.

"That night I was so mad. I had a date to the movies with this guy I had a huge crush on. I told Mom and Dad I was going out with friends because he was Mexican and they'd have hated that. This was going to be our first time together alone. And then they made me stay home with you. I blamed you. So that's why I gave you that chocolate."

"You only gave me a little. I ate the rest of it."

Tears formed in her eyes again. "If you'd have eaten the rest of the sugar-free chocolate Mom bought for you, it wouldn't have hurt you a bit. But I gave you real chocolate. I thought it would make you feel sick. I was going to keep my eye on you. But then that guy called and I forgot about you."

It took me a few seconds to process this. "You tried to get me sick?"

She sniffed back tears. "I'm sorry. I was seventeen. I know it's not right, but that's the way teenagers are."

I had two kids. I'd been a kid. I understood that. But she'd let me carry the guilt of our parents' deaths for so long. I didn't know what to do with her confession.

"I know not telling you the truth was selfish of me."

"Eating the last piece of cake is selfish. Using the family's last dollar on a treat for yourself is selfish. I don't know what this is."

"I couldn't face what I'd done so I tried to forget it, go along with it being your fault. And then, when I unloaded on you this morning, when I'd crossed the line by trying to destroy your marriage, I knew I had to make it right." She let out a sob and wiped the tears falling down her face. "I nearly didn't get the chance."

Now was not the time for this. "Someone tried to kill you," I said quietly. "The same person who killed Manuel and is setting up Chris."

Ann stopped crying and stared at me. "What are you talking about?"

"Someone took the ladder out of the pool. On purpose."

She shook her head. "No. That can't be."

I wanted to slap sense into her. "Someone used Chris's gun to kill Manuel. The only time Chris didn't have it was when he put it on your fridge. I thought maybe you had done it."

"What?" She drew back from me. "You thought I could kill someone and pin it on my brother?"

I allowed a small smile. "Well, you told me how much you hated me this morning. Just now you admitted to letting me take the whole blame from Mom and Dad's death. I'd say you might be able to pull a trigger if you thought it necessary."

She frowned at me and her eyes showed a carousel of emotions. Perhaps, like me, she decided now wasn't the time for confrontation. "If someone took Chris's gun, he'd have known it."

"Not if they substituted it temporarily for one that was just like it."

"But a gun is like a baby, isn't it? You'd know if someone switched them out."

"Not necessarily. If Chris hadn't cleaned it or shot it before it was switched back, he'd never know."

Ann thought a moment. "Oh my god." She pushed herself to her feet. She grabbed my arm. "Help me." She leaned on me and directed me through the kitchen to her bedroom closet where she let go of me and tried to reach to a high shelf. She wobbled and grabbed me.

"There." She pointed. "See that blue shoe box? In there."

I lowered her to sit on the bed and rushed back to the closet. My fingers closed on the box and I expected the heft of a pistol, but it came down too easily. I flipped the lid off and it landed on the closet floor. "Empty."

Ann's face lost what color it had gained on the trip from the backyard. "No." She sat on the bed looking at the empty box. "I don't know where it could have gone."

"Is it the same kind of gun as Chris had?"

"Exactly the same." She got that judgmental look on her face. "Fritz has had it for years. Not long after we were married, when we had even less than we do now, certainly not enough money to waste, Fritz made Chris go gun shopping with him. He wanted the same model of gun Chris had for patrol. He's always trying to keep up with Chris. Like that stupid pickup. I had a used one all picked out and he went and bought this without even talking to me about it." She stared at the floor.

I had no time for her whining. "What about someone from Mi Casa? You don't keep your doors locked." If I'd known they had a gun stashed in their house, I would have been more forceful about the locks.

She scowled at me. "You are so ready to assign nefarious intentions to those poor people. They've been through so much. They aren't looking for more trouble."

"Not everyone who comes to this country is innocent." I avoided giving her the short list of people who had stolen from Mi Casa or the very few who had been violent. Most of her clients were grateful for her help, but it only takes one bad person.

"No one from the center took Fritz's gun." She left no room for argument.

"*Hola*?" Sophia's tentative voice came from the back door.

"In here," I shouted.

A thumping like stampeding elephants sounded down the hall and Tomás jumped into the room, holding out his hand with Batman clutched in pudgy fingers. He wore a towel tied around his neck for a cape. "Freeze!" he yelled in Spanish.

Even with the tension thick, I couldn't stop my laughter. "You scared me."

"I do not mean to scare you. I am here to save you." With that, he launched himself into Ann's lap, throwing them both back on the bed.

Sophia rounded the corner and gasped. "Tomás!" Her string of Spanish went by me so quickly I only caught *Señora Ann* and *naughty boy*.

He scrambled off the bed, a horrified look on his face. "*Pardone*. Did I hurt you?"

Ann pushed herself up but Tomás's escapade had brought a smile to her lips, as well. She finger combed his fine hair. "I'm fine. You didn't do any damage."

Tomás turned his attention to me. "I am going on a trip."

"Is that right?"

Sophia shook her head when I glanced at her. She slowed her Spanish, probably so I could understand. "Efrain. He says he's taking me and Tomás away. He wants to go to Mexico. Oaxaca."

I stared at the empty box sitting next to Ann, trying to figure out who could have taken the gun.

Ann cocked her head. "Oaxaca? When did he say you were going?"

"Today or maybe tomorrow," Tomás said. He bounced in front of me. "It's a place in the mountains with lots of trees and Efrain has a big family there. He will teach me how to fish in the lake and to make tamales."

Ann questioned Sophia with her eyes. "He can't cross the border. He has no passport or visa. They won't let him back in."

Sophia shook her head. "I cannot tell you if Efrain is serious about going to Oaxaca. He says he is not happy here. Even though he was a little boy when he left Mexico, he tells me he misses the mountains and his village. He says it has not been good for him here. But I am not going back to Mexico if I can help it. And Tomás is not going."

Tomás let out a whopping, "Aw," as if he'd been denied a second helping of cake. But he didn't argue, probably hearing the finality in Sophia's voice. Coming to the United States was still a big adventure for him; he may not be too excited to travel again.

Ann looked worried. "He didn't say anything to me about not being happy here. Is it the money? Fritz and I will help him if that's what he wants."

Sophia offered a strained smile. "I do not know him well. He has been very nice to me, and especially to Tomás. But Efrain, he is maybe moving too fast for me. It is all so new here."

Ann looked serious. "What do you mean?"

Sophia answered quickly and I concentrated to translate it all. "Efrain is helpful and generous. He will do anything for us. I believe that. But it has only been a few days of knowing him. Too soon to think about going away with him."

"But you do like him," Ann said.

Sophia looked at her feet and answered in a quiet voice. "Yes. But I need to know him better. His moods ..." She trailed off and glanced up at me.

"What moods?" Ann demanded. "What are you talking about?"

Sophia took a step back. "I should not have said anything. I do not know him well, that is all. You have known him a long time."

"I know he cares about you," Ann said.

Sophia's face colored. "Thank you. I would like to take some time to learn more about Efrain." Her statement sounded like a confirmed vegetarian telling a rancher she'd like to learn to eat steak.

Ann's mouth flattened. "Are you stringing him along? Using him to support you and Tomás until something better comes along?"

"Ann," I warned. "Back off."

Sophia's polite smile wavered and she held out her hand to Tomás. "Come, *mijo*. We need to go home." She started to walk out. "I am glad to see you are not hurt."

Ann sat up straighter. "Sophia, will you send Efrain over? I want him to take the ladder out of the pool."

Sophia turned around. She looked first to me, then to Ann. "Efrain is not at Mi Casa."

"Where did he go?" Ann's manner had grown militant and gruff.

Again, Sophia looked to me, as if unsure how to answer. "He did not say. Tomás and I were waiting in the courtyard because he had promised Tomás he would play catch with him. But when Tomás greeted him, Efrain hurried by and ignored him. He looked upset and left out the front door." Her forehead wrinkled in worry. "He took my car."

Ann glared at Sophia. "You let him drive? He's not legal."

I guess she ignored how many times Fritz had Efrain run errands or take Ann to an appointment.

"I did not know what to do. I have seen Efrain angry before. But never like this. I was afraid."

Ann huffed. "I can't imagine anyone being afraid of Efrain."

Sophia focused on me. "He said 'There will be more deaths.'"

The air rippled with those words. People don't spout things like that casually.

Ann's lips pursed again, showing she clearly doubted Sophia. "I've never seen Efrain angry. I'm sure you misunderstood him."

Sophia's quick glance at me showed her uncertainty. "Yes. As I said, I do not know Efrain well."

She reached down for Tomás's hand. "I hope you feel better." She hurried out, and seconds later the back door slid open and closed.

Ann's reaction to Sophia speaking about Efrain seemed way too defensive. "Where do you suppose Efrain was going?"

"How should I know?" She stared down the hallway. "Sophia is a troublemaker. One of those pretty women who get men to take care of them. I wonder if maybe she did cause problems at the hotel."

Sophia's comments about Efrain set something off in Ann, like a mother bear protecting her cub. I poked at her. "Efrain had access to your house. He's been here many times when you've harped at me and Chris to put our guns on the fridge."

"I do not harp."

Oh honey, Harp is your middle name. "You never lock the gate or your back door. He could have slipped in and made the gun switch a million times."

"It's not Efrain."

"Sophia hinted that he's been moody."

"It's not Efrain."

"The only problem I have is why Efrain would want to set up Chris. He's been a friend. And even if he only set up Chris to get suspicion away from himself, what possible motive would he have for killing Manuel?"

Ann slapped the bed. "It's not Efrain. Are you listening to me?"

I narrowed in on her. "What makes you so sure?"

She looked away from me. "I just know."

I grabbed her chin and made her look at me. "Why?"

She gave me that old lady stiff mouth. "Because I've known him since he was five years old. He loves me and Fritz. He's like our son."

"Five? I don't remember him from that long ago. He came to work here about ten years ago, didn't he?"

"He's always been a sweet boy. And grateful."

I watched her, urging her to continue. "Your son. Is there more about Efrain you haven't told me?"

"It wasn't him. It couldn't be. We brought him up with love and compassion."

"You brought him up?"

Her eyes traveled the room like she searched for a ticking bomb. I grabbed her arm and held onto her hand. "Ann. Take a breath. Then tell me."

She did, keeping a connection with our eyes. "You've always talked about a little boy."

I nodded, my mind galloping ahead.

Her head gave an almost imperceptible nod when she saw what I'd guessed. She said, "Efrain. He's the little boy."

Click. The boy clutching something to his chest. A sock monkey. No wonder they always gave me the creeps. I associated it with that awful night. Efrain was that boy. The one watching the ambulance load his mother. The one who vanished into the night. I tried to picture the little boy's face on Efrain. It could be.

I heard the blame in my voice. "You always knew there was a boy? You tried to tell me I'd made it up."

Her face looked ready to crumble. "You couldn't find out. If you told anyone, he could get deported."

"They don't deport children."

Her eyes snapped to mine. "No. But they put them into the system. Fritz and I are better than any foster home."

"What about his aunt?"

Ann waved her hand. "She didn't love him like we did. She was happy to take the money we gave for him. But when he turned fifteen, she kicked him out."

His aunt seemed truly happy to see him the other day. I didn't imagine that look of adoration on her face.

"How is it he's here? I don't understand."

She squeezed my hand. "You already know Fritz was there that night. He'd made friends with the people in the camp weeks before. He'd been helping them get jobs with the farmers around Marana. So he knew Efrain and his parents before the accident. For years he gave Efrain's aunt money and he took Efrain to movies and sports games and things."

"When did you know he was the boy from the accident?"

Her eyes glistened. "He was sad at first. Those bottomless brown eyes scared and lost. But he was sweet, even then, so helpful."

"If his aunt didn't want him, why didn't you and Fritz adopt him?"

Her eyes flashed at me and she indicated her legs. "I'm a cripple, remember? No court was going to give us a child. But we cared for him, taught him right from wrong. He was always part of our family."

"Fritz was okay with that?"

"He felt guilty. Responsible for Efrain losing his father and mother. He thought the accident was their fault for chasing the car." So she knew about everything.

"Did Efrain know they were at the accident?"

Ann seemed sure. "No. Fritz wouldn't tell him and no one else knows who Efrain really is."

"Ann, listen. Killing Ortiz and framing Chris would make sense if Efrain knew who was in the car that night."

"You can think what you want, but Efrain would never kill anyone. He wouldn't do this. He wouldn't." She started to sob.

I paced the room. "But if he was out for revenge, he's taken care of Ortiz and Chris. He could be after Fritz."

She shook her head. "No. He wouldn't. He loves Fritz."

I couldn't work it out. "The blackmail."

Her eyes flew to my face. "What blackmail?"

"The investigators think Ortiz was being blackmailed. Would Efrain be blackmailing Ortiz? With his eyes on a political career, Ortiz might pay a lot to keep anyone from finding out he chased the car on the desert and caused the deaths of three people."

Ann wiped her cheeks and thought about it. "No. If Manuel knew who Efrain was, he'd have used it somehow. Chris and Manuel never knew there was a child. Fritz was the only one."

I reached for my pocket and my phone. The pool had done what pools do to phones. I hadn't realized I'd been dripping all over Ann's bedroom carpet. "Where's your phone?"

"What? Why?"

I scrambled for the kitchen table where she kept her phone. "We have to call Fritz. Warn him."

"Warn him about what?" Her voice followed me down the hall.

"That Efrain is coming for him."

"He's not. He loves Fritz. We're family," she repeated, as if that said it all.

I grabbed her phone and raced back to the bedroom to toss it to her. "Call him."

"No. If you're right and it is Efrain who did this, he had plenty of opportunities to hurt Fritz and he didn't. I swear to you, Fritz is not in any danger."

"Efrain pulled the ladder away from the pool. He meant to kill you."

Wild eyes met mine. "No. He wouldn't."

"Who else? It has to be Efrain."

Her fingers trembled over the phone. "Fritz," she whispered. "'There will be more deaths.'" She sat on the bed and stared at the phone.

I kept talking to her, but convincing Ann of Efrain's guilt proved impossible, even with all the evidence pointing directly at him. She wavered a moment, then declared his innocence. I couldn't drill through her stubborn resistance with any information about how childhood trauma can carry into adulthood and result in violence.

In the end, she refused to call Fritz. I took her phone and dialed myself. He answered on the third ring, puffing as if he'd run to pick up.

"Where are you?" I blurted.

"Michaela? Is it Ann? Is she okay? What's happened?"

Hearing my voice on Ann's phone must have frightened him. "Ann's fine. She's sitting right here. I'm concerned about you. Are you okay? Are you at the Hot Spot?"

He drew a relieved breath. "Good. Yeah. I'm at work. I needed to make a booze order."

"Have you seen Efrain?"

Now he sounded curious. "No. Why?"

I paced down the hall to look out the back door. "I think he's the one who killed Ortiz and set Chris up. And I think he just tried to kill Ann."

Propping herself on the wall and furniture, Ann finally made it to the kitchen and plopped into a chair.

"What?" He let out a laugh. "That's a stretch." Maybe he just realized what I'd said. "Wait. Kill Ann? How? What? You said she's okay."

"She is. She's fine. A little rattled, but okay." I filled a glass with water and set it in front of her.

"What happened?"

I explained about the ladder and everything Sophia said. "I'm afraid he's coming for you. Lock the door. I'm on my way."

"No. Stay with Ann. I don't want her to be alone. I'll lock up here and head home. We can figure out what to do from there."

I hung up and tromped outside to retrieve Ann's crutches from the patio. Standing at the kitchen counter I spoke out loud. "Efrain had plenty of time to get to the Hot Spot. But he wasn't there. Where would he go?"

Ann sat at the table with an untouched glass of water in front of her. "Give me my phone."

I handed it to her and she punched a saved number and put it on speaker. It rang several times, the tinny noise loud in the quiet kitchen.

Efrain answered. "Ann?"

She let out a sigh. "Efrain. Where are you?"

He didn't answer.

"Listen to me. Come home. Whatever is bothering you we can talk about it."

I lowered myself into a chair quietly.

He sounded like he spoke from a moving car. "I am not coming back to Mi Casa. There is something I must do."

"It can wait. I promise. I need you here. Please come home."

"You have been very good to me. Always helping and giving to me. I'm sorry I did not say goodbye to you. But there is one thing more I must do and then you will not hear from me again."

"Wait, Efrain. I—" Three beeps signaled the end of the call. Ann punched the number again, but he didn't pick up.

I sat watching her, trying to think. When I caught sight of the number she dialed, I lost my breath. I grabbed her phone. "Is this Efrain's number?"

I must have alarmed her because she grabbed the phone back, eyes wide. "Yes. Why?"

I pointed. "That's the number Jared showed me. The last one on Ortiz's phone. You got Efrain a burner phone, didn't you? No contract?"

She stared at her phone. "Yes. But why would Efrain call Manuel?"

I didn't bother starting back in about Efrain's guilt. We needed to figure out where he was. "'One thing I must do'," I said. "Kill Fritz."

Ann glared at me. "No. He's going to Mexico and he's saying goodbyes. He has one more to do."

I got it. "Tia Alma."

"She's all he has here," Ann said. "Go there. Stop him."

"Do you know where? The address?"

She pounded a fist on the table in frustration. "Somewhere south of Marana. I was only there once a long time ago. I don't know."

I thought back to the day I saw her with Efrain in the parking lot. He'd said she loved the metal sculptures and had them in her front yard. She lived down what road? What had he said? It came to me. "I know the road," I said. "I'll leave as soon as Fritz gets here."

"Go now. I'll be fine. You need to stop Efrain before he goes for the border."

27

The traffic lessened the farther west I drove, so I sped up. Annoyed with the condition that required almost constant monitoring, I checked my blood sugar and grabbed a protein bar. Driving and snarfing and worrying. The road wound out of the city, twisting between mountains down a narrow two-lane blacktop. When I was a kid, we lived down a dirt track, hidden from the paved county road by Palo Verde, mesquite, and saguaro cactus. Summer rains brought the biting smells of creosote and damp sand floating through our windows. That area was now covered in cookie-cutter neighborhoods feeding Tucson's growth. South along Sandario Road, acreages still cluttered the desert, in many cases hidden from their neighbors by the desert scrub. A wide variety of places pocked the area, from crumbling trailers and slump block mid-century ranch models to spacious pueblo-style new builds.

Efrain said his aunt had lived out here for twenty years. I hadn't thought much about the timing when he'd said it. Now I knew she'd been at the camp that night. She'd seen what happened.

I turned on Molino Road and forced myself to slow down to look for metal sculptures, specifically a blue javalina. In most cases an acre or two separated the houses with swathes of desert between them. One yard was filled with the skeletons of old cars decaying slowly in the dry desert sun.

Another yard contained nothing but tall, brown weeds and a broken pane in the home's front window. It looked abandoned. The cinderblock fence of another was painted a pale apricot. How far down the road would his aunt be?

Past several houses with bright paint, one with plastic flowers stuck into dirt beds, one with a plaster Virgin Mary shrine. I hit the brakes. There it was. A doublewide trailer with a narrow driveway and carport, and a yard full of metal animal sculptures. The javalina guarded the driveway close to the dirt road.

I pulled in and climbed out of the car. Leaping up the steps of the faded redwood deck, I banged on the door. "Hello. Alma."

A scuffling at the side of the trailer made me turn.

Efrain's aunt walked around the corner of the yard, gardening gloves on her hands, a wide straw hat shading her head. "Hello?" She stared at me a moment, her mind working. "Oh. From Efrian's work, sí?"

"Yes. I'm Michaela Sanchez." I descended the steps and hurried over.

Her face went from curious to alarmed in a flash. "Is he okay? What's wrong?"

I must have looked as frantic as I felt. I tried to dial it back. "I just need to see him. Is he here?" Of course he wasn't, if she'd reacted that way. "Do you know where he is?"

I hadn't done a good job seeming calm. Alma focused on me. "No. I have not seen him since I was at Mi Casa the day I saw you."

"And you haven't talked to him since then?"

She nodded vigorously, obviously worried. "Oh yes. He calls me most days. But he didn't call me yesterday."

"Is that unusual?"

She pulled off her gloves and stepped closer. "Yes. I'm the only family Efrain has here. We are very close." She shifted from foot to foot. "If you're here, there must be a problem. Please what's wrong with Efrain?"

"I don't know. Probably nothing. It would be good to know where he is, though."

That didn't seem to mollify her. "He hasn't been himself lately. I am worried about him. Why are you looking for him?"

I couldn't tell her he'd murdered Manuel Ortiz and I was afraid he might kill Fritz. "He left Mi Casa a couple of hours ago and Ann has something she'd like him to do."

Alma's face closed down. "Of course."

"You don't seem happy about that."

She waved a hand. "No. It is good. Efrain is lucky to have people who care so much for him."

"Efrain said they paid for Catholic school."

Alma's smile seemed a little less than grateful. "It is so kind. Efrain is doing well."

"But there's a problem."

She sighed. "Yes. At first, I was grateful for them taking Efrain to live with them when he was a teenager. He wanted to go to the school in Tucson, instead of having to ride the bus to the big one out here. He liked working at Mi Casa, helping all the people. He especially liked helping the little ones."

Tomás. Efrain wanted to take him back to Mexico. I nearly threw up thinking of all the times Efrain had been around my girls. Two days ago he'd been alone with them all day.

"There's something you don't like about this?" I pressed her.

She looked down before making eye contact and forcing a smile. "It's okay, really. I just worry they work Efrain too hard. He is always doing something for them. All night he takes care of Mi Casa, helping the residents with every little thing. Efrain works all the time. I feel like they maybe are trying to keep him from coming home to see me."

"He's at the center whenever I'm there. Maybe he ought to ask for time off."

"Oh, Efrain would never do that." She paused. "I'm being ungrateful. I can't work as much as I used to. They pay Efrain enough at Mi Casa so that he can help me out. I know that's one reason he works so much. I tell him I'd rather he work less and spend time with me, but he wants to pay me back."

The thing is, Efrain *wasn't* making good money at Mi Casa. Blackmail could supply a chunk of change, though. "Oh? I thought he mostly got room and board."

She acknowledged that. "That is why he was able to save up so much.

And this is proof of what a kind and generous boy he is. He is using all of his savings to buy me a new house. It will be delivered in three weeks. Can you believe it?"

No. I couldn't believe it. "He saved up enough for a down payment on a new house?"

Her eyes sparkled. "Not a down payment. The whole thing. A manufactured home. Twice as big as this. I even got to pick out the colors for the kitchen and carpet."

If Efrain saved every penny he earned at Mi Casa and robbed a convenience store once a week, he'd never be able to save up that much.

She retreated to her house and plopped down on the steps to the deck. "It's the heat," she said. "I can't stand it like I used to."

The clock ticked. If Efrain didn't go for Fritz and he wasn't here, where was he? "I think Efrain might be in some trouble," I finally said.

Her hat shielded her eyes when she looked up at me. "What kind of trouble?"

I couldn't say what I thought. She'd never believe me. "I think he's upset with Fritz and might want to hurt him."

Alma sat back and blinked unbelieving eyes. "Oh no. Efrain would not hurt anyone. He is a sweet boy. Always has been."

"You said he's been upset lately."

She smiled at me. "He gets upset when he sees people doing wrong. That boy has always had a sense of justice. Ever since his parents were taken from him. Other boys might grow up with revenge in their hearts, but not my Efrain. He forgives. More than I'm able."

"What is it Efrain had to forgive?"

Alma dropped her head and stared at her hands. "Efrain lost his mother and father in a terrible way. He carries that pain with him always."

As gently as I could, I said, "I know about the car accident and that Chris Wright, Manuel Ortiz, and Fritz were on the scene that night."

Alma's eyes carried sorrow. "Efrain's mother was my sister."

"Can you tell me about that night?" I stepped closer, unable to quell my impatience and sit, but needing to hear what she said.

She lowered her head, her face blocked by the wide brim of her hat. "Fritz came to the camp, like he did many times. But he brought two men with him. My cousin, she liked the men, but not me. While my sister and her husband wanted to stay up and drink, I only wanted the people to leave and for everyone to go to bed. I took little Efrain to a quiet spot and we settled down to sleep."

This would be when Chris had climbed over the hill with the girl, who was probably the cousin Alma mentioned.

"I was nearly asleep when the idiots shot the gun. Efrain woke up afraid and I held him. The gun went off again and I heard my sister scream."

As her words spilled faster, my heart rate climbed.

"I jumped up to see and ran to the campfire. And—" She let out a sudden sob, as if it caught her off-guard. "There was my beautiful Elena bleeding in Carlos's arms. He was running for the car. I picked up Efrain and followed Carlos. He laid my sister in the front and all I could do was watch."

Shot. Rodriguez was taking his wife to the hospital.

"The men were yelling and trying to get Carlos to stay. It was all so confusing. I remember setting Efrain down behind me so he wouldn't see his mother hurt. I leaned in to tell Elena I'd take care of Efrain, and when I stood up, I couldn't find him."

Her panic from that night twenty-five years ago seemed alive now.

"I don't know how he got into the car without me seeing. But when Carlos tore away from camp, I saw Efrain's head in the backseat."

"And he saw his mother die in the car crash."

Fat tears coursed down her cheeks and she sniffed. "No. His mama was dead before she left the camp."

Efrain's mother had been shot and killed before the car accident. I wondered if sweet gentle Efrain knew that, or if he still blamed Ortiz and had decided to blackmail him. When that didn't work, he'd used Chris's gun to finish him.

I didn't want to tip my hand to Alma. "Maybe Ortiz's death upset Efrain. He might want to forget that night. Maybe he wants to get away from Fritz and Ann but doesn't know how to tell them."

She gratefully accepted that. "He is so kind. Confrontation is hard for him. We've been talking about him creating some distance between them and him. But he doesn't want to hurt them. He is afraid for Ann. Thinking maybe Fritz would hurt her."

The one doing the hurting was Efrain. "Do you know where Efrain would go if he was upset?"

She shook her head. "He would come home. He likes his cat." She looked up at me. "He has no animals at Mi Casa. He has always loved animals."

"Anywhere else?"

She thought a moment. "When Efrain was twelve, his dog died. He didn't come home that night and I went to find him. He was at the old camp."

"It's still there? Not paved over in a neighborhood?"

A small smile played on her lips. "No. Because of the petroglyphs."

I thought I knew where she meant. Not far from our old house. A new subdivision crowded at the base of a mountain but couldn't climb any higher because of the protection of antiquities. As a kid, we'd played around the area, riding bikes and hiking, creating all kinds of adventures. I'd taken Josie and Sami out there to see the indentation in the stone where countless generations had ground corn.

After trying to reassure Alma that all was well, I thanked her and took off. It was a short drive and I knew I'd hit the right place when I spotted Sophia's rusty blue Cavalier at the parking area. My flip-flops weren't ideal for hiking, but the trail wasn't a long one. This parking area, just a half mile from the paved road, might have been the exact spot of the camp. Hills to the right would have hidden Chris and his girl. The dirt lot was flat with brush and desert trees outlining it to provide some shade.

I hurried along the narrow trail toward the petroglyphs. The sun beat down and on the trail between the hills, the heat radiated, no breeze to dispel it. Elephant ear cactus threatened on either side of the trail while the sunny yellow and brilliant pink prickly pear blooms burst against the colorless desert floor. Fresh pods on the chollo cactus dared anyone to get close. There's a reason they call them jumping cactus. Long practice of living near the desert taught me to keep bare toes and legs safe from the hostile landscape.

I made it to the clearing in front of the stone wall with the petroglyph panels. The powdery dirt of the space billowed around my ankles. The clearing opened up in a circle the size of Ann's pool, with brush around the edges. A few boulders scattered about and hikers often perched on them to contemplate the drawings of the ancient desert dwellers.

I cast about, looking for any sign of Efrain. Behind the brush, a spot of dark blue, maybe a T-shirt, showed between the dense yellow curtain of a blooming Palo Verde tree.

"Efrain." I tensed, anticipating his attack.

He turned, Fritz's gun clutched in his hand. "Don't."

"Put the gun down. Hands up."

Tears had traced tracks down his dusty face. "Leave me alone. Please."

I didn't see Fritz, but he must be on the ground in front of Efrain. What words could I offer to keep Efrain from shooting him? "You don't need to do this."

Efrain closed his eyes. "It's too late. I am sorry people have died. I never wanted it."

I tried for calm and reasonable. "I know you didn't mean to kill Manuel. But don't make it worse."

"It's my fault," he said. "I only wanted to help Tia Alma."

"No more killing. Please."

He turned around to face me. "I can't live with this. I should never have agreed to help him. But Tia Alma. She worked so hard all her life and now she is tired. I wanted to give her the house. So I said yes. I would help."

This wasn't going the way I expected. "Help who with what?"

"Getting the money from Manuel Ortiz. When Fritz told me Manuel was the one who shot my mother, I wanted to forgive him. But it isn't fair a man like that should have so much. It didn't seem like such a bad thing for him to pay for Tia Alma's home. He took so much from us. So I said yes."

"You blackmailed Manuel Ortiz for the shooting. And when he stopped paying, you killed him."

Efrain's eyes sought mine. "No. I mean, yes. I took money from him. I did not kill him, but I didn't stop it. I was afraid." His hand shook as he raised the gun.

I needed to keep him talking, both to stop him from shooting himself and to find out what happened. "Why didn't you tell anyone?"

His face filled with regret and despair. "Ann needs so much and has so little. She gives away what she has. She is in pain. And the doctors say her lungs are going bad. I could not stop her from getting what she deserves."

"So you thought it would be better to end it for her quickly. Is that why you tried to kill her?"

His mouth dropped open. "Kill her?"

"By pulling the ladder from the pool."

"No. Oh, no." His shock was genuine.

"You didn't kill Ortiz?"

He shook his head. "No."

"Who then?" It was coming to me. With an escalating dread, I nearly shouted, "Who killed Manuel Ortiz?"

Efrain's face crumbled. "Fritz."

28

"Give me your phone!" I shouted at Efrain.

Shocked, he reached in his pocket and handed it to me.

I called Ann and she answered immediately. "Is Fritz there?" I nearly shouted.

"No." She swallowed. "Is he okay? Is Efrain okay? What's going on?"

Efrain followed me as I ran back to the car, filling Ann in between panting. "Lock your damned door. Use the chain and don't let Fritz in."

I took Efrain back to Ann's. For once, Ann's front door was locked and we waited, hearing her slow progress on her crutches and her struggle with the chain and door lock. When she saw Efrain, she threw her arms around his neck. Her crutches clanked to the tile floor and Efrain's arms circled her waist, holding her up.

He helped her to the kitchen and eased her into a chair. Then he dropped into one.

She zeroed in on me standing in her kitchen, Fritz's gun in my hand. "On the fridge."

"Oh for god's sake. I'm hanging on to it."

She hadn't seen or heard from Fritz

"You were right," I said to Ann, not even minding giving her credit. "Efrain didn't kill Manuel."

She patted Efrain's hand, but he didn't look up. "I told her you wouldn't hurt anyone."

His voice was muffled as he spoke into his chest. "It was my fault. I did things I shouldn't."

"Oh, I'm sure it's not as bad as you think." This is the Ann who was so good at helping people.

He started slowly and told her the story of the blackmail and how he eventually ended up in the desert, planning to take his own life.

Tears filled Ann's eyes and ran down her face before she wiped them away. She'd defended Efrain against any suspicion, but she didn't protest accusations against Fritz. "I'm so sorry," she said to Efrain.

We sat in silence a moment before she spoke again. "I knew Fritz felt that life had passed him by. He tried to hide it. But when he found out Manuel was going to run for office, it set him off. Maybe knowing Chris and Manuel were working together drove him over the edge."

I wouldn't let her get away with minimizing the situation. "He murdered Manuel Ortiz and set Chris up for it."

She rubbed Efrain's back. "He's had a hard life. We need to forgive him."

I couldn't stay quiet. "Forgive him? He tried to kill you."

Ann looked at me. "Not kill. He wouldn't do that."

I wanted to throttle her, instead, I addressed Efrain. "Can you stay with Ann? Lock the doors after I'm gone."

"Where are you going?" Ann asked.

"Fritz hasn't shown up here, so my guess is that he's at the Hot Spot. I'm going to confront him there."

"I don't think that's a good idea."

"I do. Keep the doors locked."

* * *

I wasn't far from the Hot Spot when I noticed the flare and flash of fire engines. Traffic slowed, as it does when there's something to see. I knew before I saw the flames that the black smoke was coming from the Hot Spot. I wouldn't be allowed close and wouldn't try to talk to the firefighters now. I executed a u-turn and drove by again but couldn't see if Fritz's pickup sat outside the bar. All I could do was turn around and go back to Ann's.

No blue pickup was parked in the driveway and I hoped that meant Fritz hadn't come home. But it might mean Fritz had gone up with the Hot Spot. Maybe he'd tried to do what Efrain had attempted, end it all before it caught up to him.

This time Efrain responded when I knocked and hollered from the front porch. He had the door thrown open quickly and I rushed past him to the kitchen. "The Hot Spot is on fire."

At the table Ann paled, her mouth wide.

"He's desperate," I said.

Ann held her hand out to me. "Give me the phone."

I pulled it back. "Why?"

"My husband's business is burning. I need to call him."

"He tried to kill you!"

She didn't answer but continued to give me the Ann-demon stare that had made me do anything she asked since I was old enough to understand words. I dumped the phone in her open palm. She dialed and in a few seconds Fritz answered.

"Are you okay?" Ann asked, concerned deep in her voice.

I wanted to rip the phone from her. The man had killed Manuel Ortiz, framed our brother, and tried to kill her. He'd almost destroyed Efrain. She acted as if he was still the mild-mannered guy who needed nagging to get out of bed in the morning.

I motioned for her to look at me and mouthed, "Speaker," so I'd be able to hear.

"Ann?" He sounded surprised. "I thought it'd be Michaela again. Always protecting you."

"Honey, the cops called. They said the Hot Spot is on fire."

He breathed heavily. "It needed to go."

Her eyebrows drew together. "Go? What are you talking about?"

It sounded as though he spoke using the hands-free device in his pickup, the rattle of road noise muffling his voice. "It was the last of it."

"I don't understand," Ann said. By the way she clutched the fabric of her shirt, I thought she might be starting to.

"Twenty years. No, more than that. My whole damned life. It was always your family. The Wrights couldn't do any wrong. Chris pretended to be my best friend, but he couldn't wait to be rid of me. And you, I got saddled with taking care of you."

Color drained from Ann's face. "We took care of each other, honey. You and me."

He laughed. "Right. You were a cripple and Chris couldn't take care of you *and* Michaela. He chose Michaela, but I figured taking care of you would make me one of the family. Like Chris's true brother. I was stupid to think I could do it. Stupid to even try. What's so great about the Wrights? Self-righteous do-gooders."

Ann's fingers pulsed at her neck, squeezing and releasing her hold on her blouse. "We love you. We always—"

"Don't. You loved having a hired man at your beck and call. Until Efrain grew up enough to take on all the jobs and then you didn't need me. And I was an okay friend for Chris when he quit school, until Manuel came back into the picture. Then it's bye-bye Fritz."

"This is not you. Come home. We can talk about it."

"This is the real me, princess. I'm done being your legs. Done playing daddy to a kid who is biding his time until he can take my place. Done trying to be the best friend to a guy who sees me as dirt."

Ann slouched, defeated. "Please don't hurt yourself. I love you."

Maybe she was only trying to placate him, but hearing her talk of love to someone so dangerous made me want to gag.

"Hurt myself? Oh, that's rich. I've got other plans."

She clutched the side of the table. "Don't come home," she warned, and I wanted to jump across the table and strangle her for telling him where she was. "The cops are watching the house."

"I hadn't planned on coming home ever again. What's the point? You shouldn't have made it out of the pool alive and now that you are, you know what I've done."

"I forgive you, Fritz. I know that's not the real you. It couldn't be." The tears rolled down her face. "You're the only one who ever loved me. We're a team. You and me. The two who were left out. But we showed them. We made a good life together." She sobbed. "Don't ruin this. We can still be together. Don't leave me." She faltered, letting her sobs take over.

"Come on, Ann. Face it. No one ever loved either one of us. Not even each other. We tolerated and took care. But even that didn't last after Efrain grew up. I'm taking care of everything for you, as usual."

Something about the way he said that brought the hair up on my neck. "What do you mean?"

"Michaela? Is that you?"

"Yeah, it's me. Nice job with the Hot Spot."

He laughed. "I'm glad to talk to you. I wanted to make sure you know that all of this is your fault. From the very beginning. You caused the accident. Because of you and I ended up with this wrecked life of taking care of a cripple. I could have had a fancy bar like those new downtown jobs. A pretty wife who treated me nice. I wouldn't have been an unpaid servant to a bunch of wetbacks at a crappy shelter."

"You piece of shit," I said.

"You couldn't let Chris go to jail, where he belongs. No, you had to stick your nose into everything and bring it all up. It was easy to convince Efrain that Manuel shot his mother, but you'd have figured it out eventually. Because you're so damned smart."

I thought about it. "You shot Efrain's mother." I paused, putting it all together. "Sorry, Fritz, I hadn't figured that out."

He shouted through the line. "It was an accident. I was aiming at a rabbit and she stepped in front of me. She was drunk. I never meant it."

"Murder has no statute of limitations, you know. And now I have your confession."

"Your word against mine."

"And Ann and Efrain."

"Oh? Efrain is there, too? A tight little family gathering. What you Wrights are famous for. Get used to the smaller group, though. When I'm done, this is all that's going to be left."

My heart slammed into my chest. "What are you planning?"

He sounded gleeful. "Those little nieces of mine love me. They'll go anywhere with good ol' Uncle Fritz."

He hung up the phone, and I gripped the table and tried to catch my breath. "I've got to get to my house. Fritz is on his way there."

Ann shook her head. "Your family isn't there."

Hearing her say it out loud helped calm me. "But Fritz doesn't know that."

Her pale face stared back at me. "I told him they were going to Bar C."

29

I waited at a stoplight, fighting the urge to charge through the red. It wouldn't help anything if I ended up a pile of raw meat on the road, but the delay sent alarms clanging in my brain. Deon had taken the girls away to keep them safe and now they were exposed and vulnerable to a killer.

The light finally turned green and my tires squealed as I barreled around the corner, dodging in and out of traffic on the busy street as I made my way to the onramp for I-10.

I had Efrain's phone and called Deon over and over, getting voice mail. Maybe he'd left the phone in the cabin while he and the girls went for an evening ride. Or maybe he refused to answer. The image of my family lying in blood tried to push itself into my mind. No. They were fine.

I got trapped between two asshole big rig drivers clogging the lanes driving side by side four miles above the speed limit. As soon as the road opened to three lanes, I popped out and around them both, not bothering to flip them the bird as I muttered every curse word I could conjure.

How much of a jump did Frtiz have on me?

I pressed the accelerator to the floor, driving the speedometer above 90 mph. It seemed the world folded on itself like a terrifying origami, twisted and mangled, angles forming and disappearing. Sami running with her hands cupped in front of her for hooves, neighing with her shrill little girl voice. Josie, her beautiful mane of black hair billowing behind her as she crouched in the saddle. Deon, his open and giving smile behind twinkling dark eyes.

I finally veered off the Interstate and navigated several miles of light traffic on a two-lane highway. Finally I was bumping onto a gravel road. Dusk fell and I squinted through the windshield, searching for the turn-off to the ranch.

It finally came into view. Another couple of miles on a twisty, dusty road brought me to the ranch headquarters as the sun dropped below the western peaks. I didn't see Deon's car and wondered what cabin they'd been assigned. I hated having to stop to find out.

I skidded on the gravel when I braked in front of the office and sprinted inside. Of course, no one manned the desk. I banged on the bell sitting on the counter. The front office was festooned with typical ranch decor. A wagon wheel light fixture and antler chair completed the look. I banged the bell again and shouted, "Hello. Hi. Anyone?"

Still no one showed up. I slipped around the front counter and into the back room.

Bingo. A map on the wall covered in a clear plastic sheet showed boxes representing the cabins. I located the box with Sanchez written on the covering with erasable marker. Cabin 18, located at the end of the loop, as far from the entrance as possible. In seconds I was back in the Pilot, leaving a trail of dust floating into the hot, still air.

I slammed on my brakes and whipped the Pilot behind Cabin 16. I was glad for the weight of Fritz's gun in my hand as I slid from the car and started toward Cabin 18.

I wanted to barrel inside, guns blazing. There wasn't an ounce of doubt I'd kill Fritz if he'd touched my family. But running blindly into a dangerous situation wasn't a smart move. With caution and my gun drawn, I moved as quickly and quietly as possible.

Fritz's new pickup sat beside Deon's Audi outside the cabin. No lights shone through the windows. I crept toward the front door, trying to keep my footsteps silent, my breath light.

Soundlessly, I moved up the porch steps like a snake sliding across the desert floor. I stopped to listen, holding my breath. I moved to the front window and slowly raised my head to peer above the sash. Through the darkness, I made out the front room with its pine table and chairs overturned, an antler-legged coffee table with the glass surface shattered, and debris scattered throughout the room.

The door to the bedroom opened opposite from the window. The room was dark. I scanned from the galley kitchen on my left across the breakfast bar, through the living room, which was mostly a view of the back of the couch, to the wall on my right. No Josie. No Sami. No Deon.

It took no time to go to the front door. Still without much sound, I grabbed the doorknob and pushed the door open. I eased inside, holding my gun ready.

The girls' backpacks lay on the floor by the front door. Their shoes were kicked closed by. They'd have donned their cowboy boots first thing upon arrival. Maybe they really were out riding.

But no. Not past dusk.

The door to the bedroom was open and darkness pushed out thick and deep. I took a slow step and heard a rustle, as if a shaky breath. That was followed by a weak moan. With slight movements, I worked my way to the doorway and even more slowly, I reached my hand up the wall until I touched the light switch. Aiming my gun at the spot where I'd heard the sounds, I inhaled and flipped the switch.

It took me less than a heartbeat to recognize Deon in the narrow space between the wall and the bed. I flew to him, squeezing against the wall. I dropped my gun and leaned close to his face. "I'm here. Are you hurt?"

He moaned and opened his eyes. "The girls."

"Fritz. Oh my god, where are they?"

He opened his mouth and his throat clicked before words sounded. "Don't know. Shot."

That's when I noticed the pool of blood under his back, making slow progress under the bed. "Deon! No." No blood seeped from his abdomen, so the bullet hole was probably underneath him. I jumped up and ran for the bathroom. With a towel in hand I knelt next to him again. Without juggling him, I leaned close, finally seeing blood soaked his shirt somewhere around where the kidneys might be. I wedged the towel underneath him and applied pressure. I pulled Ann's phone from my pocket.

Deon managed to croak, "No."

I stopped at 9-1 and looked at him. "You need an ambulance."

"Find our girls." He panted. "If he hears the ambulance, he'll ..." He faded off, probably not willing to finish with the terrible thought.

I hesitated. He might be right. But I couldn't let him bleed out. "I won't let him." I finished dialing. Trying to keep my voice as steady as possible I recited, "Suspected gunshot injury. Male, thirty-nine years old." I gave them the address and, despite the dispatcher's pleas to stay on the line, I punched it off. The whole time I kept my eyes on Deon.

His eyes remained closed and his chest heaved with an effort to breathe. "He ... knew you ... were coming. He wants you ... to suffer. He took Josie ... and Sami."

I leaned close to Deon, fighting tears. "I have to leave you. I need to find Josie and Sami."

He opened his eyes. "Save them," he whispered.

I kissed his cold lips. "I love you."

That little twinkle lit his eyes, but it faded with his pain. "Always," he whispered.

30

I slipped out the back of the cabin. Where would Fritz take the girls? A half moon hung low in the eastern sky, not giving much for guidance. A hiking trail wound from the dirt at the backyard toward a ridge in the west that protected the corrals huddled below it. If they'd gone to the corrals, the horses or other animals might be agitated or making some noise. All seemed peaceful, so I guessed they'd gone up the hiking trail.

The girls would be upset because of Deon. I listened in the quiet, hearing only crickets and the *whee* of a male quail warning his family of trespassers. I knew I could travel faster than Fritz herding two frightened and reluctant children. I trotted up the trail in my flip-flops, keeping my gun ready and not using a flashlight.

After about ten minutes, a squeaky sound stopped me. I held my breath and tensed, all my energy going into my ears. Listen.

There. A small cry. Sami. The tiny wail, not more than the *whoo* of a mourning dove, sank through my skin. It was the sound she made in her sleep, when the dreams swelled into nightmares and I'd make my way down the hall to her side. We'd turn the pillow over to the good dream side and she'd drift off again.

Nothing could keep me from her side now. I hurried on, my grip on the gun more sure. I would kill the bastard for this.

The trail crossed the valley and took a steep climb up the side of the mountain. A few switchbacks brought me to the top of a tall bluff with a sheer wall. The ragged cliff fell two hundred feet to a rock-strewn valley.

My eyes had grown accustomed to the darkness, so I had little trouble making out the shape of Fritz with one hand on Sami's shoulder, forcing her to sit at the edge of the cliff. He held Josie with an arm circling her ribs, pressed close to his side.

If I lunged out of the darkness, it could trigger Fritz's instant reaction to shove the girls off the cliff. They'd fly down and smash on the rocks below. My two broken daughters, flesh, blood, and bone smattered on the desert.

The only solution I could muster was to shoot him. But I couldn't risk hitting Josie.

I called out to Fritz from the darkness. "It's over. Put your hands on your head."

"Mommy!" Sami cried and stood up to run to my voice.

Fritz shoved her back and she screamed as she fell on her butt. Josie shouted, sounding almost calm. "We're okay, Mom."

Fritz whirled around to me. He raised his hand, showing me a gun. "Come on out, Michaela."

I stepped from behind a boulder. "Put down your gun. You know I'm a better shot than you."

He pivoted and pointed the gun at Josie. Both girls screamed. "I don't need to be fast to shoot one of them. Toss your gun over the edge."

I hesitated. He started in. "One ... two ..."

I threw the gun away. It clanked on rocks and came to a stop somewhere below.

Fritz motioned for me to join Sami while he kept his hold on Josie. When I got close, Sami launched herself into my legs, bawling and hugging me until I couldn't move. I put my hands on her head and held her. Josie and I made eye contact. Tear streaks showed on her dusty cheeks and her eyes glimmered with fear, but she gave me a nearly imperceptible nod to show me she held strong. "Good girls," I said.

"I'm glad you could join us," Fritz said.

"The cops are on their way. Why not quit now before it goes too far."

He shook his head. "It's already too far. I'll never get out of jail when they figure out I killed the great Manuel Ortiz, protector of the undefended, this generation's Martin Luther King."

There was not much I could say to counter that. "You could still have a good life. With a plea bargain, you might not do much time. I've seen it happen."

He shoved the gun at me. "Shut up. I'm not going to jail. I've had enough of trying to make a good life out of ashes. I'm going out now, on my own terms. And I'm going to take your kids with me. Live with that, sweet sister-in-law."

Josie's quick inhale was followed by a squeak of fear. Sami kept crying, probably not following the conversation or even listening.

Below us, the wail of the ambulance floated on the quiet night and soon the flash of red and blue lights broke the darkness as it made its way to the cabin.

Fritz glanced down and back up. I'd let my thoughts bounce to Deon and lost the opportunity. Fritz said, "Not much time to dally." He paused and laughed. "That's one of Ann's favorite words. She's always telling me not to dally. What a silly thing to say to a grown-assed man."

I hugged Sami tighter against me. "They're coming to take care of Daddy. He's going to be okay."

Fritz's face fell. "Okay? You saw him?"

I nodded, releasing my tight hold on Sami and pushing her away a few inches. I focused on Josie, hoping she could read my thoughts. "He lost some blood but basically, no big deal."

"Damn it!" Fritz yelled and it echoed across the canyon. "First Ann, then Deon. I won't make that mistake with you."

"See?" I said and pointed down the trail as if he could make it out from here. "He's walking out by himself."

It was a long shot and I couldn't believe it when it worked. Fritz turned his head to look and I leaped, shoving Sami backward. Josie ducked and pushed back and before Fritz could react, I grabbed at the arm holding Josie and she slipped free. "Run!" I shouted in Josie's direction.

Fritz wrenched his arm from me and swung it around to clobber me in the face. I lunged away and it swooshed over my head.

Out of the corner of my eye I saw Josie grab Sami's arm.

That's all I spared as I reached for Fritz. I reached for him as he pulled the trigger. Thank god I ruined his aim enough the bullet zinged into the night, pinging on a nearby rock. "Run!" I screamed again to the girls.

Fritz pulled his gun up again and shot into the night. Sami screamed but it sounded far away. They'd made it out. Whatever happened now was between me and Fritz.

My police training had taken place more than a decade ago, but I knew what to do. Fritz swung the gun around in wild arcs. With my arm, I slammed down on his forearm and at the same time I brought my knee up, knocking his aim to the ground again. The gun discharged. But the contact with my knee loosened his grip. I grabbed for the gun, but his finger remained on the trigger and he squeezed. Another round shot into the night. I slammed his fist into my knee again and this time it loosened his grip and the gun fell into the sand.

We both lunged for it and I got to it first. I scooped it up and flung it away. It flew toward the cliff edge in the darkness.

"You ruined everything," Fritz shouted into the night, a sound like an animal's howl. He pulled his arm back and with surprising speed, slammed his fist into my jaw, knocking me backward. I stumbled on a rock the size of a football and fell on my tailbone, momentarily paralyzing me.

He lunged for the spot where the gun had fallen but he didn't get more than a step away before I threw myself at him. I wrapped my arms around his legs, sending him crashing face first into the dirt.

He rolled over but I straddled him before he sat up. My fist slammed into his cheek and something cracked and gave. I ratcheted my arm back and fired my fist into his face again, almost relishing his howl of pain.

He wriggled from side to side and threw his hands over his face, whimpering and moaning. "It's not fair. I took care of everyone. I gave up my whole life."

I raised myself up and yanked on his shoulder, rolling him to his stomach and with practiced ease, stretched his arms behind his back.

He reduced himself to sobs, words nothing more than jumbled syllables.

Habit and training had me reaching to my back where my cuffs would have been on my utility belt. No cuffs, just me in a skirt and flip-flops. Guess we'd wait for backup.

Below me, the ambulance's lights danced on the hillside. Josie and Sami would be there soon.

31

Sami danced through the kitchen, stopping for an arabesque. "Dad says he needs a fizzy water." She made her way to the fridge on the tips of her toes.

Ann's tired face practiced a grin. "Giving up softball for ballet?"

Sami pulled the can from the shelf and performed and not-so-graceful spin that sent her crashing into the island counter. "I'm doing both." She resumed her spin, tiptoe, arabesque out the back door to the patio.

Ann sat at the counter, elbow on the breakfast bar, head resting against it. Her gaze followed me as I rubbed seasoning into the pork loin. I wanted to ask about Fritz. What his attorney planned for defense, how he was faring in jail. But Ann wouldn't welcome the inquisition. "How are things at Mi Casa?" I asked instead.

She blinked and focused on me as if she'd been miles away. "Oh. Good. Manuel Ortiz left a big chunk of money in his will for the center. So far no one has contested the donation. It will keep us afloat for a while."

That determined, take-no-prisoner attitude of Ann's had sunk beneath layers of sadness over the last couple of months. I could only pray she'd find her way back, that Fritz wouldn't claim another victim before this was finished.

Ann didn't seem to struggle with forgiveness. Sometimes I thought maybe she had more to forgive herself for than she had to forgive others. Still, if she held a grudge against me for accusing her of murder and of setting up Chris, she didn't show it. She visited Fritz regularly. Chris also didn't appear to be holding any grudges. I'd worked through my feelings about Ann letting me take the blame for the accident. We'd all suffered enough over that. And even Deon hadn't brought up the Jared debacle.

Forgiveness seemed to be the order of the day. The only one hanging on to old grievances was me. I needed to forgive myself. Maybe that would happen someday.

Josie thudded down the stairs. She sidled up to Ann and thrust her iPad under Ann's nose. "Do you think we can make this for my final project?"

Ann's forehead crinkled as she studied the screen. "If you get the lumber and nails, I've got some chicken wire left over from the garden fence. Efrain can probably help with the design."

Josie lifted her head behind Ann's and winked at me. She hadn't mentioned a final project to me, and I was sure she'd invented it to distract Ann.

I had to look away to keep either of them from seeing my tears. Family takes care of each other.

The front door opened and Chris shouted from the foyer. "Who's going to help me with this ice cream?"

Sami appeared from the backyard again, apparently the words *ice cream* traveling like a dog whistle to her ears. "Me!"

Josie spun around and hurried after them. "Is it homemade?"

"You have to turn the crank," Chris said, entering the kitchen carrying a plastic bucket filled with ice and a metal canister inside.

A smiled teased Ann's lips. "It's electric."

He shrugged. "Be grateful I got this much done. I was up all night study-ing. I ought to be sleeping in."

I cleared a spot for him to set the ice cream freezer on a counter next to an outlet. "How's school?"

"The LSAT is way harder than I remember, but I've talked with some professors and I think I can handle it. And those pimply youngsters are gonna a pain in the ass. But I'll get through."

He wouldn't appreciate the hug I had the urge to give him. The pride I felt for him stepping away from the Border Patrol and going back to law school in his forties flared in a sudden warmth. He was going to be great.

He plugged in the freezer and it roared to life. Ann made her way to the guest room to nap while the loin cooked, and Chris and the girls headed to the pool for a swim. I found Deon sitting on a chaise lounge in the cool shade of a palm tree, watching as Chris jettisoned a squealing Sami over and over from his arms to the deep end.

"How are you feeling?"

He glanced down at his side, where the dressing was reduced to a two-inch-square bandage. "If I told you it doesn't hurt at all, would you all quit waiting on me hand and foot?"

I took his hand. "I think it's way past time I dote on you."

He looked at our clasped hands and squeezed mine. "I would like that." He took a breath. "I think we both need to pay more attention to each other."

I started to protest.

He tugged my hand to get me to stop. "You're born to be a cop."

That stopped me.

He continued. "I don't like you being in harm's way. I want you safe, taking care of the girls, maybe having a creative hobby. Cooking would be nice."

I chuckled.

"But that's not who you are. I married an adventurist. Someone full of life. Someone who wants to help other people. It makes no sense for me to squelch the best parts of you."

"So you don't mind if I go back to the force?"

He watched Josie dive from the side of the pool. "It's like you said about Chris. He was meant to be a lawyer and if he didn't follow that dream, he'd never be truly happy."

"I'm happy being a mother and your wife."

He smiled. "Good. Because those are permanent positions. But being a cop is in your DNA. So, go be a cop, too."

Ann clumped her way onto the patio. "Too noisy to sleep." She dropped a towel on a chair and made her way to the pool, setting her crutches on the side. "And I could use a swim."

Josie and Sami shouted at Ann to get in. Chris started splashing her. She admonished one and all.

I leaned over and kissed Deon.

The Desert's Share
Michaela Sanchez Southwest Crime Thrillers #2

A MURDERED AID WORKER. A POLITICAL FIRESTORM. AND A KILLER ON THE LOOSE.

When rookie agent Michaela Sanchez receives a tip from her sister that someone has gone missing in the Tucson desert, she thinks she's searching for a lost immigrant. What she finds is the murdered defendant of a high-profile local trial.

Lacy Hollander was a humanitarian aid worker, on trial for harboring felons after she sheltered illegal border crossers. When a conflict erupts with a local vigilante group, her murder ignites a political firestorm.

Concerned about her sister's involvement, and taking heat at home from her activist daughter, Michaela takes it upon herself to investigate.

But repeated run-ins with the commander of the vigilante group and a series of escalating threats against aid workers make one thing clear...the violence hasn't ended with Lacy's death.

There is a killer on the loose. And Michaela must untangle the mystery before he strikes again...

Get your copy today at
severnriverbooks.com/series/michaela-sanchez-southwest-crime-thrillers

ACKNOWLEDGMENTS

Saying this book is written by me is like saying a garden salad is simply lettuce. The tomatoes, carrots, shallots, cucumbers, and even the dressing are what make that salad satisfying and they should get their share of the credit. That's how it is with this book. So, to all the crazy vegetables and tangy dressings in my life, I owe a debt of gratitude.

To Janet Fogg, who what ifs better than anyone I know. May we continue to have retreats to write and cook, walk and scheme, and always laugh. To Jess Lourey and her terrific book, *Rewrite Your Life*. You helped me boil down the ideas and get at what I wanted to say.

To Tim Moore, Phoenix cop and generous collaborator. Thanks for keeping me legit. To Kate Matthews, for listening while we tromped up mountain tops and down to the desert floor, through cold beers and more than our fair share of bourbon. Friendship and encouragement are the best inspiration.

To Terri Bischoff, editor extraordinaire. And Nicole Nugent who tackles those pesky details. I apologize for never understanding commas. To Amber Hudock, who runs herd to keep me in line. Keris and Jason, and everyone at Severn River Publishing, and especially Andrew Watts for getting this book into the world. It is a fine thing you do.

In a fortunate series of seemingly random decisions, I somehow ended up in Tucson. I love my adopted city and send virtual hugs and kisses from the Catalinas to the Santa Ritas, including the Tucsons, the Rincons, and Baboquivari range.

When I had babies I assumed I'd always be the Mom, giving sage advice, being wiser and more mature than my children. It's been one of life's fantastic surprises to realize my daughters have surpassed me in every good way. By a miracle of genetics I helped make two of my best friends. You continue to push me to be a better writer and a better person.

Always, the biggest gratitude goes to Dave. Thank you for somehow keeping your eyes from glazing over as I endlessly work through plots and characters, ruining perfectly wonderful sunsets and relaxing hot tub sessions. Thank you for not believing me every time I say I'm going to quit.

ABOUT THE AUTHOR

Shannon Baker is the award-winning author of *The Desert Behind Me* and the Kate Fox series, along with the Nora Abbott mysteries and the Michaela Sanchez Southwest Crime Thrillers. She is the proud recipient of the Rocky Mountain Fiction Writers 2014 and 2017-18 Writer of the Year Award.

Baker spent 20 years in the Nebraska Sandhills, where cattle outnumber people by more than 50:1. She now lives on the edge of the desert in Tucson with her crazy Weimaraner and her favorite human. A lover of the great outdoors, she can be found backpacking, traipsing to the bottom of the Grand Canyon, skiing mountains and plains, kayaking lakes, river running, hiking, cycling, and scuba diving whenever she gets a chance. Arizona sunsets notwithstanding, Baker is, and always will be a Nebraska Husker. Go Big Red.

Sign up for Shannon Baker's reader list at
severnriverbooks.com/authors/shannon-baker